TANSY'S ACRES

"Love more, hate less."

by
Holly K. Szurpicki

Tansy's Acres
Copyright © 2022—Holly K. Szurpicki

ISBN: 978-0-9992323-5-4
Library of Congress Control Number: 2022918338
Szurpicki, H. K., 1976–

Text Design: Lisa Simpson
Front and Back Cover by Colleen Szurpicki
Colleen Szurpicki: border art

CONTENTS

DEDICATION

To my glorious Heavenly Father, My Husband, My Mother, My Daughter and My Son. I couldn't do this without you! Special Thanks to: An extraordinary editor, Karen.

INTRODUCTION

Mary Ann Waller was determined she would not be stuck in the small rural town of Kettlesville, Kentucky, her entire life. After graduation she planned to leave because she had dreams. Big dreams. She wanted to run her own business and be the best pie baker the world had ever known. Well, at least the best Kentucky had ever known!

But life rarely turns out the way we think or hope. And life definitely had thrown Mary some curves. She was ready to give up and had absolutely given up on God. What was the point of praying when prayers didn't get answered? That is, until Tansy reentered her life—the person who taught her some things she didn't know and introduced her to a God she didn't expect.

Tansy helped her open her heart again and reminded her that love is never a closed door and how the heart always looks for a place to call home—especially for the holidays!

CHAPTER ONE

TO BE YOUNG

*S*ometimes you just have to take a leap of faith. It can be risky business. It would have been easier to just walk away. Perhaps you feel that way as well? In my world, I overthink everything. So, I thought, why tell my story anyway? It feels strange to talk about my life to other people. What will they think? I can hear the words of Tansy ringing through my head, "Pay no mind to others' opinions of you. Be the best version of you!

Originally, I wished I could forget it—my past, the pain, my dreams, but it is who I am! Then it hit me. How can anyone care if they don't know the whole story? However messed up it may seem, believe me, this story is definitely worth telling.

It's all because of Tansy that I have finally let my guard down to share my heart with the world. She has been like

a mother to me. She is the one who helped me through a great time of sorrow. We like to think life is going to be an easy street in which luck or chance can happen to all of us. But I am here to tell you, life can be hard. And it can be even harder if you really want to achieve something. But that doesn't mean you give up when it's hard. Rather, you press in more to your faith and get ready for twists and turns, the valleys and the mountain tops—and never forget your strength in the difficult times in between.

I hope that by sharing my story, someone, somewhere— perhaps you? — may learn to love more, hate less, and achieve something important with your life.

My cotton T-shirt stuck to my back. I wiped my forehead for the tenth time and sighed. How could it be so humid and sticky? I sniffed the stuffy air. More rain was coming, but actually that didn't bother me a bit. I'm content whenever I watch the huge Kentucky moon shimmer in the night sky. Especially as I sit next to the guy of my dreams. There's no place that I, Mary Ann, would rather be than right here with none other than the infamous Keith Walker.

How can I describe him to you? He's more than handsome. He smells good, too—at least to this country girl. I breathed in deeply the smell of fresh grass and soil that is like a permanent cologne on his skin and clothes. Keith is really smart and is one of those people who will get ahead in life. Right now, Keith worked at the local sawmill and mowed lawns for a living on the side. It didn't pay much, but it kept gas in his truck and enough for pizza from Kenny's gas station now and then for our date nights.

As we sat together on the tailgate of his truck, his hand tightened around mine while we listened to the night sounds. I could tell Keith was tired and fighting sleep. It had been a long day. He closed his eyes for a moment, which allowed me an opportunity to stare at his long eyelashes. I'm so jealous! Daddy says they remind him of black fly swatters. (*He's joking by the way.*) But I love how they reached up and touched Keith's eyebrows and offset his full head of hair. Ladies, if you have any thoughts about claiming him for yourself, he's strictly off limits. I've already claimed him—he's mine!

I snuggled up next to him. I was content. I know things are right in our little world for now. Yet, it hasn't always been that way. But I'm getting ahead of myself . . .

I drove myself crazy thinking about where to begin my story. So how about the beginning? I'll take you to where it started— Morton Peak, the mountaintop of the country. The skyline is beautiful. It is a place where you can perch, rest, and dream. But it's a place where you have to be careful when the wind blows. Otherwise, you'll catch a nice whiff of cow manure. Trust me, you get used to it when you grow up on a farm.

Morton Peak is where Keith and I had our first date. (*He was so cute! Sometimes he would catch me staring at him. Then he would flash me one of his charming smiles and make me blush.*) From the top of the mountain, you can see my house. It's a white farmhouse with painted wood shutters. While it may not look like much to some, it is everything to my family.

We didn't come from money as some folks around here do. Farming was the family business, and it's plain hard work! People think farmers are rich, and some are, but the rest? Well, at least where I'm from many are poor, but they work really hard. That is for certain.

Daddy bought our old farmhouse from his granddaddy right before Granddad died, rest his ornery old soul. All twenty acres of good soil for corn and haying. I was born here, raised here, and hopefully, by the grace of God, I won't die here. Don't get me wrong, it's a nice place to raise a family, but I prefer the city. Daddy always said he would build Mama a house, but she knew better than that. He loved the family house and wasn't going anywhere. It wasn't in him.

Keith and I dated through my senior year. He had graduated a couple of years before me. We attended some of the football games, basketball games, and the school dance. But country kids don't always have the opportunity to do the same things most kids do in high school. Our lives revolved around planting and harvesting, which meant being outside—a lot. Do you know what being outside in a humid climate does to me? It gives me frizzy hair! But Keith didn't seem to mind. He loved me just the way I am—down-home fried, frizzy, and sassy.

"You know, you're the only girl for me," Keith said shifting slightly on the truck tailgate as he opened his eyes and caught me staring at him. With a big old grin on his face, he leaned in close. I could tell he was falling for me big time shortly after we started dating. He tried to hide it at first, but his eyes gave him away. Daddy says the eyes are like a window in which you can see all the way to the soul of somebody. I have to agree with him. From even the beginning of our relationship, I could tell Keith was hooked!

I snuggled in just a bit closer and smiled at Keith's comment. Secretly, I was in love with him as well, but I was too young to want to get so serious. It was about having fun. Mama said that I had plenty of time, and I tended to agree. I would tell myself that I was in no rush to get married.

Keith put his arms around me, and I felt I could have died. I was so content there I could have stayed resting in his arms all night long. Awe . . . it felt so good to be young and in love. I glanced at my watch and realized the time—I should have been home already! Daddy was going to be furious with me. But really what else was new? It was so hard to want to leave on such a perfect night.

I closed my eyes for another moment and allowed my mind to drift. That's a habit of mine actually. Bottomline, I daydream. Mama thinks it's because I am dramatic. Who me? Mary Ann Waller, dramatic? Daddy, on the other hand, swore I should have taken drama class. (*I agree with him!*) And speaking of dreaming . . .

Picture this—Keith as a knight in shining armor during the 1800s. Me? I'm a peasant woman with ragged clothes and my hair up in a bun with a cloth pinned behind it. I imagine myself picking wildflowers in a beautiful field by a mountain when, off in the distance, I spot a horse and rider galloping toward me. The wind blows and so does my hair. (*It reminds me of a hair commercial on television.*) I can't see too far off because I don't have glasses, but as the rider comes closer, butterflies stir in my stomach, (*Oh Lord, he is handsome. What a man!*) The weird part is that his hair is slicked back. (*Where did he get styling gel in the 1800s? Even in my dreams, he looks better than me. I hate him!*)

As he and his horse come to a halt in front of me, he reaches for my hand to pull me up onto the back of his white stallion. I feel a sense of relief that finally I would be rescued from the bugs and field rodents. I notice he has a great smile (*and, thankfully, all his teeth.*)

I want to pinch myself. Could this really be happening? I reach up to take his offered hand but realize my hands are dripping with sweat. (*That tends to happen when I feel nervous.*) But

I'm certainly not going to destroy the moment and wipe them on my skirt. No way! But I should have. As Keith starts to pull me up onto his horse, my hand slips from his and I plummet to the ground. (*Actually, I fell on my butt, but I thought* plummet *sounded better.*) Luckily, a lush cushion of grass is directly underneath my bottom, which helps to break the fall.

I look up from my humiliating position on the ground as Keith says, "Ah, my love, maybe next time." With that, I watch him ride off into the sunset. I stand up, with grass sticking to my face, and look on in disbelief.

I shook my head as I came back to the present but was irritated. Are you kidding me? Why was Keith such a jerk in my daydreams?

Still remembering how he had behaved in my musings, I glared at Keith with daggers in my eyes.

"What?" he asked, obviously confused.

"Don't 'What' me! If you saw me in a field and I fell off a horse, would you help me?"

"It depends," he replied.

"On what?" I demanded.

"Well, on how far from my horse and if it required I get off my horse to help you." *(His hint of a smile annoyed me—sort of.)*

"Keith Walker!" I said with mock anger while nudging him in his side. As I did, I squinted to see the time displayed on his digital watch. Precisely ten o'clock. I needed to be home right then, and we still had a good fifteen-minute drive ahead of us! Good Lord, I was going to be in trouble—again.

"We better get back to the house. I am supposed to be home by ten, remember?"

"Oh, I remember! And your daddy is going to be mad at me again." Keith still was not moving.

I grabbed his hand and jumped off the tailgate. "Let's go!" I insisted. We scurried towards the front of his old Ford pickup, jumped in, and within seconds were blazing down the dirt road kicking up dust the whole way!

This is exactly why my folks were always irritated with Keith. No matter how many times we tried to obey their rules, it seemed we always lost track of time and ended up breaking them. Mind you, it wasn't always Keith's fault. Time just seemed to stand still when we were together. It didn't bother me, so why should it bother them? I was a daydreamer under the willow tree and okay so I ran away from home one time… Regardless of any reasons I may have had, they felt he didn't respect their rules. Somebody needed to take the blame and I didn't want it to be just me!

But one thing I loved about Keith is how he let everything roll off his shoulders. He never seemed to have a care in the world. I admired him for that. On the other hand, I worried about everything and picked apart every little detail of an issue. I could almost drive myself crazy.

Keith was a couple of years older than me. Daddy thought that was two years too many! Really, I think it was because they were just worried. Mama said I looked at Keith the same way she looked at Daddy before they were married. I think they were concerned that we would elope, although I told them countless times that I'm not getting married. Period. End of story! (*Of course, secretly, I wanted to marry Keith Walker. I just wasn't saying that to anyone but God. He knows my heart.*)

Part of me believed what I told my folks. Me? Get married? This little country girl? Puh-leez. No man was going to hold me down. (*At least that is what I told myself.*) I had my whole life

ahead of me. I didn't plan to stay a country girl. I was going to move to the city and have a career. I wanted to make it big and have my name in lights. Once I'd made enough money, I planned to leave for good and never look back. (*That's me, dreaming again.*)

I envisioned myself dressed in a royal gown like a princess. All eyes were upon me. I glided down a strip of red velvet carpet and waved as photographers snapped my picture while journalists asked me questions: "Mary Ann, can you tell us how you felt to be chosen for The Wealthiest Woman of the Year award?" one reporter asked.

I smiled and nodded, "Well, maybe one day, darling!"

Someday I'd like to travel to the Mediterranean Sea or Paris. Or perhaps even end up on a deserted island filled with decadent desserts while sipping sweet tea. As I said, I wanted to live in the city, and Keith dreamed of moving to the city one day as well. For now, we both were content to settle for these familiar old country roads and the smell of cow manure.

Kettlesville, Kentucky, was made up of a post office, a dairy farm, and a diner with some of the best breakfast around. It was known as a sleepy town because everything was closed by six o'clock. Truth be told, that took a little getting used to when I first got here, but I'm used to it now, and it's not all bad.

My mind snapped back to the present as Keith pulled up to the house—10:12 p.m. He made good time, but I was still late. Before I could even get out of the truck, I saw the light from the wraparound porch flicker. It was the signal that my folks had been watching for us. Keith turned off the headlights and leaned over for one last kiss. As he did, the porch light flickered again.

I knew exactly what it meant. I was in for "the talk." I could repeat it by heart I'd heard it so often. I wondered what my punishment would be this time. Grounded from seeing Keith? Extra chores? Life without parole? Seriously, whatever the price it was worth it because this girl was in love with the man of her dreams.

"I'll pick you up tomorrow after school," Keith said as I jumped out of the truck. "Do you want to head over to Fowler's Creek and go swimming?"

"Of course! You think I want to miss you swinging from that old farming tire?" I responded, giving him a final wave. (*Keith had me wrapped around his finger.*)

"Bye, I love you." He grinned as he winked at me. (*Those baby-blue eyes got me every time.*)

As I reached the porch, I brushed my fingers through my hair and straightened my dress, trying to look as presentable as humanly possible. Taking a deep breath, I turned the doorknob. I figured I was as ready as I'd ever be. Bring it on!

I had convinced myself that I would blame Keith for this one. I mean, he had a watch too, and Daddy told him to have me home on time. For heaven's sake, I don't even have my driver's license yet! So, clearly this wasn't my fault. Besides, Keith was gone and here I was. I crossed my fingers, closed my eyes, and waited for the inevitable impact. But it was quiet.

I opened one eye and saw Mama. She was sitting in her rocking chair quietly crocheting a kitchen towel. She didn't even make eye contact with me. Then I noticed Daddy laid out on the couch, snoring like a pig, with a blanket covering him.

"Mama?" I whispered. Her only response was to rock faster.

I rolled my eyes and waited. Still nothing. "Okay, I know, I'm late. It's after ten o'clock. So, what's my grounding?"

Mama glared at Daddy, who was still asleep. I knew the look well.

"Shush!" she whispered back. "You go on upstairs, and don't you go waking your Daddy up. He's been working all day. Go on up to bed and we'll talk about that boy Keith in the morning." Then she went back to her crocheting.

I tried to defend myself. "Mama, it wasn't his fault. It was mine." But she wasn't having any of my explaining.

"Go on up to bed," she replied sternly.

"All right, Mama. Good night," and I turned toward the stairs.

"Good night." Her sternness lessening, she added in a sweeter tone, "I love you, baby."

"Love you too, Mama." I breathed a sigh of relief. Everything was going to be okay.

I turned my lamp on by the bed, but it flickered back off. Something was wrong with the bulb. I reached up and tightened it, but three different times it blinked on and then back off. This was a problem for sure. You see, after Keith dropped me off from our dates, he would always stick around until I turned on the lamp in my room. That was the signal that everything was okay. Then he would honk his horn to say, "I love you!"

I cringed as I heard him honk for the third time. Oh crap! He didn't know the light bulb was loose and kept honking his horn! It woke up Daddy.

"That's enough of that! Go on and get out of here, boy!" he yelled, then slammed the front door as he came back inside.

"That boy is trouble!" he hollered.

"Yeah, he is," Mama agreed. "He's just like you!"

"He's not for our Mary Ann," he responded. I could hear the irritation in his voice.

"Oh, let her be. She's in love. I like Keith. He's not that bad."

I smiled as I listened in on their conversation. Mama was such a pure heart.

"You may be right, but I still don't like him, and that's that!" Daddy wasn't backing off, but Mama was smart. She knew Daddy well. It was time to change the subject, because once he got started on something, he was stubborn and didn't want to let it go.

Mama cleared her throat.

"What are you making now?" Daddy asked.

"I am crocheting a pair of pants—for you," she said sweetly to defuse his sour mood.

"Woman, I'm going to bed!" Grumbling, he turned and headed for their room.

I heard Mama laugh as Daddy shut the bedroom door. He would never wear crocheted pants! She knew that and was just giving him a hard time.

Upstairs, I tossed and turned. The air was still muggy, and I couldn't get to sleep. I pulled one leg out from under the covers in an effort to cool down as my mind sped up. The truth is, I think too much. (*Way too much!*) In my mind I pictured what tomorrow might bring. I saw myself slowly walking down the stairs. Daddy and Mama were waiting for me, and Daddy would say just three words: "No More Keith."

Dramatically, I would fall to the ground in utter agony. "I can't live without him. Please reconsider, Daddy. I'll do anything you ask," I would beg. "I'll even try harder to be on time with my curfew. I promise! Anything, please, anything!" I would plead repeatedly, but he would not budge! The decision would be final. No more Keith! I shuddered at the thought of what might happen and finally recognized that situations such as this need prayer. So that is what I did.

Dear Lord, please help Mama and Daddy to like Keith. Amen.

Just as I finished praying, there was a gentle knock on my door. "Baby, it's me," Mama said quietly. I am sure she had heard me praying, even in my soft voice, to the Lord.

"Mama, come in." She came over to the bed and laid down next to me and twisted my curls away from my face.

"I know you love that boy," she began.

"Yes, Mama, I do. With all my heart."

"I see the way you look at him; it's the way I looked at your daddy before he asked me to marry him. I want you to know that you have my blessing, darling. Do you think he's the one?"

"I do, Mama." My eyes teared up as I said it.

"Then, I do too!" she said. "Daddy, on the other hand, is a different story. It's going to take him awhile to get used to that boy. Now, you pay no attention to him when he gets angry like that. I'll smooth things over before he goes to work in the morning."

"Thank you, Mama, I love you." I gave her the biggest hug. It was nice to have her on my side. That was one of the many things I loved about Mama. She was always there for me and knew how to calm Daddy. She was an absolute saint!

"I love you, honey," she whispered as she kissed me on the forehead and left. Mama always knew how to make things right!

The next morning as soon as I got up, I ran to check if Daddy had left for work. His truck wasn't in the driveway. Just the oil stains from its perpetual leak.

I smiled and did an involuntary happy dance. Breakfast would be peaceful. I walked back in and was greeted with the smell of hot buttery biscuits on the counter beckoning me to eat them! Mama knew the way to my heart. The great part about being an only child is that all Mama's cooking was all mine . . . every bite.

Mama was at the sink washing the dishes as I came in the kitchen and sat down in an old rickety chair.

"Morning, Mama," I said softly.

"Morning, darling. Go on and eat some breakfast," she insisted when I offered to help.

She didn't have to tell me twice. I stuffed my mouth full of homemade goodness, and my cheeks filled like a hamster. I glanced at my watch as I crammed another bite in my mouth and reached for my schoolbooks.

"Bye, Mama. I've gotta run to school."

"I love you, my sweet baby girl," she replied. I kissed her cheek and was off.

"Thank You, Lord," I said under my breath. Breakfast had worked out just the way I wanted it to—with no drama!

Before you get the wrong idea about my daddy, I should tell you that he didn't always drink alcohol. But when he started, he never stopped. He was a very kind man when he wasn't drinking. When he was, he never hit Mama or anything like that, but he sure yelled from time to time. Daddy had a lot of unhealed places in his mind, soul, and spirit. Some say it was demons, and I don't disagree. He never truly healed from deep hurts or disappointments of his past. All the emotional pain left unresolved made him angry and bitter towards himself and life. He didn't mean to hurt Mama, but he did. She never pushed him to change, and she never pushed him away. Rather, she chose to love him

unconditionally, accepting him the way he was. Prayer helped her cope with the losses, and their love grew with each passing year. A heart filled with love covered it all.

Mama told me Daddy began drinking heavily after they lost their first baby, my brother. Mama was nine months along when her water broke in the early morning. Once they arrived at the hospital the doctors discovered something was wrong. They immediately whisked her off to the operating room, and Daddy was left in the waiting room all alone.

For several hours he waited. No one came to give him any information, and he had no idea what was going on. All he could do was nervously pace the floor and pray. Finally, the doctor came through the doors and gently broke the news that Daddy's baby boy had been stillborn.

Mama said that the look on Daddy's face when he walked into the room and saw his son lying on the bed right next to her was heart-wrenching. He fell on the bed sobbing, and from that day on he was never the same.

They named my brother Daniel. Daddy said that no son of his would die without having a name. Daniel weighed only five pounds. Mama said it was hard when she came home with no baby. Daddy went straight to their bedroom and shut the door, and that is when he pretty much disconnected from life.

Mama had church folk praying for him, and she prayed for him every night. Of course, it was hard on her too! But Daddy had pretty much given up on God as well. Eventually Mama wanted to try to have another child. But Daddy didn't know if he ever wanted to again after the pain of losing his baby boy. Over time Mama convinced him to try one more time.

It took three years for her to become pregnant with me. She said she was the happiest woman on the earth! Secretly, Mama wished for a little girl that would be just like her. Daddy had kept his emotions shut off, and she longed for someone she could be close with. The baby's gender didn't seem to matter either way to Daddy; he just wanted Mama to be happy!

Even after I was born, Daddy's drinking continued. As I grew older, I avoided coming home whenever possible. Daddy wasn't mean all the time, just disconnected, and I ran from him. Having Keith in my life was a good excuse to get out of the house, and I did every chance I got. But Mama recognized what I was doing and didn't like it. She tried to discourage me by admonishing me on more than one occasion. (*But I didn't listen.*)

"Mary Ann, you can't run from your problems. Just because you go away doesn't mean your problems will do the same. You got to deal with them."

She was right, of course. I was always running from something and that something would eventually catch up to me. (*I realize that now.*)

CHAPTER TWO

WILLOW TREE

*B*eing young is never easy, especially when it comes to receiving any sort of discipline. No one likes discipline, but we all know we need it from time-to-time. I was a good kid, but stubborn. As a result, Daddy and I butted heads and he often grew impatient with me. I learned from Mama that his father was harsh with him. The stories Mama told me I dare not mention. When Daddy would get like that, instead of running far away from home, I ran under the willow tree. For me it was a safe place where I could dream and imagine. A place where prayers were lifted up in hopes they would one day be answered. Mama said, "It was a tree of wonder" and I don't disagree.

Daddy believed in the Bible way of discipline—spare the rod, spoil the child—and he followed it. But the Bible wasn't referring to beating children! Daddy yelled at Mama from time to time and was verbally abusive, but never physically abusive to her. His anger was taken out on me. He said that he loved me and that's why he disciplined me. But how can you hurt someone you love?

He wanted me to be disciplined, he would say, and not act wild like some kids he knew around Kettlesville. But I swore that whenever I decided to have a family, I would never spank my kids—ever!

I didn't get spanked *all* the time. Only when Daddy was drunk. After I had done something wrong, I dreaded hearing his truck pull in the driveway. Every day he would talk to Mama in the kitchen about my attitude. One time, I heard the creak of his steps coming up the stairs. I knew I was about to get another beating and climbed out the window and down the trellis. I ran to the big willow tree near a small creek to hide. My heart was racing and I was out of breath, but I knew I was safe there. I'd sit for hours under that tree watching the branches sway and listening to the wind blow. Mama told me later that she could see my feet under the tree. But she pretended she didn't and would let me stay there for as long as I needed. It was our little secret.

The world seemed to melt away when I sat there. I guess that's where I started daydreaming. Under the willow I could imagine anything, and I spent a lot of time talking to God there. We discussed everything—from my attitude to my dreams to the deepest wishes I held in my heart.

Growing up our family was not considered wealthy, but we weren't poor either. Daddy always said that we were just the right class. We had one income and that was from Daddy. He was a mechanic and knew how to fix anything. He only had to hear a sound from a machine and immediately he could tell what the problem was and then knew what to do. He was a very hard worker.

He had worked at Neil's Tire & Repair Shop for as long as I can remember. Neil sold everything from tires to candy bars. It was a family-owned business and Neil kept it that way. Although we were not related, he treated us like family.

When Daddy wasn't working, he liked to make Mama and me many things. Nothing intimidated him. He tried his hand at crafting coffee tables and chairs. There wasn't anything he wouldn't try to build. He also was an expert at fly fishing. I learned from the best! We fished the creek and caught our share of largemouth bass, and those pan fish—well, they were fun to catch!

One summer day, Daddy took me camping. He set up a green tent down by the creek while I gathered tree branches so we could make a fire. Fresh running water was an essential part for any camping site he chose.

Once camp was set up, he took me blueberry picking. Wild blueberries were a treat not just for us, but the bears liked them too. Daddy tried to scare me by rustling some bushes as I was picking berries. It worked and I jumped! He laughed his deep belly laugh and eventually I joined in and we continued picking. You'd think I would catch on to him, but he got me with that trick every time!

We caught a lot of fish that day. So many, in fact, that we threw several of them back into the water. "Catch and release" is what Daddy called it. After we got back to camp, we made a wood fire. Daddy used the cast iron pan and fried us some fish. Now, there's nothing like fresh fish. It was delicious! Afterwards, Daddy cleaned the wild blueberries we picked and rinsed them in a small strainer down by the creek. He stuffed the berries into a glass mason jar and poured in heavy cream to fill the remaining gaps. Next, he tied a small rope around the lid and tied the other end to a tall stick he stuck in the ground and placed the jars in the cold stream.

"What are you doing, Daddy?" I asked as I watched the process.

"We will let that sit in the water and stay nice and cold," he said.

"Are you sure they won't get dragged away by the current?"

"No, not with the rope attached to the stick. You'll see. In the morning, they'll be a perfect topping on our pancakes."

Those were the good moments that I never wanted to end. The times Daddy was sober, I didn't have a care in the world when he was by my side.

It was hard to sleep that night because I had pancakes on my mind. As soon as the sun came up, I zipped down to the creek and found that jar. It looked like blue cream with little chunks of blueberries throughout. I ran over to Daddy and pressed him.

"Come on. Make us some pancakes," I begged. My mouth was already watering at the thought.

"All right," he said with a laugh. "Gather some more wood for the fire."

I hopped to it and was back in no time. It didn't take long, and we were both enjoying hot pancakes with blueberries and cream. I was in heaven. If I could have licked my plate, I would have.

Afterwards, we packed up the tent and cleaned up the area. Daddy taught me that it's important never to litter in the woods or leave anything behind for the wildlife to get into. He got a bucket of water from the creek and doused the fire. Once the truck was loaded Daddy scanned the campsite one more time to see if we had left anything.

"Mary, go look around there by that tree," and he pointed to a pine tree set apart from the others. I scurried over and saw a package at the base of its trunk.

"Is it for me?" I yelled in excitement.

"Yes, darling, it's for you!" His eyes seemed to light up like lights on a Christmas tree!

"Oh, Daddy, what is it?"

"Now, I'm not going to tell you that. Go on and open it!" He was laughing.

I opened the package and inside was a wooden box. It had a small metal latch on the front. "You made this for me?" I asked, gently rubbing my fingers across the smooth wood.

"I sure did, baby, and you can put whatever treasures you find in there."

"I love it! Thank you, Daddy!" I walked back over to where he stood and threw my arms around him. The box was simple, but I was so happy with it because he made it just for me. The look in Daddy's eyes was genuine love. He *did* love me! Isn't that all a little girl wants—for her daddy to love her?

The weekend was over too soon, and when we arrived home, I had a decision to make. Where was I going to keep this box? I needed a secret place, hidden from the rest of the world. At first, I thought about maybe in the cornfield, but that could be dangerous. Especially because that's where cows often grazed, chewing the tall grass.

Then I thought about putting it under the back porch. No one would ever find it there. But then I remembered I'd seen muskrats underneath there. They would surely get their gnarly teeth around my treasures. Suddenly it came to me. Why didn't I think of it before? I knew the perfect place no one was aware of but me, God, and Mama. My willow tree.

The tree wasn't far from the house. It stood all by itself surrounded by tall grass. Once underneath the protection of its long boughs I found a perfect place. The soil was surprisingly moist from all the shade the tree provided. I remembered that Mama kept a small shovel near the back porch. I knew she wouldn't mind if I borrowed it.

Before I began digging, I gathered some small branches and leaves from around the property. That was going to be my cover to keep it hidden. Prior to placing it in the hole, I reminisced about everything inside. I washed off the shovel and returned it to the back porch, confident that my special box and its contents were safe.

I was the only one who knew they were there for now. At least, I hoped I was . . .

CHAPTER THREE

THE GREY FEATHER

Sometimes you gotta close your eyes and just jump. It's wise to be careful, but there will come a time when you have to spread your wings and fly. Hopefully, someone is there to catch you when you fall. I know angels catch you because my guardian angel is busy all the time. I cannot tell you the countless times angels have saved me. I learned from it though and now when I look back, I realize how every circumstance I faced made me who I am today. Mama always said, "Don't be afraid to try something new. It's okay to fail, but it's never okay not to try."

I turned on my side for the tenth time. I couldn't sleep. The rain pounded on our tin roof. From my window the grey sky beckoned me. Getting up, I grabbed an umbrella and slid into my rain jacket. Then I tiptoed down the stairs so as not to awaken my folks and stepped outside.

Slowly I picked my way between the puddles until I was safely underneath the willow tree. But it wasn't long before the rain suddenly stopped. I watched as the sun popped out and the most brilliant rainbow appeared with vibrant colors of red, yellow, blue, green, orange, and purple. In awe, I looked out between the willow branches, still dripping from the downpour, and pondered the beauty of God's creation.

Just as the colors of the rainbow began to fade, a grey feather fell from the sky, landing right on top of my mud boots. It was like no other feather I had ever seen, and I'm convinced it was an angel's feather. I know it to be so because there is no other logical explanation for it. Now, some people may call me crazy, but there are angels all around us.

Mama used to say that often. She had stories about how her life was saved because angels showed up—but not always with wings and halos. She said that they looked like everyday people, but they could do extraordinary tasks. They were guardians, our supernatural protectors who were sent specifically to aid us in times of need. Like this one situation that Daddy told me about a while ago.

It was dark outside and he couldn't see nothing. He was driving home late from work and with one headlight out. The fog was thick that night. Between the tree cover and the road, it was difficult to see anything.

At one point he saw a deer and slowed the truck. Then out of nowhere another deer came from the opposite side of the road. Daddy tried to swerve so he wouldn't hit the deer. What happened next could have taken his life. After swerving, he lost control of the vehicle and ended up in a ditch.

People who swerve to avoid hitting a deer don't always live to talk about it. Especially at night when you can't see well. Where we live there are no streetlights outside of town. At night, unless there is a moon, it's pitch black. And old cars with dull headlights don't really do much good!

Mama has often instructed me, "You should never try to swerve if you are going to hit a deer. It's better to just hit it. There are other deer, but there is only one you." She was right. Daddy lost control of his car that night. He hit his head on the steering wheel and passed out.

When he didn't come home, Mama was worried sick. If he was going to be late, he always called. Mama sat up most of the night praying, and just when she was getting ready to call the police to have them search for him, he pulled into the driveway. Daddy told me that although there was blood all over the steering wheel, there was no blood on his head. He was healed and didn't even have a headache. He felt fine!

Daddy believed that because Mama was praying for him, an angel came as an answer to her prayer, touched his head, and healed his wound. He never even had a slight head pain. The doctor checked him over, and he didn't have so much as a concussion. He was miraculously healed, and he knew that it was divine.

I turned the feather over in my hand. The angel must have dropped it on the way back up to the stairway to heaven. I have always believed that angels travel up and down stairways and ladders to heaven. Mama used to tell me when I was young that angels saw the face of God.

The ground was wet from the rain, so I could easily dig out my special box Daddy had made for me where I kept my special treasures. My feather would join the other pieces already inside. As I opened the lid, I saw the necklace Mama bought for me. One time when she was thrift shopping, she happened upon a red and turquoise-beaded necklace at a second-hand store. She said that as soon as she saw it, there was no doubt in her mind it was mine! I also saw the short story Mama wrote. (I always thought it should have been published.) The title was *Why Do I Have to Go to School in a Thunderstorm?* Mama jotted it down in a small black notepad, which I kept hidden in my treasure box. To this day it is my favorite story.

Inside the box I also kept a deck of cards for rainy days when I couldn't do much of anything, especially chores. Believe me, I am not complaining about that! Oh, and another box keepsake were the two necklaces made from two copper pennies flattened by a train. I risked my life to get them.

I recollect the time I went to the train tracks alone. Mama told me never to go there by myself, but in this instance, I didn't pay much attention to her. I took two pennies and placed them on the train tracks and waited. Now, I was no fool; I didn't want to mess around with trains, so, you may be thinking, why did it appear I was? But before I tell you what I did and why, I need to tell you the story that changed our small community forever . . .

Old man Stew lived in the backwoods in an old cabin. He had a son named Bum who was a troubled kid. Bum ran away from home all the time. Most often it was from his house to our back porch. In the summertime, Mama hung our clothes out on a clothesline to dry. The wind coming off the field helped the drying process. Mama said that one day she went out back to hang up our laundry and she had a visitor on the back porch. It was Bum.

"What are you doing here?" she asked him. Did you run away again?"

"Yep, I did," he stated proud of his achievement.

"Well, if you are going sit on my porch, then go grab some clothespins and help me hang up these clothes," Mama instructed. He was helping Mama hang her laundry when Old Man Stew started yelling for his son. Bum seemed to not hear; he just continued to hang the laundry.

Mama looked at Bum and shook her head. "Boy, I know you hear your Daddy yelling for you. Go on home now, you here?" But Mama didn't let him leave before giving him a cookie and some milk. Now, come to think of it, I would have run to that back porch, too, for her cookies!

Bum gave Mama a hug and headed toward home. He wasn't a bad boy. He just came from a troubled family. No one was ever allowed in Stew's house. From what the neighbors gather (and this is purely gossip), he had a fiery temper. He was always yelling—especially at Bum. Mama and I felt sorry for the boy. He didn't deserve that. I'm sure it is why he ran away all the time. It was his way of escaping, and our home was a refuge.

Mama told me one night that Bum ran away, and pretty soon Old Man Stew came over to the house asking about his son. We didn't know his whereabouts, but Old Man Stew wasn't satisfied. He said, "I found footprints on the side of the house. Bum must have climbed down from the bedroom window." My eyes were bug-eyed. I stayed quiet, listening to Stew talk with Mama. I dared not speak. Those were my footprints. I was guilty as charged from doing that and Mama knew it. Stew eventually went home once Mama convinced him that Bum wasn't hiding at our house.

We learned later that apparently Bum was planning on hopping the train. To reach the train, however, you have to walk down to the creek, known as the rushing river. The current under that body of water is so strong that even a grown man couldn't fight it.

In order to reach the train tracks, you need to first cross the creek. There were big boulders in different shapes and sizes in that water. Some were close together while others were far enough apart that you had to hop to get from one to the other.

Of course, the rocks are slippery and dangerous, especially at night when you can't see very well. It was presumed that he slipped and fell into the rushing current. They found his body the next morning.

The sheriff said that he drowned. What a horrible way to die. It just scared me spitless to think about it. When I consider losing my breath and being stuck under water as well, it makes my skin hurt.

It was a sad day for our community. Mama loved Bum almost like he was her own son. She took care of his heart and treated him with respect. After that, she told me I was never to go to the train again. "If the train don't kill ya, then the rushing river will."

You would think that story was enough to keep me out of that body of water. No sir, not this girl! I got this crazy idea to take two pennies and lay them on the railroad tracks; then when the train came, they would flatten right out. My plan was to take the flattened coins and make them into a necklace. Now, when I get something in my head, I just cannot let it go. I knew it could be trouble, but I didn't care. I was going to do it, no matter what the cost!

That night, I waited for Mama to go to bed. Sometimes she read a book, which meant I had to wait longer. But when I heard her bedroom door shut, I knew I was in the clear.

I am not going to lie, I was afraid. It was nighttime and that's a whole other world in Kentucky. Where I live, everything out late at night wants to eat ya! I quietly snuck through my bedroom window and climbed down the ivy on the side of the house. "*Oh Lord, no!*" I exclaimed when I saw the light in my folks' bathroom turn on. *Shoot, Mama is up; I'm dead!* I whispered to myself. I stayed completely still as I dangled on the side of the house and waited for the bathroom light to shut back off. I don't know how many minutes passed before the room went dark. After staying still for another minute or so, I scurried down to the ground, jumped on the grass, and headed off into the field.

Although I brought a flashlight with me, when I turned it on, I discovered the batteries didn't work. It was so dark I couldn't see a thing! My legs felt like rubber as I ran through the fields of cornstalks, eyes darting back and forth as I went. You never knew what you would run into out there—deer, bear, or even a raccoon. I hoped that I wouldn't run into a skunk; that would be horrible and smelly!

As I ran, I berated myself. I should have listened to Mama. I had the jitters, and I didn't like being by myself. The story of Bum played in my head, and I could hear Mama's voice, "If that train don't kill ya, then the rushing river will."

What was I doing? Had I lost my mind? I was insane to be out this late! If I didn't die, Mama was going to kill me!

I ran faster than I ever had before. There were all kinds of sounds coming from the woods. My imagination of what was making those sounds was growing larger by the minute.

What if it was a big black bear? A serial killer? A mountain lion? Or a pack of ravenous wolves who could devour me? I tried to convince myself that it was simply harmless squirrels or rabbits as I continued to run.

I slipped and slid most of the way to the creek. The ground was still wet from an earlier downpour. By then I was covered in mud and the thick muck slowed my progress. My heart skipped a beat as I passed by the memorial rock where Bum's family had placed a wooden cross. Someone had been there recently, as flowers adorned the ground in front of it. The memorial was one more reminder that I shouldn't be there, but I made it that far and I wasn't going to turn back no way, no how!

When I came to the rocks my heart skipped a beat again, and I said a prayer before I started across. I picked my way slowly from one rock to another. If I messed up with just one step, Bum's fate would be mine. Finally across, I breathed a sigh of relief as I climbed the bank. I felt the train before I saw it, as the ground rumbled announcing its approach. I had a small window of opportunity to get those pennies on the tracks and myself back to safety. My knees shook as I quickly placed one shiny penny, then the other on the steel rail and ran to a nearby bush where I squatted down to wait. Seconds later the train came barreling down the tracks.

My heart was still racing as I heard footsteps. Lord have mercy, I was not alone! My mind was racing as fast as the pounding of my heart. Who on earth would be out at this time of night down by the tracks? I thought of the crazy old man who lived in the woods in an underground bunker. Rumor had it that he survived on a diet of canned beans and squirrels he shot out of trees. Clearly, I was to be his next victim! I chastised myself for not listening to my instincts better. I had sensed someone following me but thought it was just my edgy nerves. I should have paid attention. *I'm going to end up with a picture of my face tacked on a pegboard at the local grocery store with my description and the date I went missing,* The thought was scary!

I turned as the rustling grew closer. It was only a raccoon. I breathed a sigh of relief as the masked creature held his ground looking at me. I'm sure he was wondering why I was in the bushes. Raccoons are inquisitive creatures after all. Mama warned me never to get too close to a raccoon. They can seem docile at first, but if they think for one minute you are backing them into a corner, they will snarl and bare their teeth. If threatened, they will even attack. I stayed still until the raccoon sniffed the air and turned to head back the way he came. Whew! After wiping the sweat off my face, I waited until my heart rate started to return to normal.

I wondered why I always thought in worst-case scenarios. For example, what if the train came off the tracks and hit me? What if some creepy guy lived on the train and jumped off and then kidnapped me? I imagined that scenario and what if my only source of food was stale corn and rusty-tasting well water? None of the what if's sounded good to me.

Just then a drop of water hit my nose. "Oh no, rain!" I exclaimed. Now I really had something to worry about and this time it wasn't from my imagination. I still had to cross back over the rocks, and the rain would make the already slippery rocks more treacherous. What if I fell in the creek and was swallowed up by the current never to be seen again? Mama would be so mad she might kill me twice!

The train had come and gone. It was short by most standards, pulling only around twelve cars behind it. I waited for the steam to clear and went to grab those pennies. At first, they were hot to the touch, but once I got them off the train track, they were fine. Both were flat as a pancake. My mission was a success. I just had to get home safely. The rain held off as I made my way back across the rocks and the creek and back through the cornfield until I finally reached the safety of our yard. My breath came in ragged gulps as I surveyed myself. My shoes were caked with mud and my legs covered as well. I began the ascent up the lattice to reach my bedroom window. Although I slid a couple of times, I was determined to get back inside before Mama realized I was gone.

When I finally reached the window, I pushed it up and flung my leg over the ledge. My shoe fell off and hit the floor with a loud thud. *Oh great,* I thought. *That would wake Mama for sure!*

Sure enough, as if on cue, Mama called out, "What's going on up there?"

"Nothing, Mama," I replied as I frantically climbed the rest of the way in and started shedding my muddy clothes.

"Are you sure?" she asked. I knew she wasn't buying it!

"Yes, I'm sure," I replied, moving as quickly but quietly as I could.

I was in trouble. Mamas know when things aren't as they should be. They just do. You can't fool them—especially mine. To make matters worse, I don't know why, but every time I try to lie to Mama, my right eyebrow sticks up. I swear, it's a sign!

Thankfully, Mama never came up the steps. Exhausted from my efforts, I crawled in bed as soon as I got changed. But in the morning when Mama came to my bedroom, it was a muddy mess.

"Well, did you have fun last night?" she asked as she surveyed the pile on my floor.

Was this a trick question? I knew I was in trouble and that I better just confess. There was no sense messing around with Mama.

"I'm sorry, Mama." I closed my eyes and cringed, waiting for her response.

"Sorry? Sorry won't do you any good, Mary Ann," she began. "Tell me where you went."

Oh no! She used my middle name, which was the signal that life was over as I knew it. I might as well of died from the plague at this point because I knew once she heard what I had done, she wasn't going to let me go anywhere ever again! I would be stuck in the house forever, never to see the light of day. Okay, maybe I was being slightly dramatic, but I knew I was in trouble.

"I told you I didn't want you down by that creek. It's dangerous!" Mama scolded. "When are you going to understand that you are all I've got?"

Mama never raised her voice, but she did this time. She was as angry as I have ever seen.

"I don't have but one child, and I don't want anything to happen to my baby girl," she yelled. "Do you understand what I am saying to you?" Tears filled her eyes and started to run down her cheeks.

It pained my heart to know I had hurt Mama. I answered her with an emphatic "Yes!" as I started to cry. *Mama hated to see me cry.*

"Come here," she said as she grabbed me and hugged me tight. "Now, you go on and clean up this room. I want every bit of that mud gone. That is your punishment."

"Okay, Mama, fair enough." I realized I had gotten off easy.

"By the way, let's just keep this between us, okay?" she said as she started to leave the room. "I don't want your daddy getting upset over it."

"Just us. Thanks, Mama." There she was again, Ms. Pure Heart—always making things right. I love my mama.

I picked up my muddy clothes and put them in the sink to soak. Next, I cleaned up the mud, which had dried to dirt all over my floor. As I did, I breathed a prayer of thanks. Mama wasn't going to tell Daddy! No complaints from me. No sir, not me. I had a sneaky suspicion Daddy already knew about my shenanigans, but I wasn't going to push it.

I waited several days before approaching Daddy to help me drill holes in the top of the pennies so I could run a string through them. I needed his help.

"Where did you get them?" he asked as I handed the pennies over.

"They were a gift from a friend," I replied as I quickly covered my right eyebrow. The strange part was that he looked at me as if he already knew where I got them. I wondered if Mama had ratted me out, but I knew she wouldn't.

I felt bad for lying to him, but if he found out where I had been, I would have been in big trouble.

It wasn't long before he had the two holes expertly drilled into the copper pennies. He had some old leather string he wove in and *wala*—the necklaces were complete. They were just how I envisioned them, and I loved them!

"Thanks, Daddy," I said as I gave him a big hug. There was nothing my Daddy couldn't do!

The next evening after supper I grabbed the two necklaces and headed to the willow tree. The willow tree was the place where God spoke to my heart. I felt I could tell Him anything! That night I had a specific purpose in mind. I pondered the conversation I wanted to lay out to Him as I walked. I had a big request, but I know He can do miracles!

I settled myself on the ground before I started. "Lord, hear me out. It's Mary, Your friend. I hold in my hands two penny necklaces, which I risked my life for. I crossed over the dangerous rocks, facing my fears and almost succumbing to death! Well, not death, but I was close." I cleared my throat before I went on. "You know what I mean, God.

"Now, listen carefully my Lord. I will place one necklace around my neck and the other one, I will leave with You here under the willow tree. Whoever finds this necklace will be my husband. But I'll let You decide who that will be." I took a deep breath before I went on.

"I am not interested in boys now. But Mama tells me that will change when I get older. I know this sounds crazy, but You have the right one for me. I believe You can do it! Thank You, Lord."

As I concluded I heard a rumble of thunder. "That must be You, Lord! Thanks for listening." Then I headed back to my room. Later that night before I climbed into bed, I placed the necklace in my dresser. Soon I forgot it was even there. I was only ten at the time. But that was seven years ago. I am no longer interested in sneaking out at night to run to the train tracks. Now I am interested in boys. Well, one boy!

Originally, Mama told me she didn't want me to date someone unless I knew in my heart that we were going to get married. "It's just a waste of time," she'd say. "You don't need to get all close to someone who isn't going to always be in your life anyway!" I tried not to roll my eyes each time she mentioned it, but seriously, there was nothing to do in a rural town but date when you got older. Come on, Mama!

Marriage was the furthest thing from my mind. At least that's what I made others think. But to be honest, I thought about it. Come on, every girl does at least once. That is where Keith came in and things began to change. I was falling and falling hard.

Even though Daddy never said anything about when I arrived home past curfew, I was still worried I might be in trouble. I hated making Daddy upset because it always caused problems for Mama. I also hated getting up in the morning for school, but I had to. It was my senior year and this day was no different. The time dragged by and I found myself watching the clock hour after hour. I sat and listened as the teachers droned on. I craved greasy cheese pizza, and I missed Keith. The worst part about it? I couldn't have either. Sometimes life stinks!

The school was small. There were only around one hundred students in the high school. Everyone knew everyone and unfortunately gossiped about them too. I didn't want any part of it. Most of the time I stayed to myself—a loner.

Finally, the bell rang. I grabbed my bags and dashed out the door. I planned to get out of this forsaken place as quickly as possible. I was almost to my locker to drop off the few books I wouldn't need when I noticed the prettiest sunflower stuck in the side of the door. Attached was a note from Keith. It read "I love you" with a misshapen heart drawn in red ink. I smiled as I closed the locker, clicked the lock shut, and headed out the door with the sunflower held gently but firmly between my fingers. How did Keith always know the way to cheer me up? No matter what I was feeling or facing he was always there for me.

"I'm home, Mama," I yelled as I burst through the door and headed for the kitchen to grab an apple before going up to my room. I mentally calculated that I had at least three hours of homework minimum. Why do teachers give us that much homework? Notice to teachers: kids have lives too!

I had much of it done by the time Mama called me to come eat. It was a quiet meal. Suppertime came and went, and Daddy didn't say a thing. I figured I might as well just let things be. I was growing up and at least sometimes it felt as if they were trying to treat me like an adult. It was a whole new chapter in my life. They were letting me go and I could feel it! They didn't argue with me as much, and Daddy hadn't even grounded me for being late. I must admit, I liked it! I wasn't a kid anymore, and I didn't want to be treated like one either!

I decided if they were not going to talk about my infraction, then neither was I. I wasn't going to dig my own grave. What is in the past can stay there for all I am concerned. I had better fish to fry. I looked at my watch—almost 6:30. Keith said that he would stop by when he finished up work. I helped Mama clear the table, went upstairs and brushed my hair, and waited on the front porch.

Keith was not from around here; maybe that is why I was attracted to him. His folks died when he was just a child. Although he was a good kid, no one ever wanted to adopt him permanently, and so he was shifted from one foster home to another all his life. I was surprised he was not bitter about it. Instead, he let it roll off his shoulders.

A woman at the local church fostered him for a few years. Although he liked her, he never considered her his mother. Once Keith turned eighteen, he moved on and moved out. It had already been two years since he graduated. Now he worked at the local sawmill and had also started his own mowing business to make extra money. There's not much going on in this quiet town. You either worked fixing cars, farmed, or chopped wood at the sawmill. Oh yes, and there was a small run-down diner where you could wash dishes, bus tables, or waitress, which is where I worked!

The weekends were when I made the most money in tips. Everyone wanted breakfast. Bob couldn't make the biscuits and gravy fast enough. It was busy and I was saving my money. One day I would leave this place—population five hundred and twenty-seven. *Fifteen of them were speckled cows!*

Keith had been promoted to supervisor and was heading toward management. He had started to make good money working at the mill. He hated that I had to work at the diner. We talked about getting married so I could quit that job. That sounded good to me.

Keith was the type of guy who would give the shirt off his back. He was generous, loving, and kind. I don't think there was a mean bone in his body. He worked hard and adored me. Life was good when I was in his arms, and all my troubles melted away. He was like a big teddy bear. I felt safe with him by my side.

CHAPTER FOUR

THE LOOKOUT

You can't plan for everything. Even when you think you're ready, you're not. We have to just let life happen. That's hard for me sometimes. I'm a planner and like to have control over everything. But it's better just to let go and give it to God. Mama said, "The world is in God's hands and He cares for each one of us."

Keith took me to Morton Peek. *To us kids it was a secret place we found—a hideout away from everyone.* When he picked me up, his cheeks looked a bit flushed, and he kept shifting his weight from one leg to the other. He always did that when he was nervous. I wondered if he was feeling okay, but we soon settled into comfortable conversation as we got out of his truck to watch the sunset. We stood side-by-side and hand-in-hand. I laid my head against his shoulder and sighed with contentment as the sky exploded in bright colors of orange, pink, and yellow. It reminded me of my favorite ice cream—rainbow sherbet.

As the sun lowered in the sky, Keith knelt on one knee. I knew what was coming. He was going to ask me! He was really going to do it! My hands were sweating, and he was trembling.

"Mary, you're the only one for me, baby. Will you marry me?"

I looked at his blue eyes and melted. I was truly the only woman he saw. He loved me with all his heart, and I loved him more. A woman knows when a man loves her. She can feel it and see it!

"Yes, yes!" I exclaimed and gave him the biggest kiss ever!

He placed the diamond engagement ring on my finger. It was gorgeous and looked good against my skin color. I had never seen such beautiful diamonds in my whole life. In fact, I don't think I've ever seen a diamond 'cuz Mama's wedding ring was a simple gold band. She didn't even have diamonds on it.

"Is it real?" I asked as I held my hand out in front of me to admire it. It shimmered in the fading sunlight.

"Of course, it is!" Keith responded with pride. "Fourteen carat gold. The jeweler gave me an authentic certificate for two diamonds."

"The ring is just beautiful." I was thrilled with it until I had an unsettling thought. "Did you ask my folks?"

"Well, not exactly," he stammered, not meeting my eyes.

"You mean you didn't ask my daddy for my hand in marriage?"

"No, I didn't." Keith said hesitantly.

"Keith, Daddy is going to be mad. You have to ask him first." I was firm about this.

"Look, I don't know how to do all this. I never had a dad." He sounded rather defensive.

"I understand. Let me tell him then," I suggested as I put my arms around him. I didn't want to spoil this beautiful moment.

Daddy didn't like Keith at first, but we had been dating for a year and Keith was growing on him. I panicked thinking how I would deliver the message of my engagement to him. I pictured myself walking into the living room. "Hi, Daddy, guess what? I'm getting married," I would say rather nonchalantly, like it was something that happened every day. Or another scenario might be, "Hi, Daddy, this is so funny. Keith proposed to me, gave me a ring, and we are getting married! Isn't that grand?" I shook my head in frustration. Nope. That would never work. *I'm dead,* I thought as I pondered this new dilemma.

Proper etiquette for marrying is to ask the daddy first. If there is no daddy in the picture, then it goes to ask the mama first. If there is no mama, then it is okay to just ask—but hey, you've got to get it right.

Keith apologized. I knew he felt bad about creating a situation over what was to be a happy moment for us. "I didn't think about telling your daddy," he admitted. "I just wanted to marry you. But I'll make it right, Mary. I'll come over to the house after I get off work tomorrow, and I'll break the news."

I let out a sigh of relief. I laughed at the thought of Keith dying over me breaking the news to Daddy. Not really, but it was nice to be released from having to be the one to tell him.

I took off the engagement ring and put it in my pocket before I got out of the truck. I hated to take it off, but if Daddy or Mama saw it on my finger before Keith asked, I would really be in trouble. "Good night. I love you," I said to the man of my dreams as I headed to the house. Everything in the world seemed right . . . but that was about to change.

That night I had a horrible dream. I was washing dishes and set my engagement ring on the windowsill. As I was washing a coffee cup, it slipped out of my hands and hit the sill. The cup splintered and the ring went tumbling down into the drain where it disappeared. Desperately I reached into the small hole to find it, but I couldn't. Each time I tried my hands would get bigger. "I will never see my beautiful ring again!" I cried out and then awoke.

You might laugh, but I was terrified. I felt my hand for the ring, which I had put on again as soon as I got upstairs. Thank the Lord on high, it was there and that was just a dream. A horrible dream, but a dream nonetheless.

I woke up again later with the bad dream a distant memory. I hummed as I got ready for school with the thought that two very important things were going to happen soon. One, I was finally going to graduate from high school! Two, Keith was going to break the news to Mama and Daddy of his plans to marry me.

Although we had planned for Keith to come over and talk with Daddy, we talked on the phone before school and decided with graduation that night, now would not be the right time. "But what about the ring?" I inquired, nervous from last night's dream. "How am I going to hide it?" Keith suggested I take it off, but after the dream I definitely didn't want to. I would just have to hide it one more day, at least till after the graduation ceremony.

I ran out the door without saying anything to Mama. The door banged shut after me, and I heard Mama run out onto the porch and yell, "Mary, Mary, are you going to eat breakfast?"

"No, Mama, they need me to be early at school. I am helping set up for graduation," I replied as I was running down the street to the school.

"Daddy and I will see you soon," she said with a wave. "We're proud of you!"

"Thanks, Mama. Bye!" I waved as I ran off.

I was relieved she didn't see the ring on my finger, but I felt horrible. Like I had lied to her. I said a quick prayer to God asking for forgiveness. I remembered what He said in His Word, "Honor your father and mother." Let's just say at that moment I wasn't doing a good job at it!

My senior year had gone by in a flash, and I was ready to be out of school. No more gross lunches with stale pizza and withered fries, or boring pep rallies. No more crusted gum wads snagging my tights from under my desk, and no more mean girls and smelly football guys. No more test or math homework late at night. Now all I had to do was work at the diner and spend time with Keith until our wedding day. We were not in a rush to get married. We had plenty of time, or so I thought!

Before graduation, my teachers had asked me if I was planning to attend college. I thought about it briefly, but most people around here never made it past high school. Mama and Daddy encouraged me to go, but I was ready to be done with school. That's not to say I won't ever go. But if I ever do, I want to get a degree in business management. I dreamed of one day owning my own business. Then I wouldn't have to answer to anyone besides myself.

There is never any real work to be done the last day of school, but especially as a senior. So, the teachers asked if anyone was willing to decorate for graduation. I volunteered and helped a small group of students line up chairs and decorate the football field. Only fifty out of one hundred of my classmates were actually able to graduate. Of course, I was one of them. Why would anyone want to stick around another year?

That night as my classmates and I stood in line to receive our diplomas I had to pinch myself. I couldn't believe that I was about to graduate. I looked out into the audience and saw Daddy, Mama, and Keith there to cheer for my achievements. It was nice to have their support.

Our principal, Mr. Besson, stood at the podium to address the class. He was a short, balding middle-aged man with the most irritating voice I'd ever heard. If you ever tried to talk through a soda straw that would be it.

"Congratulations, Seniors, you did it!" I sniffled just a bit. He began as folks erupted in applause. "You made it through four fantastic years at Kettlesville High. I speak not only for myself and our staff when we say, we are proud of you and all your accomplishments. We have worked hard with your folks to prepare you for the next journey of your lives . . ."

I don't remember much else from his speech but was brought to attention when I heard him call my name, and I walked up to the platform. We shook hands and he handed me my diploma. Moving my tassel to the other side of my graduation cap, I went back to my seat and sat down.

Before we were dismissed, he gave us a charge. "Today, each one of you holds in your hand a diploma. This is not just a piece of paper, but a key to open the door to your future. With this key you can seek higher education. It will allow you gainful employment in the world we live in today.

"You can do anything you set your mind to. Never give up and remember your roots. Never forget where you came from and who you are. We are proud of your perseverance and determination and look forward to seeing what you will do."

As he concluded, everyone stood and applauded. We stood with them as all of us graduating seniors cheered and threw our caps in the air. I had finally graduated!

I looked around and it was as if everything stood still like a moment etched in time. It was then I looked over at a childhood friend, Bubba Thompson, and suddenly found myself in an embrace. I cringed because since childhood Bubba has always smelled like peas and rotten soup. Oh well, I smiled in excitement. Anyways, we did it! Thank goodness at that moment another classmate tapped his shoulder. That was my opportunity to bolt. As I turned around, I looked over at Mama. If a look on someone's face could speak, hers did. She couldn't stop smiling and clapping. I could tell she was proud.

I kept smiling too. It felt amazing to be done with school. Although I had dreaded going year after year, somehow, I had made it through. A loud buzzing pulled me back to the present, as I felt something on my leg. You must be kidding me! A bee had flown under my gown. I freaked out and started smacking my legs to get the bee out. Probably not the best idea as I felt him sting me as I tried to unzip my gown and give him a bigger opportunity to get out!

I sensed the stares of everyone as they watched me dance, scream, and wave my hands.

Bubba said, "Looks like Mary's dancing." Everyone started to laugh.

"I wasn't dancing you idiot," I hissed. "I had a bumble bee stuck underneath my gown." Bubba was stupid as far as I was concerned and often didn't understand even simple communication. As Mama would say, "Lord have mercy!" I am not trying to be mean, but it's hard to be patient with someone who is stupid and reeks of body odor. I wish that boy would take a shower occasionally.

Finally free of the bee, I looked out at the crowd and saw Mama, Daddy, and Keith with the cheesiest grins watching me. My face flushed red. Keith walked over and gave me a congratulatory kiss. "I'm so proud of you," he said. I smiled up at him—that is, until he brought out his cell phone to show me the pictures he had captured of my bee dance. I rolled my eyes. Just what I needed. Pictures of me looking all crazy flailing like a fish spread out all over social media.

We turned to head out when Bubba came up to say goodbye. "Thanks, Mary, for making me laugh," Bubba said as he started to leave with his family.

"You're welcome, Bubba. That's what I live for—to make you laugh. Ha!" On second thought, Bubba wasn't all that bad, just smelly.

After we arrived home, Mama brought out a graduation cake she had made for the occasion. We were all sitting and chatting in the living room when Keith gave me a familiar look. I knew he was going to break the news.

"Mary, will you go get your mama?" Keith prompted, as Mama had gone back into the kitchen. Daddy knew what was going on and wasted no time to talk with Keith.

"What you got on your mind, boy?" Daddy asked with arms crossed. Keith wiped his hands on his jeans and took a deep breath. He looked up at Daddy's face, which was intimidating to begin with. That and the fact that he was six feet and four inches tall. Keith was tall, but Daddy was taller.

Keith took a deep breath and started, "I want you to know that Mary and I have been dating now for a few years. I have been respectful of her and a perfect gentleman."

"Yes, go on," Mama said, as she had now joined us in the living room her eyes beaming with excitement.

"I know I should have come to both of you first, but not having any folks, I didn't really realize how to do it. I asked your daughter to marry me, and she said yes. I gave her a ring and we are now engaged. I didn't want you to hear it from her. I wanted to tell you."

A long silence followed before Mama blurted out, "I am so happy for you both!" She turned to look at Daddy, who had still said nothing. (*She gently nudged him in the arm.*) "And your daddy is happy too."

Finally, Daddy spoke. "I understand, Keith, and I appreciate you telling me. Although I think you two are too young to get married, if that is what you want, then I cannot stop you. But don't you go breaking my daughter's heart," he warned.

"I won't! I love her." Keith was overjoyed and relieved.

"Well, are you going to show us the ring?" Mama asked as she grabbed my hand. "It is gorgeous!" She was excited as she turned my hand to catch the light.

Hugging me she said, "I am so happy for you. I knew this day would come. I just didn't think it would be so soon!"

"Don't worry, Mama. We aren't in a rush and have plenty of time."

"Darling, you'll be married before you know it, and then a family will come."

Keith was learning how to communicate with my family. I could tell he missed having parents. He didn't have anyone to run things by for advice or wisdom. I wish I could have met Keith's real parents. It seemed to bother me more than it bothered him. All I did was hear about it where he actually lived through it.

I sighed as I looked at Keith and then my daddy. Keith wanted my daddy's approval, but there was a wall around Daddy's heart, and it was hard for Keith to knock it down. Daddy didn't trust anybody, and it took a while for him to learn people. Time and staying around is all that worked for him. There was no way around it.

Keith understood what it felt like to feel alone emotionally. That is what made us strong together. We knew each other's weaknesses. Both of us struggled with a father figure. Even though my father was alive, he wasn't emotionally well. Keith never had a father and that left him feeling abandoned. It was a bigger issue than we knew, but we both had learned to shove the pain in the past and believed that being madly in love would solve all the world's ills.

Later that night after Keith had gone and I was upstairs getting ready for bed, I thought back to when I was younger. Back then, I had a notebook in which I used to doodle. I must have signed my name about a hundred times. After each one I added make-believe last names, pretending to be married. None of the names ever sounded right until Walker came on the scene. Mary Ann Walker. I liked the sound of that last name! *Yep, that's the one,* I thought back then. And now it was going to be true.

Time was passing quickly. We were both excited to get married. We decided to remain pure until our wedding day. Believe me, that was a hard choice to make. I was attracted to him and he was attracted to me, but we decided it would be better to be married first! Mama and Daddy were happy about that.

Many nights I either stayed up talking to Mama or planning the wedding in my head. I wanted it all. A fairytale wedding. Mama always said, "Mary, you're a treasure and a treasure is worth waiting for." Finally, I understood, and I agreed with her.

I thought after Keith proposed that we would wait for a few years. But Mama was right, and we decided to get married towards the end of summer. I was eighteen years old and both of us just couldn't wait. Daddy put in extra overtime hours at work to make some additional money. He wanted to give me the best wedding ever.

I remember that July he was sober for the whole month. He just suddenly stopped drinking. He didn't say anything to anyone. Mama and I couldn't figure it out. Something must have happened to make him quit, but he was being tight-lipped about the matter.

During that time, he built Keith and I a dresser. It was gorgeous with fancy wood inlays and brass handles. I loved it even more because my daddy made it for us with his own two hands. Preparations continued as July turned to August and suddenly the day of our wedding had arrived.

I stood in front of the long oval mirror in the dressing room of the church we had attended since I was small. Mama stood behind me. She was wearing a royal blue dress with white pearls. Tansy, Mama's best friend, had done her hair in curlers. The soft curls framed her face and made her look even more beautiful. She had even put on red lipstick and painted her nails for the occasion.

I continued to look at myself in the mirror. My ivory dress was simple but gorgeous. I loved the color and how it offset my complexion. "Here, baby, this is for you," and Mama handed me a beautifully wrapped box in silver wrapping paper.

"Do you want me to open it now?" I asked, "or do you want me to wait?"

"No, open it now. Go on." She clapped her hands. She was more excited about the gift than I was. I gently pulled off the paper and opened the blue velvet box. Inside was another set of pearls, which I recognized.

"Mama, these are the pearls you wore when you married Daddy," I exclaimed, holding them up to my bare neck.

"Yes, they are, and I want you to have them. They're yours now. Smiling, she took them from my hand and began to clasp them around my neck.

"Really?" I asked. I was speechless. *(Even though I smiled deep down inside, I could not help but remember my prayer under the willow tree and the two pennies I flattened down by the railroad tracks. But I knew it was only a prayer of a child. I was all grown up now, so freshwater pearls would do just fine!)* Mama connected the clasp and we both looked in the mirror. They fit perfectly with my dress.

"I have never seen you look so beautiful," she exclaimed with a huge smile. "Your eyes are filled with so much love. Keith is the luckiest man alive." Then carefully she gave me a big hug and a gentle kiss on my cheek so as not to ruin my makeup.

"Thank you, Mama. I love you and Daddy with all my heart," I said as I squeezed her hand.

"I know you do, and we love you too," she said quietly. "You ready, darling?"

"Ready as I'll ever be." I pulled my eyes away from the mirror and turned to look at her. "But I am not ready to leave you."

"I know, baby, it's hard for me to let you go!" she said as she wiped away the tears that threatened to ruin my makeup. "That old devil, Keith; why did he go and steal my baby girl?"

I gave her a final hug and then stepped out of the dressing room and made my way around back to where Daddy and I would walk into the church. He was already standing there when I arrived, smiling as he saw me. "There is my baby girl," he said. "You look beautiful."

"Daddy, thank you . . ." I began, but he interrupted me.

"No, baby, thank *you* for being the best daughter a daddy could have. You are my baby girl, and I am proud of who you are."

Tears welled up in my eyes.

"Now, don't you go crying and ruin your makeup." He put his arms around me. "Today is your day, a joyful day."

I took a deep breath and grabbed his arm as the music began to play and he walked me down the aisle.

The church pews in the chapel were wood, and Mama had decorated the ends of them with sunflowers and yellow and white bows. It was just our family and Keith's boss, along with some of the church members. A quaint wedding. Keith looked divine. He was wearing an ivory tuxedo with a yellow bow tie. His blue eyes shimmered like the ocean that day. Our eyes met as Daddy walked me down the aisle, and there was no mistaking that boy was in love with me.

We exchanged our vows in front of everyone and then had a celebration out back of the church. Daddy roasted a whole pig, and Mama and the church ladies made a feast to celebrate our wedding day. I will never forget Daddy grabbing Mama and holding her close and dancing. It had been a long time since he looked at her that way. I liked Daddy without alcohol; it was so much better.

Keith and I didn't take a honeymoon, but I wish we would have. We were trying to be responsible with our money and save for a ticket so we could get out of that small town. We lived in a tiny apartment attached to a garage and quickly fell into a rhythm of married life.

Near our apartment was a small farm owned by our neighbors, Clarence and Tansy. Tansy was friends with my Mama. I know that many young people tend to pass by older people and not give them a second glance. Not this girl! I learned that older people have lots of wisdom and stories.

Keith and I worked hard to save money; we were determined in our hearts to leave. Some months we saved more than others. That was usually my fault because I bought extra things here and there. It was hard being a newlywed couple on a tight budget; there were many things we needed but only could afford a few at a time.

I worked hard as well, but my pay wasn't consistent because tips were a large part of my wages. Being a waitress was challenging work. I remember one time a group of people came in and only left me a dollar tip even though I had waited on them for three hours, serving them soup, salad, their meal, and finally dessert. It was frustrating. I really think if people cannot tip their waitress, then they should stay home and cook their own meal.

Bob Martin owned the diner where I worked. He was a nice enough man and was fair. He came down with a bad cold that he couldn't seem to get over. Eventually, they put him in the care clinic for about two weeks. We were all praying for him. Soon after, everything turned around and they let him come home. It seemed he was going to be fine, but within a week, he got sick again with pneumonia and died suddenly.

The doctors said it was complications from the pneumonia. Bob never married and had no children to pass the business along to. Charlie and I were his only employees. He did the dishes and cleaned, and I bussed the tables and waitressed. It was a small business for sure, but that's all you needed in a small-town setting.

With no owner to run the restaurant, the diner closed, and the bank took it over. It was sad. There were already so few businesses in our town. When another closed not long after, everyone knew it was either a divorce or a death. Neither was ever good news. So, Keith got his wish because I was now officially out of work. That meant I could sleep in and have the weekends off, which sounded good.

Mama, Daddy, Keith, and I went to Bob's funeral. It was a proper burial, and we gave our condolences to his younger brother, Mark, who had come in from out of town. Mama and Daddy let him stay at the house in my old room for the time he was there.

Finally, we had some good news. A new sawmill was to be built, as the business was going to expand to the city. They needed a supervisor to run the operation and chose Keith. He was one of the hardest workers at the plant and I always knew he would be promoted. I just didn't think it was going to be this soon!

After the news about Bob, the loss of my job, and then the job transfer, I was stressed out. I carried all my stress in my stomach and felt sick for days. I didn't feel well at all and spent most of the day with my face in the toilet. I thought for sure that was the death of me. Keith was concerned and we thought I might have the flu. Keith didn't want to take any chances, especially after the death of Bob. He kept pressuring me to see a doctor. Mary Ann Walker stubborn? Yes, but I finally agreed after weeks of being constantly sick. We were not prepared for what we were about to hear.

I made the doctor's appointment for lunchtime so Keith could go with me. I was shaking while waiting in the room for the doctor. So much so that my bottom stuck to the paper on the examination table. I was embarrassed. (*I hate waiting rooms and I hate doctors.*)

When the doctor came into the examination room, he acted like he wasn't late at all. But he was, and I was frustrated. He looked me over, asked a few questions, and sent his nurse in to draw some blood. Oh, I hate needles, and I hated the additional twenty-minute wait! I was ready to go.

Let me just say that I couldn't find anything to like about the visit except the fact my husband was with me so that I was not alone. I never liked being alone. Oh, I could be by myself sometimes, but eventually I would yell for Mama. Sometimes just hearing her voice from another room was fine with me.

The doctor came in to talk with Keith and me. "It should take a few days to get the blood test back; however, I found in our first test a certain hormone. What it means is you are officially pregnant!" Well now, that made perfect sense. I considered the bloating, the nausea, and the constipation. "Congratulations to you both!" he said. I thought, *yes right, I feel horrible.*

But that didn't dampen my excitement about the baby. I was excited and nervous at the same time. The unknown of what would happen to my body was a little unsettling. Everyone tends to give advice about being pregnant. But I heard more horror stories than good ones. Keith could barely go to work whenever he had stomach issues. I couldn't imagine if he experienced the nausea, constipation, and bloating I was enduring! I could hear Mama's voice, "Lord have mercy!"

Keith and I looked at each other intently. I gave a nervous giggle. We were relieved to know that I wasn't dying after all. On the way home, though, I was purposefully quiet. Keith tried to get me to laugh by turning on the radio. He had this animated way of lip-syncing to songs. It almost always made me laugh, but nothing seemed to work at that moment for this stress bomb, including that Keith way of charming me. Nothing could get me out of this funk. Everything seemed overwhelming, and the thought of being someone's mother completely terrified me. I had always dreamed of this moment. But now that the moment was here, it seemed surreal.

"How could this happen to me, Mary Ann Walker?" I blurted out.

My dream was that I was supposed to leave this town and be a business owner or work in the fashion industry. At that moment, life hit me like a freight train. I wondered if I would ever reach my dream now. Honestly, I was doubting myself and really needed to step back and evaluate the situation.

Don't get me wrong—I wanted a family, and I loved being married. But a baby so soon? I wasn't ready at all. I remember Mama used to say, "No woman is ever ready to have a baby, but when the time comes, she will rise to the challenge and be the best mama she can be." *(Mama certainly was for me.)*

Keith took my hand, and his gentle caress assured me everything was going to be all right. I felt safe in his arms. He had a way about him to still my anxious heart, even when I was going crazy inside with so many thoughts running through my head. He kept me steady.

Unable to keep this to ourselves, we drove over to Mama and Daddy's house and broke the news. Mama screamed in excitement, "I'm going to be a grandma!" She was already dreaming of quilting patterns and baby blankets. Daddy, on the other hand, said just one word— "Congratulations!" Then he opened the fridge, grabbed a beer, and walked out the back door. I was looking for his approval, but was glad that he at least said something. After my wedding he went back to drinking. We had learned to tread on eggshells around him when he was depressed and turned to alcohol.

The door shut behind Daddy and I began to cry. It was a combination of my fear of being a mother and the hormones. Mama immediately came over and put her arms around me and consoled me in my emotional state. "I'll talk to him later, honey. Don't let him bother you. You know he is happy for you. It's just the depression he battles that makes him so moody."

Mama always kept peace between the two of us, God love her. She had the patience of Job. You may not know who Job is. He was a man I learned about at Vacation Bible School one summer when I was a child whose whole world got turned upside down. I went for one full week every day from one o'clock to five o'clock. It gave the kids in our small town something to do. One of my fondest memories is that we would play ball and eat cookies and cheddar fish crackers. Then we would listen to some stories told straight out of the Bible.

Now Job . . . well, he had a rough go of it. He lost everything and then he almost died! I remember Mama was in a car accident once, and it took her a long time to recover. She was single then, before she met Daddy, and lost everything—her house, her car, and her job! She never complained; she simply trusted God. That's when He sent her Daddy. They fell in love and the rest was history. Mama had always been strong in faith. Because of the road she'd had to walk with Daddy, she was convinced that nothing was impossible with God. The same couldn't be said about me. I always struggled with trying to understand who I was. I never doubted God, I just didn't understand why He did certain things. It was beyond me! But thankfully, it seemed Mama had enough faith for the both of us.

Over time Daddy's drinking became worse. Mama was exhausted dealing with him at times, but she never showed it. I asked her periodically, "Mama, how long are you going to put up with this?"

"Baby, he's my husband. However long it takes," she always replied. The doctors had told him if he kept it up, he wouldn't make it to his sixtieth birthday. He was fifty-five now. Nothing could sway Mama. She kept praying and believing for a miracle.

I swore to myself that I would never be like him. There was absolutely no alcohol allowed in our home, ever! Keith knew that if he even started acting like my daddy in any way, I would be gone, and our marriage would be over. I knew I couldn't tolerate what Mama did, and I was unwilling to put myself in that position. Daddy was fortunate to have such a good woman sticking by his side. I hope I can be half the mother and wife to my husband, Keith, that Mama is to Daddy.

Occasionally, we would eat supper with them, but most evenings we spent time with Tansy and Clarence. Mama always invited us over for supper on Friday nights. She had the gift of hospitality and we never knew what she would surprise us with. This week the menu was buttermilk fried chicken, green tomato pie, and butter beans. There was nothing like Mama's sweet tea, which was more sugar than water or tea. I must have consumed four glasses of it.

I completely cleaned my plate before I pushed away from the table. My belly was full, and the baby was satisfied too! "Well, Mama, we should get home. I am tired and it's been a long day," I told her as I helped her clean off the table. "Tell Daddy I love him when he gets up!" and I gave her a kiss. As usual Daddy had passed out in his chair from drinking too much. No surprise there. We had learned to live with it. Mama was so patient with him.

"Night, Daddy!" I said as I left the house. He never stopped snoring.

Mama walked us out onto the porch. "Be safe, baby! I sure love you, darling. You take care of my grandbaby in there, you here?" she told Keith and I both.

"I love you, Mama," I said, giving her a final wave goodbye.

"And I love you, baby girl," she replied.

On the way home, Keith was unusually quiet. He didn't say much at all. Then as we pulled into the driveway, he finally shared what had been on his heart. "I'm going to take that promotion and the job in the cities." (Just so you know, when I say, "the cities," I am referring to an area where there is a higher population of people. Certainly not like our rural town. The area is a few hours away by car. People travel to Kettlesville to rest and we travel to the cities for opportunities to work.) "I've been considering it and I think it will be good for us."

Sometimes you must jump when something like this comes along. It's not every day an opportunity arises, especially when you live in a rural town. When Keith first told me about the opportunity, I was happy for him. Of course, I wanted to celebrate his success. He was proud of himself and extremely joyful he would have the opportunity to provide even better for his family. It had always been a dream of his to work in the city, and he took his leadership role seriously.

"I think we should," I responded. "I am so proud of you, Keith," and I gave him a kiss. But to be honest, in my heart I had questions. We would be leaving everything that was familiar, including my folks. But I said nothing. He smiled and gave me a big bear hug!

The next morning, we talked to Tansy and Clarence about the promotion. We needed their advice. At first they seemed okay with our decision but were concerned about us being far away from family since a baby was on the way. Tansy, however, was concerned about Mama. She knew how bad she wanted grand-babies and reminded me, "No Grandma wants to live far away from their grandchildren." I knew she was right, but we needed the money starting a new family. The problem was they knew no job around here that was going to pay Keith as much as he would make in the cities. I was happy Tansy laid out her concern. In the end they gave us their blessing!

Since Keith had always been a foster kid, he never felt like the homes where they placed him was really home. Now he wanted the chance to buy his own home and have a place for his family to always live. This was his opportunity to make something of himself, and I didn't want to stand in his way just because I had anxiety about moving, or change. I chose to let him live in the moment and instead of telling him what I really thought, I blurted out, "So, when do we move?"

"As soon as we buy a house. With the new raise we will have more money than we ever dreamed."

Once he mentioned the more money part, my heart changed towards the whole situation. Money isn't bad. It's good, not to mention we needed it with a baby on the way. Immediately my heart fluttered with excitement. This meant we could finally get out of this place! But what about my mama and daddy? I didn't want to leave them. My emotions went up and down like a roller coaster about the upcoming move. Being an adult is hard at times!

Just as I was about to open my mouth with more questions, Keith placed his hands on my belly. "I haven't even met you yet and I already love you," he exclaimed. That was all I needed to hear. We were a family and ready for a new chapter in our lives. Bring it on!

CHAPTER FIVE

CHANGES

*L*et's face it—nobody likes to change. Change is tough, but life has a way of throwing you into it headfirst. Whether we like it or not, change is coming, so don't freak out. Walk through it bravely. You'll be better in the end. The main thing is, don't give up! Sometimes high winds would blow in the fields. I remember Mama would hold me saying, "That wind is howling. You know what that means darling?" I smiled, "What Mama?" "It means change is coming!"

It took a few weeks to pack up our belongings. The truck was overloaded, because Mama sent us off with boxes of canned fruits and vegetables, bags of freshly baked bread, homemade cookies, and leftovers from supper. Daddy gave me a hug. I could tell he was tired and sad. He was going to miss me!

"Daddy, I'll visit, and I want you to know, I love you," I said as I kissed him on the cheek and squeezed his hand. Hugging was a little hard with my huge belly.

"I love you, too, and I wish you the best," he replied. He tried to smile, but I could tell he was fighting back tears as well.

"Bye, Dad," Keith said as he held out his hand to shake Dad's.

"Now don't you go calling me Dad when you're taking my baby away, thinking that will make this any easier," he said with a furrowed brow.

"Oh Daddy . . ." I said as he smiled at me and winked. I was his baby girl.

A co-worker of Keith's named Buck told us of a neighborhood he grew up in when he lived in the cities. His folks had a home there and it was for sale. Evidently the houses in the neighborhood were older and less expensive than the newer homes. Perhaps it would fit our budget! We were hopeful.

Keith called Buck's folks to talk about renting their house. We wanted a big backyard for our kids. Even though we might not need it yet, we were preparing for our future. They talked for a while when suddenly Buck's dad offered to sell us the house instead of renting it to us. That was a big step. My eyes widened as I listened to the conversation on the other line. I wasn't going to miss a conversation like that. This had taken a sudden shift.

"I'll need to discuss it with Mary first," Keith interjected as they concluded the call. "I'll get back with you in a couple of days."

Looking at me, Keith said with excitement, "We obviously need to go see the house. Do you feel up to the trip?"

"Of course! I wouldn't miss it," I exclaimed. I was about five months along and my belly was getting big, but it's not like it was an all-day trip.

That Saturday we left early in the morning to head to the cities. We found the neighborhood pretty easily. It was well-kept in an older, more established community. We turned down a couple of roads until we found the house. It was a cute bungalow. There was moss green siding on it and a large porch where I envisioned putting two chairs that we could sit in outside on summer evenings. The backyard was small but perfect for us right now. Buck's folks greeted us at the door and invited us inside. It had three tiny bedrooms and a small bathroom with a tub and vanity. I was ecstatic because although small it had a garden tub. I couldn't wait to take a bubble bath. (*My own tub rubber duckie. Here I come!*)

The neighborhood was quaint and had great curb appeal. Everyone took care of their place, which, now that I think of it, was creepy. I really hoped there was no secret club for "perfect" homemakers around here. (*Having weird neighbors was not my cup of tea.*)

The bungalow was close to the fire station. That meant homeowners insurance would be less expensive. That was fine by me. Although I wasn't planning on burning down the house, but Keith said it's good to have insurance just in case!

We made the decision to take the jump and buy our first home. But after we agreed, my mind shifted to overdrive as I considered the huge responsibility. I went into utter panic. Our mortgage was going to be for thirty years and to me that was a long time. I was wondering if we would even be able to pay off the house. Thirty years? Lord help us!

When the closing day arrived, Keith helped me into our car to make the drive back into the cities where we would complete the paperwork. I should have been ecstatic, but I wasn't. As we drove, all sorts of thoughts raced through my mind. I pictured a mortgage guy with greasy, slicked-back black hair and a mustache that he twirled nervously with his fingers. "Please sign here on the dotted line," he said slyly. "This is where you sign your life away!" he smirked as he handed Keith a long pen and let out a long evil "bahaha."

Next, he shoved the contract in front of me. As I read, I realized it didn't say a thirty-year note but 300 years until the loan would be paid! "Three hundred years?" I questioned.

The greasy-haired mortgage guy pushed the pen into my hand, "Oh, don't mind that extra zero. Just sign the contract." My heart raced and the room seemed to cave in. I looked to Keith for help, but he seemed oblivious to the trap.

"Well, we will both be dead long before this loan is paid," I pointed out.

"Better now than never," the mortgage guy said as he took the signed contract.

Then my thoughts immediately came back to the present. "Keith, are you sure we should buy this house?" I was still worried about the financial commitment.

"Yes, it's perfect for us." He reached over and squeezed my hand to reassure me. He was right, of course. I was being silly. Everyone has a mortgage nowadays, right?

It took a total of four hours to get to the cities. We should have been there sooner but being pregnant I had to pee often. I never liked using the bathroom at a gas station without buying something, so I had a collection of gum, chips, and candy bars in the back seat!

The closing was uneventful, and the mortgage "guy" was a pretty woman in her thirties who completely put us at ease. After signing and putting our initials on numerous documents to the closing company's satisfaction, our realtor smiled and handed us the keys to our little bungalow. I smiled too. Finally, the excitement hit. Once we pulled up to our new home, I began to tear up. I was overwhelmed with joy. Keith thought it was because I was pregnant, but it was more than that. We were home, our very first home!

It was a busy weekend. We got our things moved in, in no time at all. It was an exhausting few days, but we were in good shape. On Monday morning I drove Keith to work so I could have the car. I was ready to decorate. Poor Keith! By the time he got home from work, I was already showing him swatches of paint colors for every room of the house!

"I'm going to cancel cable so you can't watch anymore of those home renovation shows!" he said with a laugh. But I knew he was just as excited as I was.

We painted the baby's room yellow. It was bright and sunny but gave no hint of the baby's sex. We had decided not to tell anyone until the baby was born. But that didn't stop Mama. She bugged me each time she called to chat. She hoped one day I would cave and just come out with it. But Keith and I wanted to wait to have the big reveal until our baby's birth, and that was that!

It took a while for me to get used to living in the cities. Everywhere we went people were in a hurry. I was having a tough time adjusting to this new life. I missed the quiet of our rural home. I never realized how much sound came from the freeways. Our new home was close to one and although they had built a brick wall to block the sound, we could still hear the cars as they zoomed past.

Even though I wanted out of Kettlesville, to be honest, I missed it. I regretted moving away from home. Honestly, I cannot believe that I am even saying that! But there is nothing like living at a slow pace, even with cow manure all around.

Everyone at the factory loved Keith. He was doing well in his new job, but the only problem was he was never home. His hours were crazy, and he didn't have seniority like he did back home. It felt like he was starting over, and he was determined to prove himself reliable.

It was a lonely time. With only one car, I was forced to stay home unless I got up early to drive him to work. People in my neighborhood kept to themselves pretty much. Don't get me wrong—they were nice, but not very friendly.

Where I grew up it wasn't uncommon to have a neighbor drop by for a sweet tea and visit for a while on your front porch. Our porch was the focal point of the house. Mama took extra care in keeping the white porch swing painted and pretty flowers in pots. Tears sprang to my eyes as I thought of those happy memories. How I missed my home!

Later that week I drove Keith to work and then headed to the doctor's office for him to do another ultrasound and make sure everything was fine. I really wanted Keith to be there with me at the appointment, but since his responsibilities had doubled at the new job, he couldn't leave his work as easily as he did before. I laid down on the examining table as the doctor checked my vitals and then checked the baby. "Well, everything looks really good," he began, "but based on your measurements the arrival date might be sooner than you were originally told."

I was stunned when I found out the news, and when I am stressed, I eat. Being pregnant gave me a good excuse. That night I cooked an amazing meal for Keith. I baked cheesy macaroni and pan-fried chicken. For dessert I made cinnamon apple pie topped with vanilla whipped cream. I was proud of my culinary accomplishments. I used to watch Mama in the kitchen cook for our family. Most of the time she thought I was ignoring her, but I was secretly paying close attention.

As Keith pulled into the driveway, I lit some scented candles. They smelled like raspberries and cream. I loved when I saw the headlights of his white truck roll up toward the house. It was the highlight of my day. Once my husband was home, everything made sense again!

Keith walked in and took a sniff in the air. "Something smells good," he said as he greeted me with a warm smile and a gentle caress.

"How was your day?" I asked.

"It was long. I am exhausted." He noticed the dinner table, which I had set with tapered candles for extra ambiance. "This looks good. I'm starving!" he said with a laugh. "I'm the luckiest man alive. Thanks, baby."

It was already late by the time we finished supper. Keith helped me clean up and put the food away, and we headed to bed. He fell asleep almost immediately—as usual. Not me. I found myself thinking about Mama and Daddy and all the things we had left behind. I recalled Mama's friend, Tansy, who was like a mother to me. Thinking of her dear soul brought a smile to my face. She was an incredible woman—selfless, generous, and wise.

Tansy and Mama had been best friends for as long as anyone could remember. It was Tansy's rental house where we had lived right after we had first married. Tansy was a fun-loving southern woman with a big heart. She was there for Mama through everything, and I thought of her as my second mother.

Mama and Tansy had grown up going to church together. They had baked together and even held a few classes for quilting together. As the day of the baby's birth neared, the two of them devised a plan behind my back. I knew those two were up to something, because they were pleasantly quiet with phone conversations. Anyone knows that when people get to be quiet, they are up to something! I was just waiting to find out what it was.

Suddenly the phone rang. As if she knew I had been thinking about her and Tansy, Mama called. "Why are you answering the phone?" she asked. "I thought you would be in bed by now."

"I am. Is everything all right, Mama? It's kind of late. Is there something else you want?"

"Yes, everything is fine. I just wanted to see how you were feeling."

"Good," I said. "What do you want, Mama?" I still was startled by the rather late call.

"Tansy and I have a surprise for you. We are going to throw you a baby shower."

"You are? I knew the two of you were up to something," I replied with a mock scolding in my voice.

"We always are." She was laughing. "We can talk about the details another time. I can tell by your voice you're tired. Night, darling. Talk to you soon. Love you. Tell Keith we love him too."

Keith roused slightly from sleep to say, "Love you too, Mama."

I surely wasn't going to fall asleep now that I was so excited! A baby shower! How thrilling. I was already excited to meet my little one and now could look forward to the party. It was so thoughtful of Tansy and Mama to throw it for us! A couple of weeks passed, and Keith drove me out to the farm for the shower. I felt as big as the barn on the property now that I was seven months pregnant.

When we pulled up in front of Tansy's house, we were greeted by a tower of bright yellow balloons that matched the nursery. Her living room was filled with old friends all dressed in their Sunday best. There was a table filled with beautifully wrapped gifts and another filled with quite the spread of food as I knew Tansy would do.

It was two hours of heaven. Fun activities, great friends, and amazing food. I enjoyed the creative baby games and laughed as I watched Mama and other friends try to guess at the baby's sex and name—which were both still a secret. Such a wonderful luncheon and shower. It was so nice to reconnect with everyone, and the gifts I received were heartfelt and too cute. After the shower, Keith loaded up the truck with all the gifts. As he put the last one in and started to shut the tailgate, he said with a laugh, "Mary, we are going to need a bigger house." I laughed, too, looking at the mound of presents and thought he might be right!

Tansy walked us out to the truck and handed me three freshly baked blueberry pies. Her instructions were, "Freeze one and eat the other two." Now, I can sure follow those instructions.

"You got it, Tansy," I said, giving first her and then Mama a huge hug. On the way back home, the weariness set in. I was tired of being pregnant. My stomach was big, and I couldn't see my toes. It was becoming harder and harder to do tasks that had been easy just a few weeks before, such as tying my shoes or fitting my large belly behind a steering wheel. Not to mention it was hard to extend my arms that far.

As summer ended the nights grew cooler and the leaves began to turn. I loved this time of year. And although I was trying not to rush autumn, Christmas was around the corner. I wanted to put up my tree and meet our baby. I was also already dreaming of all the pies I would make for Christmas. I liked my pumpkin pie with whipped cream and a combination of cinnamon and sugar sprinkled over the top. But I also like peppermint pie with an Oreo cookie crust and dark chocolate drizzle on top. Pies were our family's specialties, so you can understand why I was dreaming about them.

Christmas is also my favorite time of year, and I had the decorations to prove it. It always feels as if love is in the air. I love when our home begins to fill with Christmas cards with colorful stamps, candies, cookies, gifts, ugly decorated sweaters, warm snuggly blankets, Christmas movies, hot chocolate with extra semi-sweet chocolate sprinkles and a half a jar of marshmallow topping, plus mistletoe hung all over the house. I was not going to miss a kiss!

I wished our new home had a fireplace, but Keith found a CD that we put into the DVD player so we could watch a blazing fire from there. I so enjoyed this time of year! Keith and I were hoping that our baby would be born on Christmas Day. Wouldn't that just be fantastic if we had a Christmas baby? Keith's birthday was in January, something he didn't want for our child.

He said he remembered how horrible it was growing up with a birthday falling just after Christmas. No one had any money and he felt like he always got leftover or last-minute gifts. Plus, they were never wrapped in birthday wrapping paper but Christmas paper. Being in a foster home didn't help. It seemed money was always tight. He remembered many birthdays in which he often went without. So, each year when his birthday came around, I tried to make sure he felt special. I wanted him to know how much I loved him. When you love someone, you care about what they say and value their heart's desire, and so I made sure to make a big deal over his birthday to make up for the years in which no one did. But let's get to Christmas shall we? I have memories to share. Mama made Christmas magical with special touches. From decorations to the tree and candies and cookies, Daddy and I looked forward to this time of year.

When I was a child, Mama and I baked sugar cookies together. She would let me frost them with buttercream frosting in every color of the rainbow. Mama's philosophy for baking was simple: "You don't need an exact measurement when you bake with love." Now, I disagree because I *do* need exact measurements when baking, but I understand what she meant.

One time, I added too much butter and the peanut butter cookies spread out and melted like soup when they were baking. Another time, I added too much flour into my snickerdoodle cookie dough. The cookies looked pleasantly edible, but the texture was like rock candy. We tried new recipes and Daddy liked being the taste tester. Mama scolded him when he tried to eat raw cookie dough; she said he would get a disease from the raw eggs and die. That was a little dramatic I thought.

The forecast was for early snow and the bins of heaven didn't disappoint. I loved how the snow flocked trees sparkled in the sunlight. It made everything look like a fairy-tale land. Usually we only had light snowfalls in our area, but occasionally, we would get a big one. And then it seemed everyone forgot how to drive! When I was the passenger in the truck with Keith and there was any type of snowfall on the ground, I would use my imaginary air brake to try to slow the car down. Keith laughed at me. He thought it was funny as I sucked the air out of the car when someone braked in front of us. I didn't think that was funny or that he mocked my "near-death experiences." Thankfully, though, snowfall was rare, so we weren't too worried as we thought of the impending drive to the hospital when I went into labor. We were in the countdown of two to three weeks left.

We often took short walks each night down the street so I could get some exercise and to check out the Christmas lights. People in the neighborhood outdid themselves. Some even had their mailboxes decorated with lights while others put pine wreaths with red bows on the front of their cars.

Keith loved Christmas as well, but he didn't like having to decorate. I told him, "You leave that up to me." Prior to the holiday I had scouted for sales on a Christmas tree, lights, and other decorations. I grew up with red and white lights on the tree. Shopping one day I found some iridescent bulbs on sale at the hardware store. They were cheesy with the company logo, Sam's Hardware and Goods, stamped on them, but I didn't care. I thought they were pretty and the light from the bulbs made them shine. I looked around our decorated home. It was simple, but it was warm and cozy as we approached Christmas and the birth of our little one.

Just days before Christmas the weatherman began to announce severe storm warnings headed our way. There was a prediction of three to five inches of snow. Initially I wasn't worried. Keith had just bought a used machine to help shovel away the snow and we had a few shovels. It wasn't supposed to hit until the weekend and Keith would be off. That meant just him and me. We were enjoying every minute together before the baby arrived. Soon it would no longer be just him and me, it would be us.

Toward the end of the week there was a knock at the door late afternoon. It couldn't be Keith, as he wouldn't get off for another hour or so.

"What are you doing here, Mama?" I asked as I opened the door. She and Daddy were standing there, arms loaded with casseroles and food that we could freeze and a delicious meal for us for tonight. My mouth watered as I pulled off the lid of several tin containers to reveal oven baked chicken with seasonings, potato wedges, creamy cabbage coleslaw, and flaky biscuits with sweet honey and cinnamon butter. I couldn't wait for Keith to get home so we could dig in!

In anticipation of the storm, Mama had managed to whip up a truly divine meal for us and additional meals we could put in the freezer. Growing up with an amazing cook gave me a front-row seat to learn from the head chef, Mama, and I was grateful for the experience and grateful for her help.

"Now you be careful, honey," Mama said as they put away the extra meals into the freezer. "Don't get out if you don't have to." She and Daddy started to head towards the door.

"We aren't going to stay," Daddy informed me. "We want to get back home before the storm hits. We just wanted to make sure you were taken care of." Then he gave me a kiss. My heart was bursting with love for my folks and their thoughtful concern and care. It was getting hard for me to have the energy to stand and cook a full meal, not to mention Mama's cooking was always so delightful.

Keith and I lay on the couch, our bellies full of chicken, a double helping of potatoes, biscuits, and more. Keith laid the remote to the television on my big old belly. He knew if it fell on the floor, I wasn't getting up to fetch it. Honestly, I was surprised that the baby didn't kick it off as it balanced on my rounded belly. Most times, especially after eating, my stomach would move all over the place as the baby kicked and squirmed, but lately things had been more still, and there had not been as much movement. It concerned me, but Mama told me it was only because the baby was running out of room. That eased this first-time mother's mind.

As we lay on the couch, we turned off all the lights in the living room and gazed at the Christmas tree. It was spectacular. In that moment I felt life couldn't be any more perfect than this! I had the love of my life, my husband, next to my side, our first child on the way, and a roof over our heads. I was thankful to God for all our blessings.

That night, Keith and I fell asleep on the couch. About three o'clock in the morning I woke up with cramps in my belly and had to go to the bathroom something fierce. "Keith, Keith, help me up. I have to use the bathroom right now," I cried as I shook him awake.

"What's the matter, baby? Does your belly hurt?" he asked.

"Yes, it hurts, and my back hurts bad too!" In an instant he was fully awake and jumped up from the couch.

"Maybe you should just stay right where you are and let me call the doctor," he said as he grabbed his phone. I tried to get up from the couch but soon discovered that wasn't happening unless Keith extended his hand to help me. I could have rolled off the couch, but I didn't want to hurt myself or the baby.

"Oh, please, I am fine," I insisted. "I just need to go to the bathroom." But even as I said that I had to stop and double over. The cramps were getting worse by the minute. No one needed to tell me I was in labor. I also wondered why no one told me it would hurt this badly.

Keith was nervous I could tell. Even so, he tried to keep me calm with his gentle words. "Don't worry, baby, everything is going to be all right," he said as he gently kissed my cheek.

Keith started the truck so that it would be warmed up before I got in, and he brought my favorite blanket. He grabbed my bag, which we had pre-packed and had sitting by the front door.

Inside were things for me but also a new baby elf outfit complete with a hat with green and white stripped ears. I smiled at the thought that it wouldn't be long now.

Keith and I walked carefully across the now snow-covered steps and sidewalk. Large flakes were still coming down as he helped me up into the passenger seat. I probably could have enjoyed the beautiful scenery of the quietly falling snow on the trip to the hospital had I not been fighting off the panic of each contraction as it hit. Soon after we arrived, they checked me into a room. I was glad to be at the hospital, scared but glad.

Ten hours of intense labor passed. Keith stayed by my side. He helped encourage me when to breathe and when to rest, just like we had learned. I felt exhausted, though, and was certainly ready to see our baby.

The nurse continued to check me as the labor progressed. Finally, the doctor rushed in rather breathless. I assumed he had just arrived. "Are you ready to push?" he asked. What a question! I thought I had already been pushing! Just then I felt an intense pressure and had to push. "The baby is coming. Keep pushing, Mary," the doctor instructed.

"You are doing a wonderful job, baby." Keith still coached from the side of the bed as he held my hand. I felt I could do any-thing with Keith by my side. Just ten minutes later after several more pushes I felt relief as our baby was born.

"It's a boy!" the doctor informed us.

Keith beamed at me and kissed my forehead. We had gone over about a thousand baby names during the past months but had decided if it were a boy that we would name him Jason Keith Walker.

"Is it all right to say my boy is beautiful?" Keith said as he held him.

"Of course! He's our son! I am beautiful and he was in my belly, so of course he's beautiful." I said with a grin. People always say girls are beautiful, but I think my boy was beautiful too!

Keith had called Mama and Daddy as soon as I was checked into the hospital. Because of the snow conditions it took them a while to arrive, as the roads were slippery. Mama came into the room looking first at me and then her new grandson. She couldn't wait to get her arms around him. Daddy was excited, too, and proud of me. I could tell by the look in his eyes. He shook Keith's hand as he beamed from ear to ear. Keith was growing on him. He may not have liked Keith at first, but what daddy likes the boy who will eventually steal his daughter away?

Mama sat down in the chair as she held our little bundle. "Well, what's his name?" she asked.

"His name is Jason Keith Walker, Mama." I answered.

"Oh, darling, that is a fine name," she replied.

"That baby is beautiful. His head is perfectly shaped!" Daddy interjected.

"That is exactly what Keith said." I was laughing. I think Keith was self-conscience about his head. It was flat. We teased him often about it.

Baby check: Jason had ten fingers, ten toes, big blue eyes, and a head full of dark hair. He was strong, too, kicking his little legs. No wonder I was in pain when he was in my belly. Mama said, "That baby is going to be a runner. He's got strong legs, just like his mama."

They kept Jason and me at the hospital for a few days' observation. It was nice to get to rest, and I was glad to have the nurses' help. I didn't know what I was doing, and they took time to show me the ropes. I jokingly asked the nurses, "Can you please come home with us? Just until we figure this whole new baby thing out?" I'm sure they get those requests all the time.

Of course, they declined. They had more faith in me than I had in myself. At least for these couple of days I wasn't doing this alone. But nothing can truly prepare you when you bring your child home. I thought I knew all there was to know. Boy, did I know absolutely nothing!

Jason was a cute baby, which was God's gift and His saving grace. But Jason stayed up all night long and he slept during the day. Plus, he wanted to eat every hour. He had an appetite just like his daddy. No sleep makes for one tired woman. I wondered how Mama had done it. I have a whole lot of respect for her now. I never realized all the work she did for me.

When I look at my life, it still amazes me how much we can take for granted in life. There certainly are no shortcuts to wisdom, and I learned that the hard way.

After we arrived home, our lives were turned upside down. Jason struggled with colic, and it was exhausting. I never got a break until Keith came home. But Keith was exhausted, too, from working all day. However, I still needed his support. Then I felt guilty asking him to take over because I knew he was tired. This whole charm of the newness of having a baby was wearing off quickly.

Mama and I talked on the phone every day. It was nice to have someone who could answer my questions as well as someone with whom I could have adult conversation. She called one day when Jason was about three months old. "I need some grandma time, honey. Can I come over?" It was precious to see the two of them snuggling together. Mama never missed an opportunity to spend time with her grandbaby. This time she brought a gift for Jason. It was a blue and yellow blanket with his name sewn into a pocket.

I admired the blanket. "How did you know it was going to be a boy?" I asked.

"God told me," she replied.

I was never much for believing in that. When I prayed, God never talked to me, or at least I never heard Him. Mama said I needed to clean out my ears and listen. *Perhaps she was right*, I thought as I pondered her response.

Mama came alone this time. "Your daddy's drinking is getting worse," she confided. "It's really out of control." She explained that most days he spent sick in bed, depressed, and stone drunk. He didn't want any light in his room, and he insisted on keeping the drapes closed so that the room was pitch black. "He moved into the guest room and just wants to be left alone," Mama said as a tear slid down her cheek. "I don't know how to help him."

This wasn't the first time Daddy had moved into the guest room when his drinking had gotten bad. I only went in that room a few times as a child. When he was there, it smelled like an old closet. It was always dark. The windows were kept completely covered so not even a sliver of light could come through. I shuddered at the memory. It was not a very welcoming place for a child. Mama tried to get Pastor Greg from her church to visit with Daddy, but every time she asked Daddy if he could come, Daddy refused. He walked away from everything.

The visit was far too short and soon Mama was gathering her things to head back home to Daddy. As her car pulled out of the drive, I was already missing her. I was glad for phones. At least Mama could talk to me every day. I needed her advice and help now more than ever.

The first year of Jason's life went by quickly. Every month I was excited to celebrate his milestones. As his first birthday approached, Keith and I planned to throw him a party. He loved giraffes so we chose a safari theme. I made a happy birthday sign and hung balloons along the walls with streamers hanging down. And I made my very own ceiling palm trees keeping with the theme and was proud of myself the way it all turned out. I also had a giraffe cake made for him at the bakery. Keith was ready to flip out over everything until I told him it only cost forty-five dollars. He couldn't believe it and had braced himself for so much more. We were still on a budget, but things were not nearly as hard as when we had first married.

Much to our delight, Jason took his first steps just before his party and began climbing on the furniture. It scared me the first time he climbed up on our bed. He fell off a few times but, thank the Lord, he didn't get hurt! You know, I swore I would never spank my children—well, that philosophy went out the window. Jason was a handful and although I gave him "time outs" in the corner once in a while, he made it over my knee when he endangered his life!

With the first hint of spring and warmer temperatures, Keith put together a swing set in our backyard. Just the perfect place for Jason to play. It was nice to get outside and enjoy the beauty of spring. Jason's toddling walk soon turned into a run, which made it hard to keep up with him. That kid loved to play all day. Thankfully, though, between the running and the fresh air, by early evening he had knocked himself out and slept through the night. That meant this mama could get a good night's rest.

Life was flying by. We passed the toddler stage and soon our boy was getting ready to go into preschool. He was excited and looked forward to riding the bus. "You're still too little," I informed him as I tousled his hair. Preschool was half days only a few days a week. That was perfect. It gave me time to get a few things done while he was gone, plus, for this new mama, it meant I didn't have to miss him too long.

As any parent can attest to, once your kid starts to go to school, they are exposed to way more germs and illnesses. It was no exception here. Jason came down with a nasty virus and then I did too! I absolutely hate it when my baby is sick! Even worse, I was not feeling good at all either, but I was still having to take care of him.

A week passed and while Jason felt better, I certainly didn't. I made an appointment with the doctor in hopes he would give me an antibiotic to kick the thing, or a shot of vitamin B to help restore my energy so I could get out of bed. While there, the doctor suggested a pregnancy test. Uh-oh. I hadn't even considered that, as Keith and I were not even trying to have another baby. I agreed and was stuck waiting about twenty minutes until the results came back. I thumbed through a magazine absentmindedly, unable to focus on the words. Eventually, I sent Keith a text to let him know I was still at the doctor's office. "I might be pregnant," I texted. Now, that's not necessarily the news you want by text, but what else was I going to do for twenty minutes?

Finally, the doctor came in. "Well, am I pregnant again?" I asked.

"You sure are. Congratulations!" he said. Jason was happy too.

"Does this mean I get a baby brother?" he asked, wide-eyed.

"Well, it could. Or it could mean that you get a baby sister," I replied, still processing the news.

"Awe, I want a brother." He had his hands on his hips.

As the pregnancy continued, it felt different than my first one. With this one I had a ton of energy, and I wasn't sick like when I was carrying Jason. With the virus I had a nagging cough, but eventually it went away, and I felt good. But keeping up with Jason meant no rest for this mama. (*Jason had the energy level of a flying monkey.*) Thank God for coffee!

Mama thought I was having a baby girl and was already making me a pink blanket, bonnet, and booties. Keith, on the other hand, was convinced I was carrying another boy. I told her that Keith was not going to let his baby boy wear pink, no way, now how, no ma'am. She laughed at him and nodded her head in disbelief. Give me a break. Like Keith was going to tell Mama what she was going to make for her grandbaby? Please!

"I am getting my girl, my little granddaughter, Mary," she repeated over and over as she knit the soft pink blanket.

Daddy pulled himself together with the news of the new baby. Already he had crafted most of our furniture with his own two hands. I remember the wood treasure box he had made for me to hold all my beloved treasures. I absolutely adored it, especially because it was made by Daddy's hand. When I was younger, he had also built Mama a wooden curio cabinet with beveled glass and a light inside. It was an anniversary gift, which she loved. She put all the things she collected inside. It was off limits to me. My little hands were not a good match for the delicate glass angels inside.

Time sped by and in a heartbeat, it was time to deliver and meet our next child. I couldn't believe it. Where had the time gone? Contractions came like lightning. I had forgotten how intense they were and wasn't prepared for them at all. (*How could I forget the pain of contractions? I am convinced God does this intentionally just so we will keep having more children!*) Keith was exhausted from the start. He had just worked a double shift and was excited to get home, eat dinner, and get off his feet. We both had hoped for sleep, but the baby had other plans and sleep wasn't one of them.

I was in pain and the contractions were getting closer. "I think I need to get you to the hospital," he said as he timed my contractions. I nodded. I was fine with that. I called Mama and told her to come. She left shortly after we hung up the phone and would meet us at the hospital to get Jason. On the way I was scared and excited all at the same time. Keith's eyes were bugging out of his sockets. He was on no sleep and now straight adrenaline.

Once we were at the hospital, they checked me in and handed me one of those wonderful gowns with no back, only ties. That is just what I want—my bottom hanging out the back end. When will they fix them?

I was sure my baby was going to be here soon, but not soon enough. That baby was stubborn just like me. I was staring at the clock, waiting for Mama to arrive. I knew she had a long drive, but I wanted her to be there. I was hoping Daddy was coming with her too.

Three miserable hours passed, and I was ready to be done with this whole labor thing. Just when I was about to push, Mama and Daddy came rushing in the room.

"Praise God, we didn't miss it!" Mama exclaimed.

"You don't know how fast I drove to get here baby. Your mama had a fit the whole way," Daddy said as he turned to Keith and shook his hand.

"Thanks for coming, Dad." Keith said as he reached out to shake the extended hand. Tired as I was the small interaction brought a smile to my face. It seemed Daddy had finally accepted that Keith was part of our family and here to stay.

"I've missed a lot of things in my life, but I wasn't going to miss this," Daddy said as he gave me a thumbs up.

"Go downstairs and get the gift in the car." This was one of the few times Mama gave the wrong instruction because as Daddy left the room, I was ready to push!

"Come on, Mary. You can do it," Keith encouraged as he wiped the sweat from my forehead. Three to four pushes later, it was finally accomplished and Gracie Ann Walker, our beautiful baby girl, was born.

I pushed so hard that I was surprised the doctor caught her. The baby shot out like a football. Gracie Bear was ready to be in this world and nothing could stop her!

In the end, Mama's prediction was right, and she got her grandbaby girl. I looked down at the small bundle as the nurse placed her in my arms after cleaning her and bundling her up. She was precious. She had a headful of blond hair, blue eyes, and long eye lashes, which she obviously inherited from her daddy. Lucky girl. Jason, who had been sitting in a chair, made his way over to the bed and crawled up. He leaned over my shoulder to peer at his new little sister. It was clear he absolutely adored her.

"She's so little, Mama," he exclaimed with big eyes.

"Can you believe you used to be this little once?" I told him.

"There is no way I was *that* little." He was gently fingering her small hands.

"Yes, you were and just as cute as your sister." I kissed him on his head as Daddy lifted him back down. "Love you, baby," I told him as he continued to stand there completely in awe of the miracle in my arms.

Now, Keith was different with this baby than he had been with Jason. It was as if she had *fragile* written all over her. "She's beautiful, Mary. She looks just like you," he said proudly after I handed her to him. (*By the look on his face and the way he handled her so delicately, it was apparent girls are much different than boys.*)

The labor had been tough. Harder than I remembered with Jason, and I was in a great deal of pain, but once I saw my Gracie everything went away.

By the time Daddy made it back to the room with the gift, little Gracie Ann was already here. His face showed both surprise and disappointment that the baby had been born in his absence. "The security gestapo stopped me," he said with frustration.

"Did you grab my bag?" Mama was on a mission.

"Yes, ma'am." He laughed and gave a mock salute. "Everything is right here."

"Thank you, dear," she said as she took it from him. "I'm so sorry you missed the actual birth. I wasn't thinking!" She gave Daddy a kiss. "Now hand over my granddaughter. I want to hold her," Mama said as she held out her arms. As soon as Keith placed her in Mama's arms, she walked over to the chair by the heater and wrapped the warm blanket she made around her new grandbaby.

"Keith, grab my camera and take some pictures of Mama and Gracie," I instructed. Keith took several pictures as I continued to quarterback from the bed. Yet, I will never forget the look of love in my mama's eyes as she stared at our baby girl.

"She's precious, Mary. She looks just like you the day you were born." Mama said as tears welled up in her eyes and ran down her cheeks. "I've been waiting for 'my Mary' all these years, and God finally answered my prayers." She made a contented sigh.

Daddy pulled up the only other chair in the room and sat down next to Mama. It did my heart good to watch them as they poured out their love and adoration on little Gracie.

My eyelids were heavy as I looked back and forth at my two babies. Early on it was just Keith and me against the world. Now we had two precious children. My heart was full as I drifted off to sleep.

Once they released Gracie Ann and me from the hospital, Mama sent Daddy back home and she came to stay with us at the house. It was nice to have her around to help with Jason and Gracie Bear. As any mama knows, it takes a few weeks to heal and start feeling like your old self again.

During the visit with Mama, I noticed she moved slower than before. It seemed she got out of breath just walking from the kitchen to the dining room. At first, I thought it was because Gracie Bear was keeping her up all night. *(I forgot to mention that Jason came up with the nickname while he was rocking her.)* She was getting about as much sleep as I was. I asked her if everything was all right. I knew Mama never worried about herself but was always concerned with the needs of others. I shrugged it off. We had our hands full between taking care of Jason and the new baby as I got my strength back.

I didn't want to say goodbye to Mama when the time came for her to return home. I was feeling semi-normal but still tired from being up and down all night with a newborn. But I knew she needed to get back home to Daddy and her own bed.

Keith had arranged to get off early that day so he could drive her back to the house. "Bye, Mama, I love you," I said as I hugged her and tried not to cry. Jason climbed up on her lap and gave her a big hug and a kiss on the cheek. Next, Mama kissed the top of Gracie's head and handed her back to me.

I could tell Mama was struggling as much as I to keep the tears at bay. "Come and visit Daddy and me, and bring my grandbabies," she told me emphatically before climbing into the car. The three of us watched from the porch until Keith backed out of the driveway and the car pulled out of sight. Already the house seemed empty now that she was gone.

Jason surprised me with how naturally he took on the big brother role. He hugged his sister any time he could. We loved her nickname "Gracie Bear." It fit her perfectly, especially since she loved to hold onto each of us so tightly.

After Mama visited, I really missed her. Although I was busy all the time, it didn't lessen the ache in my heart to see her. We only lived hours away from each other, but that didn't stop the days from seeming long and the nights even longer. Being busy in my own life, I didn't even realize Mama wasn't doing well. She didn't like to worry me with her problems, so she stayed tight-lipped about it. We visited a few times and she seemed to be moving slower and her vision was going just a bit. I could also tell she was a little wobbly on her feet.

Sometimes she came to visit without Daddy, and I noticed she slept longer and later than she used to. I figured it was because we tired her out running to the park, shopping, and chasing the kids. Maybe she just needed a vacation! I know I did. It also crossed my mind that since Daddy started drinking again it may have stressed her out.

As always, it was hard to let her go, but we lived in two dif-ferent worlds now. I watched as she drove away and deep inside, I knew this was the season Mama was aging and that meant I would have to face something I dreaded—watching her get old. I don't know why it bothered me so; after all, age is a blessing and everyone has to age. But not my mama! I needed her. She was the rock I built my security around. She was my everything, a pure saint from heaven above.

I knew that Mama wouldn't tell me her true woes, but I could always count on Tansy to spill the beans—with a little coaxing, of course. Tansy was loyal to Mama, and I understood that. But I hoped she would provide some insight. I waited until the kids were both quiet before I tried to call her. Thank goodness they both still took naps. I knew I had about a half hour before they would awake, but for now it was quiet in the background.

"Tansy, it's Mary Ann. Is there anything going on with Mama? I know she's getting older, but she has sure seemed to slow down all of a sudden. I'm concerned." Tansy and I talked for several minutes, and she filled me in just a bit. She mentioned Mama was dizzy and was losing energy. That was totally not like her, and it was a bit worrisome. "Is there anything else?" I inquired. "Oh child, you haven't heard. Clarence died!"

I was stunned and I couldn't believe that no one had told me or Keith.

I didn't want to be mad about it so I held my tongue and instead gave heartfelt condolences. "I'm sorry Tansy. Is there anything I can do?"

"No child, there is nothing you can do. Just promise this old woman that you will live your life to the fullest and take care of those grandbabies for your Mama. Tansy will be fine!" And with that we were back to talking about Mama. "I'm going to encourage her to go the doctor," Tansy told me. "I think they need to run some tests to make sure nothing is seriously wrong."

True to her word, Tansy prompted Mama and the next week Mama went to the doctor. After he ran some blood work, he had her check in the hospital for further tests. "It may be nothing," he said. "I just want to make sure everything is fine."

That weekend Keith watched the kids so that I could visit her in the hospital. Her church friends had bought her beautiful flowers and made her heartfelt cards. That was nice of them to cheer Mama up. There was an infection that had started in her leg. Initially, the doctor couldn't get it under control, and at one point we thought we would lose her. But she made it simply fine. She said that it was because everyone at church was praying for her, including her best friend, Tansy.

I started to believe she was right. The doctor had told me about that severe infections like what she had rarely end up good and could result in death. Thank God she was okay. She was my rock. I could always count on her, and whenever I needed something, she was there. What if I lost her?

CHAPTER SIX

NO WAY OUT

*T*here is a reason the Bible says don't worry about tomorrow—because we don't know what each one of us will face. That was me, worrying about every-thing. Why? I had all I needed, but I let worry get in the way too many times. Life happens and as unfair as it is, we have to walk through it. We have to learn to deal with it and not worry about tomorrow, as that never does anyone any good.

With two growing kids and lots of toys, we were out-growing our starter house. Thankfully, Keith got a raise. So, whenever we had a chance, we would load the kids in the car and drive around looking at bigger homes, dream-ing of our future. We were dreaming, praying, and hoping.

I never thought we would collect so many toys and other things. But between birthdays, shopping trips, and "I want" buys, we had picked up a lot over the years. I

looked at the mound of stuffed animals that filled Gracie Bear's room. There were enough to start a small stuffed animal village. Now at the age of two she loved to pretend she was a cook and so Keith bought her a pink mini kitchen set. I wish my kitchen were pink!

We had lots of fun together. From shopping, to garage sailing, thrifting, playing at the park, and having picnics, we didn't miss a beat! I can tell you, spend time with your children. We only have them for a short while and then they fly!

I recall one hot afternoon we found two plastic eggs and a small cooking set at a garage sale for pretty cheap. They were only twenty-five cents apiece and Gracie Bear loved them. Kids are so smart today. When I was little, we didn't have all the fancy, electronic-type toys they had today. We made our own toys from whatever we found outside. Now, that's making me seem old. I think Gracie liked watching me cook; I may have been the inspiration for her banging on pots and pans. One of her favorite meals to "cook" for me was a plate of these two plastic eggs with two Lincoln logs for sausage links. It was very nutritious too. No calories, but a little hard on the teeth.

It was such a joy to have the kids home, but Jason was growing fast and so was Gracie Bear. Mama said it was going to go this way, and like a stubborn teen, I thought she was out of her mind. Who's crazy now?

One Thursday morning during summer break I decided to let the kids sleep in. I needed some beauty rest and a day without our usual routine. Keith was getting ready for work. I opened one eye and watched him as he brushed his teeth and hair. Although we had been married several years already, he still made my heart flutter. When he finished, he walked over to the bed, gave me a kiss, and whispered, "I love you." He never left in the morning without kissing me and the kids goodbye. That's another thing I loved about Keith—he really valued the present.

His beard tickled my nose. "When are you going to shave that beard of yours?" I asked, rubbing my cheek. (*To be honest, I hated that bushy thing.*) After he left, I rolled over to get some more rest, but I couldn't go back to sleep. I stretched and threw back the covers. So much for my beauty rest. After pulling on a pair of jeans and T-shirt, I headed to the kitchen to make myself some coffee and fix a bite to eat. At least I would have a little bit of quiet before the kids woke up and our day began.

I sat at the table and listened to the coffee maker drip. Why is it that when you want a cup of coffee in the morning it seems like the coffee maker drags on and on? Amazing how still and quiet the house was at that moment. Looking out the window, I could see the sun peeking over the horizon. I sighed with contentment, but a moment later it felt as if a cool wind touched my arm. It startled me. We were indoors. It sent goosebumps down my body. I got up to pour myself a mug of coffee and tried to shake the eerie feeling it had given me. Just then the phone rang.

"Hello," I answered.

"Ma'am, there has been an accident at the factory." My heart dropped as Keith's manager identified himself and continued to speak. "Three men have been taken to the hospital. Your husband, Keith, is one of them. You better get down there as quick as you can." I grabbed the counter to steady myself. I couldn't believe it. It seemed like Keith had just left!

I hung up the phone and tried to call Mama. My hands were shaking so bad I misdialed twice and had to start over. Finally, the call went through, and she answered on the second ring. "Mama, Keith has been in an accident. I need to get to the hospital. Can you please come and watch the kids? Please hurry, Mama. I need you!"

"I'm on my way, baby," she responded without a moment's hesitation. After disconnecting, I noticed our neighbor Wilma was outside watering her garden. I dashed out the door and ran to the fence.

"Will you sit with the kids? Keith has been in an accident, and I need to go to the hospital."

"You got it, Mary. Go. Don't worry about the kids. And I'll be praying." She was already turning off the water and heading over to our house. My heart was racing. In the pit of my stomach was a pain I never felt before. I thought I was going to throw up.

I ran inside, grabbed my purse and keys, then hurried outside and jumped in our car. Thank God we had been able to become a two-car family a couple of years before. I drove like a madman to the hospital, found a parking spot, and sprinted inside to the information desk.

"I'm the wife of Keith Walker. He was brought here from an accident at the factory," I informed the receptionist.

"Have a seat and someone will be with you shortly," she replied.

That wasn't good enough for me. I wanted to see my husband—and I wanted to see him *now*. "I need to see him right away," I stated firmly and perhaps a little loudly. "I don't want to wait! He is my husband. Don't you understand?" I felt panic beginning to set in. I desperately needed to see Keith and ensure he was okay. Just knowing he was there in the same place, but that I couldn't touch him or see his face suddenly made it all unbearable.

The receptionist looked at me with compassionate eyes. "I understand that you are worried. Please calm down. As soon as I can get you back there I will."

Mama always told me not to worry, but worry was setting in. I was thinking about how the children would wake up without their mama. I worried that they would be worried. Worse, I couldn't stop thinking the worst. I was in full panic.

I sat down hoping it would calm my frazzled nerves. I tapped my foot, looked at my watch, and then looked up to the ceiling. "God, if You are there, I need You," I whispered. Almost immediately a calmness settled over me just like it had earlier that morning as I waited for the coffee to brew. But this was different. I had never felt this kind of peace before. Not like this. It had to be supernatural. I can get so agitated that normally I needed Keith to calm me down. But at that moment my mind was at peace and the fear abated. There was no explaining it—except God. Why hadn't I reached for God sooner? But I guess sometimes that's what we do. We reach for Him when its dark, painful, and scary. This time was scary for me. I felt like a little child completely helpless.

Why is it that time goes by so slow when you are waiting? Fifteen minutes passed, but it seemed as if it was an hour when the double doors finally pushed open, and the nurse called my name. "The doctor is ready to see you," she said as she held the double door open to allow me passage inside.

What? my mind screamed, *the* doctor *was ready to see me?* I wanted to see my husband not the doctor. But I said nothing while I followed the nurse as she led me down a narrow hallway. I felt the walls closing in around me and everything seemed as if it were moving in slow motion. Deep in my soul I knew something was seriously wrong, but I tried to hang on to hope and the peace that had come upon me moments before. Where was it now?

The nurse led me to a small sterile waiting room with one picture on the wall. It was hardly warm and friendly. I absolutely hate the smell of hospitals, and every time I am in one it makes me feel sick.

"The doctor will be in shortly," she said as she headed back out. *Great,* I thought. *Hang in there, Mary. Don't give in. Don't be negative. Take a deep breath and just think positive,* I said to myself. But it was not helping.

I felt numb. My nerves were shot, and my heart felt like it was beating out my chest. If someone didn't tell me what's going on soon, I felt like I would have a panic attack. How long can someone remain calm on the outside while dying on the inside?

Finally, although it felt like forever, the doctor walked in. "Mrs. Walker? Are you okay? You're very pale."

I nodded, thinking, *thanks for the compliment, doctor.* Sheesh! "Yes, I am Mrs. Walker. And yes, I'm okay. How is my husband?" I asked, not sure I wanted to hear the answer.

"There's been an accident at the factory as you know," he began. "A steel crane broke free and hit your husband in the left side of his head. That type of traumatic brain injury has resulted in a cerebral hemorrhage. So far we have been unable to stop the bleeding. We have done everything we can do. I'm sorry, Mrs. Walker. If you have family, I recommend you call them, and then we need to discuss the decision of when to pull him off life support. He has no brain function left and will not get better."

"Isn't there anything we can do? Anything?" I asked him. "This cannot be the only answer. I mean, with all the medical technology we have today, there is nothing left?" In my mind I wanted to scream so loud it would break every window in the room. Instead, I sat there with my hands folded tightly in my lap.

"Let me try to explain this the best way I can, Mrs. Walker," the doctor said patiently. "Without your brain your body won't know what to do. You only have one brain. Your husband will never be able to live on his own again. I know you wouldn't want to see him like this for the rest of his or your life. He is in a coma for now. I'm so sorry."

I covered my mouth in horror and shock. "Oh my God, help me!" I cried.

"Again, I am so sorry, Mrs. Walker," the doctor said as he started to exit. "A nurse will come give you instructions as to when you can see your husband."

"Wait a minute. What are you saying, doctor? Keith is going to die?" I asked, trying to make sense of what the doctor had just said. Surely I hadn't heard correctly. I was in total disbelief. This couldn't be happening. I could still feel the scratchiness of his beard on my cheek as he kissed me goodbye earlier that morning. Now I was in a hospital listening to a doctor tell me that the love of my life, my husband, was unresponsive?

The dam holding back the tears finally released. How does anyone process such news? The doctor tried to console me, but it didn't help. I needed my mama. No, I needed my husband! "Doctor, can I see him?" I begged.

"Yes, but be prepared. He is badly hurt and may be unrecognizable to you."

I didn't care, I just wanted to see Keith. I wanted to touch him as if I could make him better. This had to be a dream. Just maybe he would respond to me and this nightmare would all go away.

Despite the doctor's warning, nothing could have prepared me for what I was about to see. I walked into Keith's cubicle in the ICU and was immediately overcome by the noise of all the machines whirring and monitoring him to keep him alive. It confronted me like fingernails on a chalkboard, and I cringed at the sound.

Keith's face was swollen and completely deformed. Already there were dark bruises from the impact he suffered. He didn't even look like the man I married. I thought I could prepare for everything in my life, but not this. I couldn't have prepared for this even if I tried.

The left side of his face was crushed, and his skull wrapped in white bandages was partly caved in. How could this have happened to him? To us? One moment we were the happiest couple and parents of the most amazing children on earth, and now I looked at my unconscious husband and was told he would die.

"Mama, where are you?" I cried out, needing her comfort and support.

I had no strength left to hold back the tears. I felt like my heart was breaking into a million pieces. I watched Keith's still form unable to hold me or touch me. I felt like my heart was breaking as I stood there helplessly. Since we met there was not a time his eyes didn't light up when he saw me. How on earth would I survive without his arms around me? I never felt so safe then when he held me. The reality I was faced with was one I never saw coming. I wanted this nightmare to be over! I wanted him back and for all of this to just go away.

I fell into a chair near his bed and grabbed his hand. "Keith, I love you. If you can hear me, please squeeze my hand," I whispered. I waited and waited. But there was no response. Mascara ran down my face and my nose dripped. I was a sobbing mess. Just then I felt a hand on my shoulder. I looked up—it was Mama.

"I'm so sorry, baby." Mama exclaimed as she held me close.

"Mama, the doctor said Keith is going to die. They cannot help him," I blurted out between sobs.

"Only God can help him now," she whispered as she stroked my hair.

I looked up at her and screamed, "Where is God at anyway? How could He let this happen?"

"Oh Mary, don't blame God. He didn't do this. Hold on. Take a deep breath," she encouraged.

I fell to my knees unable to take the emotional stress a moment longer. Mama dropped down beside me and prayed until I had no more tears. Eventually we both stood up, but now I felt like I was going to throw up and ran to the bathroom. "God, where are You?" I sobbed.

My neighbor Wilma brought the kids to the hospital. This was going to be hard on them, but I couldn't let them believe Keith just floated away. They needed to know. They needed to see their dad one more time. Clearly, they didn't understand, but I let them touch his hand and give him a kiss and say goodbye.

After much contemplation and further discussion with the doctor, I agreed to let them disconnect him from life support. The doctor told me there was really no "life" left in him since his brain was dead. This was a decision I never contemplated I would ever have to make, and I felt paralyzed. Wilma took the kids home. She knew I needed to say goodbye as a wife. She was a good friend. Gracie Bear hugged me. Oh, how I needed that love.

She asked me, "Dida okay?" in her toddler language.

Jason interrupted, "Come on, Gracie Bear, let's go cook something!" He looked up at me and smiled. His eyes were wet with tears, but we knew each other. In his little heart, he had made his peace with his dad, and he was ready to help his baby sister.

Despite the situation there was my son, just like his father. He remained unmoved, unworried, cool as a cucumber. I had some amazing children; I am a blessed mama for sure.

I sat down by Keith's bedside and sighed. Rubbing my fingers through his hair with tears rolling down my cheeks (*this was so hard*), I took a deep breath. I wanted this to just be a horrible nightmare in which I would wake up eventually and everything would be okay. The hospital staff walked in and out of the room, but I ignored them. There is no peace and quiet in a hospital. I just wanted them to leave me alone as I spent the last few minutes with my husband.

"It won't be long, Mrs. Walker," a nurse informed me as the whirring of the machines stopped and the room grew quiet. Within minutes Keith passed peacefully into eternity. Just like that, my life changed with no warning.

During our entire relationship Keith had always been a gentleman. He had always waited for me if we were going somewhere.

Except this time.

CHAPTER SEVEN

LETTING GO

*N*umb. *That was the only thing I felt now. I couldn't really tell you how I was going to go on, but something in my spirit kept pushing me forward, whether I wanted to or not. I knew all the right words to say and the right way to feel, but all that fluff flew out the window as I faced the cold-hearted truth. Life is unfair.*

After signing the papers at the hospital, I walked slowly to my car. The sun hadn't risen, and the sky was as dark as my heart felt. I drove the short distance home and crawled in bed, pulling the covers up over my head. I sobbed until I finally fell asleep. I woke to the sun coming through the windows and to the noise of the kids in the next room. How dare the sun come out when my husband had just passed away. It seemed so wrong. I walked out into the kitchen where Mama was clearing the table from breakfast.

The kids were already in the living room playing, oblivious to the fact their dad was never coming home again.

I didn't feel like eating. I didn't feel like doing anything actually, but there was much that had to be done. I got dressed, ran a brush through my hair, and kissed Mama as I grabbed my purse. "I'm heading over to Cumberton Funeral Home to make the burial arrangements. I'll be back soon," I said flatly.

Once I pulled up to the building, I couldn't make myself get out of the truck. How does one go about making plans to bury their best friend? The funeral director was very kind and helpful and guided me through the arrangements. Keith's boss had called to say that the expenses would be covered by insurance, so at least I didn't have that to worry about. But honestly, I don't remember any of the details of that day. It was like I was walking in a fog.

At the service I held Gracie Bear in my arms. Jason stood next to me and Mama. Daddy then came and stood by Mama and put his hand in mine. Daddy looked frail. I think the drinking was getting to him. Why couldn't he just give it up?! I'll never know.

The preacher started the short service. "Dearly beloved, today, we mourn a son, a father, and a husband. We mourn the loss of Keith Jason Walker. Death reminds us that each one of us will experience it. Our flesh is only a temporary housing, but our souls are eternal. One day each of us will stand before the heavenly Father, our God, and His Son Jesus Christ. It is there we will have to give an account of our life. Our promise is secure in God, and He promises to comfort all those who mourn. We will always hold dear the life of Keith in our hearts!

It was overcast the day I buried my sweetheart. As they lowered him in the ground, I felt like a piece of me died and was buried with him. It was surreal. I was alone and it happened so fast.

After the funeral Mama and Daddy took me and the kids out to eat. I pushed the food around on my plate. My stomach was in knots. Later that day Daddy went back home, but Mama stayed with me for a few weeks to give me time to get things in order and process. Keith had a small life insurance policy, but it was only ten thousand dollars. Because the accident was a work-related death, there would be some type of insurance payout for me and the kids. I just didn't know how much. There was a question on whether the company's policy was up-to-date which left me with more questions than answers. At least there was enough to get us by for now until I figured out what I was going to do.

I knew my first order of business was to get a full-time job. I went back to the only thing I really knew and got a job as a waitress at a local breakfast joint named Clyde's. Clyde was a working owner, which meant he worked morning, noon, and night to keep the business running. I learned that he was a widower just like me, having lost his wife to cancer three years before. It seemed he was now married to his restaurant to fill the void. The restaurant was popular because everything was made from scratch. Clyde was up at four o'clock in the morning slicing potatoes, making batter for pancakes, baking muffins and croissants and whatever needed to be done. He ran a tight ship, but that was fine by me.

Keith's Chevy truck had become a precious treasure. There were oil stains on the driver's seat that made me smile and think of him, so I left them. Each time my hands touched the steering wheel it was as if my hands were touching his. It was the vehicle where we had spent hours talking, kissing, and dreaming of our future. A future that had been cut far too short.

Three years passed and yet grief was still my constant companion. Since Keith's death, well-meaning friends would encourage me that over time I would get over it. Well, guess what? The pain seemed as fresh as ever. Although I kept a smile on my face and tried to move on for the kids' sake, when night came and I was alone in our bed, the sadness descended, and the grief was all too real.

My heart was broken. While the kids brought much joy to my life, the love of my life was gone. I never pictured this could happen to me. My life had become something I expected to read in a book or watch on a sad movie. I could feel myself spiraling down into depression but wasn't sure how to get out of it. I talked with Wilma. She insisted I was still grieving and needed time to process the loss of my soul mate. Maybe she was right. Whatever was going on, I still didn't feel like me. I constantly felt run down, mentally drained, and emotionally caput.

By now Jason was in second grade and Gracie Bear was a kindergartener. There had been so many "firsts" without Keith. So many times, I had wanted to share a special moment with him. At least I had my neighbor Wilma. She often watched the kids so I could make a quick run to the grocery store and have a moment to myself. Sometimes she would invite us over for dinner or I would invite her. It was nice to have company and the kids loved her.

One morning as Wilma and I were having breakfast I received a phone call. Wilma could tell by the tone in my voice and the look on my face it was not good. I started to dread answering the phone. It was Mama. "Mary, are you sitting down?" she asked.

"Mama, what is it?"

"Daddy died last night, baby. I found him this morning."

"What? Mama, I'm sorry. I will be on my way shortly," I told her before disconnecting. I was stunned, completely unable to process the news. Wilma had heard and looked at me with compassionate eyes.

"Can I help?" She was already in motion beginning to clear the breakfast dishes to allow me to go pack. I called Clyde soon afterwards. I had the best boss on the planet. After I told him the news, he not only gave me the time off, but shoved $50 in my hand for gas money and sent me on my way back home.

The kids were bickering in the car most of the drive, which set my already fragile emotions on edge. I had so many questions. When we finally arrived, the kids jumped out of the car and ran off to play in the backyard. Mama met me on the porch as I lugged our two suitcases up the steps.

"The drinking finally caught up to him," she stated as she grabbed for one of the cases. "He went to bed drinking, and according to Dr. Ross, had a massive heart attack and died instantly. I found him around 7:00 a.m. I knew something was wrong when he didn't come out of his room for breakfast." She started dabbing a tissue at the corner of her eyes. Even though it had been three years, I was still grieving the loss of Keith. And while I was sad about Daddy, it wasn't the same. Our relationship had been distant for the last few years as his drinking increased. I told him I wasn't willing to bring the kids around when he was drinking, and so the times we had been to their house had been few and far between. I had mixed feelings about the whole situation. But what was for certain was that Mama needed me and the kids.

I helped Mom with the funeral arrangements and other decisions. I wasn't looking forward to attending another funeral. I'd had it with death!

The funeral was small, with just a few church folks. Trying to keep herself busy, Mama made most of the food. Lord have mercy, she must have been up half the night cooking. There was no shortage of mashed potatoes, beef roast, fresh baked bread, fried chicken, pasta salads, sweet jelly salads, and jumbo chocolate chip cookies. The women at the church insisted that they wanted to cook for her, but she kindly refused their offer. She wanted to do it, as it helped take her mind off losing Daddy. The women understood and surrounded her with prayer and hugs for her and the family. After it was all over, though, I could see the weariness hit her like a ton of bricks. Thankfully I wasn't the only one, as the women stepped in to help clean up the mess she had made of the kitchen. They were grateful to help, and everyone pitched in until that kitchen was squeaky clean.

Over the next few days I helped Mama clean out Daddy's things. We built a fire out back and burned the old dusty drapes that had been used to keep the light out of his bedroom. Why someone would ever want to live in that kind of darkness, I'll never know. After we emptied out his stuff, Mama watched the kids while I painted it. I also put together a few shelves I bought from the local sawmill. It was a long day, but as the sun set, I looked around the room and breathed a sigh of accomplishment. Daddy's old room had been transformed into a sewing room, perfect for crafts and a space for Mama's colorful fabrics and quilting supplies. I built some shelves and even made her a desk.

I decided on the spur of the moment to make a special design on one of the walls. I poked my head out of the room to ask Mama to take the kids along the ditches to bring me some of the wildflowers that grew there. I didn't tell her what I was up to. I hadn't allowed her in the room yet, as I wanted it to be perfect before I opened the door. When they returned, Jason knocked on the door lightly. After opening the door, he held out a huge bouquet of multi-colored wildflowers. "Those will be perfect," I informed him, giving him a kiss.

I used the flowers as stamps and made designs all over the walls. It reminded me of spring. The room went from dreary to fabulous in a matter of hours with a little fresh paint and a lot of hard work. I made Mama put on a blindfold before I allowed the kids to take her by the hand and escort her into the old bedroom.

"Mama, what do you smell? I asked.

"Well, I smell fresh paint. A lot of it." She took off her blindfold and turned in a slow circle to see the entire room. What had been the dingiest room in the house was now the brightest one. She loved how I organized her shelves and fabrics, and most of all she loved the peaceful sea foam green I had chosen for the walls. Mama cried tears of joy!

The kids and I stayed for a week. But I knew it was time for me to get back to work, school, and our home. Mama was sad to see me go. Despite the sorrow of why I had been there, we still had a fun time together. The kids weren't quite ready to leave and so she agreed to keep them through the weekend. I knew they would provide a good distraction for her so the house wouldn't feel so empty. Like most good grandmothers she spoiled them rotten. Which is exactly what grandmothers are supposed to do. Mama told me that having grandchildren was like a second chance at being a parent. Right now, I knew it was like a medicine to her soul.

The next few days, while the kids were with Mama, it allowed me time to process. Although Mama had always tried to prepare me that Daddy would die prematurely if he refused to stop drinking, it didn't make it any better. The truth is there is only one way out of addiction and that is death. With both Keith and now Daddy gone, I didn't realize it, but I was angry at God. It had slowly crept in my heart as I argued at why life was so unfair. I didn't understand why I had to face all this death. I asked for forgiveness because I knew my heart wasn't in the right place. I needed healing and it was going to take some time.

When Sunday came it was time for me to pick up the kids and for life to return to normal, whatever that meant. After we got everything loaded into the truck, Mama walked to the driver's side window so she could say a prayer for me and the kids. I didn't want to pray, but I was not going to stop her from praying for me. Her prayers were always sweet and from her heart, and they made me feel better.

"Dear Lord, I pray You would bless my daughter and my grandkids. Keep them safe and help them to turn to You. In Jesus's name, Amen." She patted my hand as she finished and blew a final kiss to each of the kids.

"Love you, Mama," I said, trying to keep my emotions in check.

As I backed out of the driveway Mama waved goodbye from the front porch. While we headed home, I pondered all that had happened in such a short amount of time. This was it. A new chapter in my life. The two men I loved the most were gone. I wiped away a tear as I turned out onto the road.

A few months passed. God and I didn't talk much during that time. Normally I would have a talk with Him every now and again. But lately, not so much. My life was busy and being a single parent consumed most of my waking hours.

It was two more days until Friday, I thought as I wiped down the counter at the restaurant. Thank the Lord, I had the weekend off and that meant I would be relaxing and watching television. I was excited as it had been a long week. The restaurant was getting busier. Clyde's reputation for making everything from scratch was picking up more business. As I ended my shift, I hobbled to the car, ready to be home with the kids. My feet were very sore and I was ready for bed. I fed the kids a late supper of jumbo shrimp and grits. They ate heartily as they filled me in on the events of their day. They were both chatty and so I didn't have to say much, which was probably good. It took all I could do just to keep my eyes open. Finally, with full bellies, it was time for bed.

Gracie Bear was giving me a tough time, but eventually she went down to sleep. She never wanted to miss a thing. I think she secretly thought I was having fun in the midnight hours. If she only realized that the extent of my fun after working all day was drooling on my pillow. Pretty exciting, right? I picked her up and rocked her to sleep. I could tell she was actually as tired as I was. When her eyes finally closed, I laid her down in her bed and tiptoed out the door after quietly clicking the door shut so as not to wake her. When I got to my room, I didn't even bother washing my face or changing my clothes. I fell into bed and like Gracie Bear was out like a light.

The last few months since Keith and Daddy's deaths, I had been so busy working and caring for the kids that I had no time to even think to take care of myself. I was dealing with anger in my heart, and I was still grieving. In frustration I said, "Well, God, You took my husband and my Daddy, so, I guess that means two down and one more to go."

I grabbed an iced tea, slammed the back door, and sat on the back step of the house, brooding. The phone rang. My heart dropped as I pondered what I had just said. A chill ran over me, and I intuitively felt something was wrong. Plus, it was rare that anybody called me during the day unless they were a telemarketer.

"Please don't let it be Mama. Please, God, please!" I said as I answered the phone just before the answering machine got it.

"Hello, may I speak to a Mrs. Mary Walker, please?" the woman said after identifying herself as a nurse from the hospital.

"This is Mary Walker," I replied as my hands began to shake.

"Mary, your mother has suffered a massive stroke and is in ICU," she began.

I hesitated, then said, "Oh no! Is she okay?"

"Well, I don't know the answer to that right now. I am sorry. We are watching her and don't have any report yet from the doctor. Mary, I would get here as soon as you can." There was compassion in her voice, which I appreciated, but which also put fear in my heart. I couldn't lose Mama too!

"Thank you for calling. I will be there as soon as I can," I replied. I felt as if my legs were going to give out, and I slid to the floor after I hung up the phone. I was stunned. Think, think, think! My brain felt numb. A sense of panic washed over me and my whole body began to shake. Somehow, I had the sense to call my neighbor. She answered on the first ring. "Wilma, please come and sit with the kids. Mama had a stroke, and I have to get to the hospital. I am freaking out!"

"Calm down, Mary, I got this! I'll be right over. Don't worry," she replied.

My calm friend—what would I do without her? I knew I could count on her for anything!

I drove like crazy all the way to the hospital. I was surprised I wasn't pulled over and given a speeding ticket. I wanted to get to Mama and see for myself what happened. When I arrived at the hospital, nothing could have prepared me for what I was about to hear.

"Hi, um, I'm Mary Walker. My mama was brought here earlier today. They called me and said she had a stroke."

"Oh yes, have a seat in the lobby, please. I will call the nurse and get you back there as quickly as I can. There are water and cookies if you want some," the receptionist said as she waved her arm at a table along the side of the waiting room.

"Thank you," I replied, although the thought of food made my stomach turn. She went back to answering the switchboard, and I was alone with my thoughts. They weren't very encouraging.

I sat down and grabbed a magazine for a distraction. I flipped through the pages, completely unable to concentrate. Here I was back again in a hospital awaiting bad news.

"Mrs. Walker, the nurse is ready to speak with you now."

The nurse came out to the lobby wearing blue smocks and a blue cap over her hair. "Mary, your mother has had a massive stroke," she began. "She is paralyzed on her left side and right now is unable to speak."

I began to sob uncontrollably. The pent-up dam from the loss of Keith, my dad, and now this news of my mom was too much. The nurse tried to console me the best she could. Until then I never realized how hard a nurse's job could be. You cannot pay them enough for what they see and experience when working at a hospital.

"I know this is hard and that it's going to take some time to get used to seeing her this way. Strokes can happen suddenly without warning and leave permanent damage. I wanted to let you know before we go back, to prepare you the best way I can. You will have to see for yourself." She held the door open for me now so we could go to Mama's room.

"Mama!" I said entering the room. Her bed was elevated, and her eyes were open. That's a good sign, I thought. "Mama, look at you. You're sitting up. Can you hear me?" But there was no response.

The bed was elevated because her throat was swollen, and they didn't want her to choke. She couldn't speak or do much of anything else.

Her face was swollen and drooped on the left side. She looked so different, and it scared me. The nurse explained it was the aftermath of a stroke. Up to this time Mama had always been so energetic and on the go. Now lying still and quiet in the hospital bed, she seemed small and vulnerable. I never thought I would see her this way. I ached to hear her voice again and wondered if I ever would.

I stayed at the hospital with her that night. The nurse's assistant brought me a sheet set, a scratchy blanket, and a pillow for the expandable chair. I swear that pillow was filled with cement instead of memory foam. They must not want visitors to stay for extended periods of time because they surely don't make you feel comfortable. All night long I stayed close to her, looking at the clock every hour, hoping for improvement. I thought she would wake up and this nightmare would all be over, or she would reach out her arm to hold my hand or speak to me. I was holding out in faith although the circumstances seemed grim.

By morning my head hurt from lack of sleep. I rubbed my neck and stretched my arms and back. They were all killing me. On top of my worry about Mama, I missed my kids and I wanted my own bed. I sighed as I tried to fold and put away the blanket and pillow from my makeshift bed when Pastor Greg walked through the door with his faith and his Bible. "I'm here if you need me," he said with a hug. He patted Mama's hand and prayed over her and then quietly slipped out into the hallway where I heard him praying again for her.

"Oh, Lord, have mercy and bring healing. Send a miracle!" he cried. He knew this was a sensitive situation and handled it with such grace and respect. I wanted a miracle just as badly as he did. I wanted Mama to rise out of that bed and be completely healed. I just didn't feel like she was going to. I still didn't want to lose hope, and I couldn't give up believing for a miracle. Sometimes you just know that you know something is about to happen. It's God's way of preparing you in advance. But it doesn't make it any easier to face, that's for sure.

The nurse brought me a complimentary dinner. I picked at my food. My nerves and worry removed all signs of hunger. The nurses came in and flipped Mama from side-to-side every few hours to prevent her from getting bed sores, but other than that, I was alone with her in the silent room except for the beeps and whirring of the many machines connected to her. Exhausted, I eventually fell asleep next to her. Around three in the morning, I awoke to a loud steady beep coming from one of the machines. The next thing I knew the lights were flipped on and the room filled with hospital staff. In the chaos, they asked if I would step out into the hallway. Scared and half asleep, I left the room. I cracked the doorway wanting to be with Mama. It was clear she had stopped breathing and a doctor was doing CPR compressions to restart her heart. "Breathe, Mama, breathe!" I whispered, willing her to live.

I watched as the doctors tried feverishly to make her heart beat again. With each time they pressed on her chest, my heart sunk. Tears streamed down my face as the doctor declared time of death. It was here and now I had to say goodbye. It all felt so very cold and final.

Keith and I swore that we would be there for each other in times like these. I felt abandoned and alone in that moment and desperately wanted him by my side. I never thought I would have to walk through life alone. I mean, I had my kids, but they cannot fulfill the longing for love and belonging of a mate. A heaviness passed over me. It was as if someone had covered me with a weighted blanket and I felt smothered. It was as if every organ inside my body seized. I couldn't speak, I couldn't feel, and I couldn't move. My head began to spin, and I slipped into what seemed a dark tunnel.

When I came to, I found myself all alone in a hospital bed. I looked around trying to get my bearings, but my vision was blurry. I noticed a figure, a man in white linen, slowly walking towards me. His face was bright and his eyes sparkled with so much love. Then my eyes dialed in, and it was Keith, "Oh baby, I've missed you," I said as I reached for his hand.

"It's not your time, Mary," he said. "Mama is here in heaven with me. There is no point to return to the past. What was once, is no longer. It has been undone and now made new." With that Keith's voice began to fade and so did his body.

"Don't go! Please, I love you," I begged.

"You will live again, Mary," I heard as he disappeared.

I burst into tears. I missed Keith dearly and at that moment felt his presence in that room so strong. I was grateful for the vision and that Mama was with him. I wanted to be with them, but the children needed me.

I told the nurse about seeing Keith. She thought it was a hallucination, but I disagreed. I know it was a vision from God. He knew I needed strength. Mama often said, "God will always help you when you feel like there is no way out."

Every time I wanted to give up, the Lord would put someone else in my path to help me. I would have just enough strength for the task ahead. That is supernatural provision.

The hospital staff told me that after Mama died I blacked out. I learned later that Isabelle, a woman from church, had come and stayed all night in my room and prayed for me. She was my angel. An angel God sent to me to help me in my time of need.

Isabelle was a close friend of Mama's. She was an older woman in her late seventies who raised seven children and had ten grandchildren. Even though her complexion was dark, her eyes were blue, and her hair was long and white as snow. She had stayed at the hospital to pray for me even though her health was getting bad, and she had just had knee surgery. It was humbling that an older woman, who had her own health issues, would take time to pray for me. Who does that?

Now fully awake I picked up the phone and called Wilma. She had been worried since it had been a couple of days and I had not checked in. "The kids are fine," she confirmed. I told her the devastating news about Mama. She had figured as much.

"Let me get checked out and I'll be over to pick up the kids," I told her. The weight of responsibility suddenly settled on my shoulders as I said it, thinking of what needed to be done. After I picked up the kids, I would have to break the news to them that their grandma was now in heaven. Then I would have to plan her funeral.

"Honey, now don't you worry," Wilma instructed. "I'll bring the kids as soon they are out of school."

Whew, that was a relief. I was so grateful for Wilma's friendship. She always knew what to do and never made me feel uncomfortable asking or that I was a burden.

As I sat and waited for the nurse to announce my discharge, Isabelle came in my room. She was carrying a bouquet of yellow sunflowers. It was something Keith would have done. Their bright colors and her thoughtful smile made me grin in spite of everything. "How are you feeling, Mary?" she asked.

"Well, Isabelle, it was the saddest day of my life. I thought losing my husband and Daddy was sad, but this has been the worst. I don't want to feel anymore. It's just too much to bear! My God in heaven, I can't stop crying," I confessed as I grabbed another tissue to wipe my face.

Isabelle placed her hands on my face. "Darling, your mama loved you with all her heart. She's with Jesus now and you can take comfort in that. But you aren't going where she is just yet. You hear me? You got to live again, girl. You gots to love again. You got babies who need you. Don't give up, Mary!" she encouraged me, taking a breath before she started again. "Your Mama's time done come. Nobody knows when that day will be. So, we got to make sure every second counts. We all start out in heaven and some of us come to earth. But one thing is for sure, we all going to see God one day. Every one of us. Do you hear what I'm saying to you?" She was looking me in the eyes intensely.

"Give this to Jesus, Mary. This is a burden you were never meant to carry." She sat beside me, put her arms around me, and held me quietly for a long time before she spoke again. "Remember, His burden is light, baby, it's light."

I knew she spoke truth, but I was angry—especially with God. First Keith, then Daddy, and now Mama. It wasn't fair. He wiped out my whole family. Who was to blame? God, of course; He's the One in charge, right? I blamed Him for taking my husband, for letting Daddy die in his addiction, and now for taking Mama. She was the glue that had held our family together. I felt so alone.

I knew deep down that Mama was struggling for a while, and Daddy's death broke her heart. It's not uncommon for spouses to die shortly after the other dies. Maybe that is what happened to her. Lord, help my kids if that be the fate of my life.

Isabelle let me cry and rant as she kept her arms around me. "Tomorrow is going to be better, Mary. Tomorrow is your today. Don't waste it."

I knew what she said was right, but my heart turned cold that day. I didn't want to listen. I knew she was a praying woman and begged her to pray for me. Perhaps God would listen to her. Because He sure wasn't listening to me anymore.

"Oh, baby girl. It would be my honor. Your mama prayed for me often as I raised seven kids. She helped me through plenty of trials. I want you to know I'll be on my knees till I can't be on my knees no more. Nothing is going to stop me from kneeling before God and praying for you. He made a way for me, and He will do the same for you. Keep your faith and never forget death is life, Mary. Death is life."

Shortly after Isabelle left the nurse came in and completed the paperwork so that I could be discharged and head home. I was ready to go. I needed out of this place that reminded me of death and how I missed my babies.

"Where's Mama?" I asked before she left. She informed me that the funeral home had already picked her up. She instructed me to go there as soon as I could to decide on a plan for her burial. I nodded and headed to the parking lot. Right now I just wanted to get my kids and be home.

When I walked through the door, Jason jumped in my arms, "Mama, I missed you." I gave him a huge hug as I felt Gracie Bear tugging on my leg. Setting Jason down, I picked her up next and gave her an equally big hug.

"Mama, can we go home?" Until then I hadn't realized how unsettling this time had been for them as well.

"Yes, Gracie Bear, it's time to go home. I gave her another squeeze, told them both how much I had missed them, and then thanked Wilma again.

But before we left Jason handed me a card he made. It was a crumpled piece of paper and he had struggled with the writing. But his face beamed at his handiwork.

"What did you make for me?" I asked.

Jason blushed, "A poem, Mama. Read it."

He had written, "Mama is great. Mama is fun. Mama is my sweet. She is the only one."

"Awe, you wrote this all by yourself for me?"

He nodded. "Yes, and I even dotted the i's right this time."

"I am so proud of you. Thank you. I love it." Tears filled my eyes for the hundredth time that day.

"Mama, what about me? I made you something too," Gracie Bear whined in her baby voice. It gets me every time.

"Oh, I am sorry, baby girl," I said as I turned my attention to her. "I could never forget you." I took the card she had made and saw that she had scribbled flowers all over it along with three words woven in-between them. It read, "I love you, Mama." There were a few more m's than there should be, but it wasn't about the grammar. It was the thought that counted. She made me proud.

I gave Wilma a final hug as we walked next door to our home. Walking through the door released a flood of emotions in me once again. I realized we were all alone. "Why are you crying, Mama?" Jason asked.

"Come here, kids." I led them to the couch so that I could sit between them both. Without fanfare I told them that their grandma had died.

Jason was so sweet. He held me and said, "Mama, it's going to be all right. Grandma is with Jesus."

"How do you know that?" I asked, surprised.

"An angel told me," he began. "Last night he came into my room."

"Where did you see it? What did it look like?" I was caught completely off guard by his response.

"I didn't see the angel," he told me, "but he talked to me, and he left a single feather near my bed."

It was then I recalled the time when as a young girl, after a rainbow faded, a feather had fallen from the sky. "May I see the feather?" I asked. He pulled it from his pocket and opened his little hand. I gasped. I ran to my room and found the treasure box Daddy made for me all those years before. I opened it and stood amazed. My feather was identical to Jason's.

"What is it, Mama?" Jason asked as he followed me into the room.

"It was an angel, Jason." He smiled because I believed him. I marveled at how God spoke to us both in those moments but then wondered why He hadn't answered my prayers to heal Keith and Mama.

It was hard to get through the funeral. The kids kept me distracted, but all I wanted to do was hear my mama's voice again. After it ended I wanted to head to Mama's. At least there I could feel close to her again. I needed to walk through the house one more time before I buttoned everything up.

"Do you mind sitting with the kids while I walk around the property one last time," I asked Tansy once we had changed. She nodded, understanding my need for some alone time.

I pulled up to the property and sat in my car for a few minutes before getting out. There were so many memories flooding my mind as my feet slid through the tall grass out back of the house. Standing still for a moment, I closed my eyes and took a deep breathe. I didn't know when the next time would be that I'd return to this place. Glimpsing up at the old vines wiggling up the siding to my window, I could see the hole I made in the screen with my finger. I wonder why Daddy never fixed that? Out of the corner of my eye, my old friend the willow was waving to me. She beckoned me back to my secret place.

It had been years since I had sat under the protection of her wings. I stooped down beneath the branches and crawled underneath. I was certainly taller now, but the feelings I felt as a child came back vividly. I sat and closed my eyes. This was the one place where I always felt safe. This was the place I came when everything fell apart. This place was where I wished, I dreamed, and I believed God could do anything!

The breeze gently caressed my face as I watched the branches sway in the wind. I was caught in a memory that captivated the moment. It was warm outside, summertime, and bees were buzzing around. The familiar cries of cows grazing in the field all lulled me right back into a world of imagining and dreaming as in times past.

I remembered when I imagined myself as a magical princess twirling about in a colorful sundress. Dandelions displayed over the countryside and I couldn't resist picking up a few and setting them in the curls of my hair. The soles of my feet were black from dirt and tree sap. I'd been playing outside all day and had been under that tree making my wishes to God. Back then, I wished away all the bad in everyone's life. I wished that Mama and Daddy would stop fighting, Daddy would quit drinking, and I even wished for a puppy.

The specific breed of dog I had in mind was a golden retriever. I had already chosen her name as well—Sammy or Sam for short. I desperately wanted a dog because I never liked to be alone for long. I dreamed how we would sit under the willow tree together. Every now and then I would peek from under the leaves to ensure Mama was nearby. She always was either hanging laundry, working in the kitchen, or sweeping the porch. But neither Daddy nor Mama were agreeable to my getting a dog. It became a forgotten dream.

Even so, I would imagine I had one as I sat under the willow tree. When Mama stood in the kitchen washing dishes, I could see her face through the window. She pretended not to see me, but I knew she knew I was under the tree. It was our little secret and no one was to know but us. I thought she would have told Daddy by now. She didn't tell him everything, but I know she told him some things.

My imagination faded back into reality. I let out a big involuntary sigh. Mama was in heaven. I wished for just one more time to hear her voice. I missed the warmth of her smile and the way she held me. "Mama, if you can hear me, I miss you. I love you!" I said with my face lifted to the sky. I don't know what I expected, but what I didn't expect was the grey feather that floated down to the ground and landed by my feet. I cried like a baby. Mama must have sent an angel. I knew that I knew she had heard me and my heart leapt with joy.

I looked around the yard and then climbed the steps up to the porch. It really needs a good coat of paint, I thought as I opened the door and walked inside. It was so very quiet, missing the quality it held when Mama and Daddy were alive. I wandered around taking it all in. I wanted to grab a few things before I left. One thing was for sure, I wanted her favorite mixing bowl and rolling pin along with a rooster fan I coveted, which she always kept on the kitchen counter.

Wilma came back with me the next day. She helped me box up the rest of Mama's belongings and household items and then covered the furniture with sheets to keep the dust off. Then she helped me clean and board up the house. It was tough to do, but I got through it. In life we do hard things, don't we?

I walked around the property one more time before getting ready to leave. It was strange not to see Mama standing in the kitchen window where I had always looked for her.

CHAPTER EIGHT

STARTING OVER

*R*aising kids is hard work and don't let anyone tell *you any different. It is the toughest job on the planet whether you stay at home or work a full-time job—which just adds to it. Daddy and Mama had instilled in me a good work ethic. And working hard had always served me well. I liked the end result knowing I had completed a task well, but sometimes it just left me plain exhausted.*

After Mama's death, next I had to deal with packing up her house and tying up all the loose ends that come with the finality of closing out a life. But then it was back to the normal grind. Wilma helped me with many things. I was so blessed to have her in my life, plus she was a good singer too. A few times she even made me go to karaoke with her. I was reluctant at first but eventually gave in. Once I got passed my own insecurities, I had fun! Each morning she came over faithfully with a smile on her face to help me get the kids up and around. She would always start a pot of coffee.

"What you up to today?" she asked one morning.

"Well, since this is my day off, I thought maybe I would take the kids to the apple picking. You want to come with us?" I hoped she would say yes, so I added, "I was thinking of picking up cinnamon sugar donuts and apple cider while there."

"Now, you know I don't need any extra donuts. Have you seen my behind?" She started to laugh. About that time Jason came in the kitchen, his hair spiked up—morning hair.

"Morning, Mama. Hey, Wilma," he said.

"Looks like you slept good last night," Wilma giggled.

"Guess what? I had a dream last night," he stated as he pulled out a bowl for cereal and opened the refrigerator to grab the milk.

"You did? Well, I want to hear all about it," she said with an encouraging smile.

"What was it about?" I asked as I sat down at our kitchen table holding a mug of steaming fresh coffee. Boy, it smelled good.

"I was a pitcher with my own baseball diamond in our backyard," he began.

"You had your own baseball field?" I questioned. That was strange, but dreams can be, so I kept listening.

"Yes, ma'am, I sure did." He had a big grin. Jason had always dreamed of playing professional baseball, and I could tell the dream encouraged his heart.

"Well, I hope one day you make it big and are a wealthy man," I told him. "Then you can afford your own baseball field. But if you want to be a professional player, then you are going to need to eat your breakfast. You need nutrition for those muscular arms you're going to need to catch those balls and swing those bats!" I squeezed his bicep to make my point.

Gracie Bear had wandered into the kitchen and crawled into my arms. She was so not a morning person.

"Mama, can I have a sip of your coffee?" she asked.

"Absolutely not!" I told her playfully. "But I'll pour you some milk and we can put some chocolate syrup in it and that can be your coffee. How would that be?" Gracie Bear nodded vigorously.

"You just sit right there and I'll make it," Wilma said, allowing me a few more moments of snuggle time.

After she drank her milk and Jason finished his cereal I instructed them, "Go in the bathroom and brush your teeth and get ready. I am taking you both to the apple orchard today!"

They were ecstatic and showed it by jumping around the living room. Now, normally I don't allow them to jump on the furniture, but on this occasion I didn't care. If I thought I could jump on the couch without destroying it, I would have too! They had so much energy it made me smile. It reminded me of Keith. I always needed coffee in the morning to get me going. Like their daddy, they didn't need a thing.

Finally, the jumping slowed and Jason walked back in the kitchen trying to grab a cup of coffee for himself. Wilma teased him with a gleam in her eye. "Now Jason, you know if you drink coffee, you'll grow a ton of facial hair."

"Really?" he asked. "Then I guess you need to stop drinking coffee, Miss Wilma." Jason responded, sticking his tongue out in a playful gesture. He had a quick wit just like his daddy.

"Oh, you stinker!" Wilma scolded as she jumped up from the table and chased him around the house. When she finally caught him, she tickled him till he was in tears. I watched the two in play. Every day Jason looked more like his father.

"Mama, aren't you supposed to defend me?" He was laughing so hard he could hardly talk.

"Well, I had just got out of bed. I can't even defend myself until I have a couple more cups of coffee," I explained with a smile.

The entire day turned out as delightful as the morning. The weather was beautiful and we had a great time picking apples, enjoying the day, and eating the cinnamon donuts I brought home for dessert.

That night when I tucked the kids into bed, Jason asked if he could pray. It wasn't our normal routine at night although it should have been. *(Guilty as charged!)* I had pretty much given up on prayer, as it seemed God just didn't answer mine. Life hadn't been fair or kind to me and I was tired of trying to pretend it was. But if Jason wanted to pray, I wasn't going to stop him. I remember how I used to when I was little.

"Sure, go ahead, baby," I told him as I sat on his bed. Jason closed his eyes and folded his hands. "Dear Lord, You know I love baseball. And I believe You can do anything. What do You say we work together and build a baseball field? Well, how about You build it, and I will play the game. What do You say, God?"

"Amen. That was a great prayer!" I complimented him, and meant it. Honestly, I loved his faith. Adults like to make things complicated, but Mama always said all we must do is simply ask! It was the waiting that was the hard part, though. I realized that more now than I did at his age.

It became a more regular occurrence that Jason and Gracie Bear both wanted me to pray with them before bed. I thought it was a great idea and we did it occasionally. But I knew God was tugging at my heart, through my kids, to do it more. They believed in Him as I once did, and I didn't want to take that from them. It was important they understood about God themselves. Their prayers were heartfelt and sweet. Jason even prayed for a puppy! Now, that was going take a miracle.

The kids were growing up quickly. Jason joined the baseball team at school. And before I knew it, one year had led into another. Boy, time never stops for no one. Jason ate, slept, and drank baseball. Like I wasn't busy enough, the daily practice and games became my new schedule every week. It seemed I was always running here and there.

Gracie Bear loved going with me. She was her brother's biggest cheerleader in the bleachers.

"You get them, Jason. You can do it! I believe in you," she would yell from our position in the stands.

As he had always dreamed, Jason was the pitcher—and he was good. Each time just before he threw a pitch, I saw him look at us. He was like, "Yes, sit back and watch, I got this!" His goal was simple on the field. Cut the batters. I thought he did a rather good job of it. Now, I didn't understand the game like Keith did, but I gave it a full effort.

Many kids tried out for the team, but the coach only selected a few. This made some folks irritated. I wasn't bothered by it because Jason made it with no problem. I was a proud Mama. I loved his spunk and determination. He was a hard worker just like his daddy.

There was this one kid named Barry. No matter how many pitches Jason threw, he still couldn't strike him out. He walked Barry every time. But he refused to give up and one of these days he would get Barry out. Jason and Keith both had a thoughtful and caring heart and a deep sense of humor. Both put the needs of others before their own. When I heard Jason laugh, it always reminded me of Keith. How I missed Keith's laugh.

I've heard some say that kids will be opposite of their folks, but in my case that wasn't true. Jason was just like me. When he set his mind to doing something, he wouldn't walk away until it was finished. And if you want to be a player in the game of baseball, then that's just how you need to be. Coaches don't like lazy players or you're outta there!

After his game on Friday, I took the kids out for pizza. That was a real treat for them. What's not to love about gooey cheese, spicy pepperoni, and garlic butter crust? It was a treat for me as well, as it meant this Mama didn't have to cook. It was a nice break. I had the weekend off and even got a chance to sleep in, which was rare in the world of single parenting.

Monday morning, I dropped the kids off at school and headed to work. Work had been a place of frustration because for the last few months, I felt my pies were complete flops. *(Why are we women so hard on ourselves?)* I knew my crust recipe was s something, and I just couldn't seem to get the measurements right. I worked so hard to perfect the pie crust. And then suddenly, one day it clicked. The customers noticed and so did my boss, Clyde. He was proud of me. I wondered why it couldn't have clicked back like three months ago. But I had finally perfected a rich buttery crust for our signature apple, cherry, and wild-berry pies, and all my pie testers where pleased about it.

The restaurant was always busy, and I could not make enough pies to keep up. It seemed my hands were always stained with berries. We sold two hundred pies a day. That was fifty pounds of various fruits, ten bags of all-purpose flour, fifteen bags of sugar, and a whole lot of lard mixed up by one good woman, me, Mary Ann Walker!

It was time for a break, and a much needed one. I thought about taking the kids to an adventure park, but I didn't have the money for that in our budget. It took every dime I had to pay rent, insurance, food, and gas. It wasn't easy living on just one income. Being a waitress and pie baker at the restaurant didn't pay that much!

Although hoping for some time off with the kids, I received a phone call from Marley Thickens. She lived in a small cottage just behind Mama's old house. The grass needed to be cut and the place needed some minor repairs. I cringed. I was sure everything was overgrown at the house since it had been all boarded up and no one living there. Kettlesville was small, and so things like that didn't go unnoticed. Each neighborhood had their own neighborhood watch. No one got away with anything. "As soon as I have the money I'll head back over and take care of the outside of the house," I informed her. I needed to figure out what I was going to do with the property. But just the thought of it overwhelmed me.

When I made it over to Mama's the next week, I noticed Marley's cottage. The outside was meticulously kept. Why, I don't believe even a spider web could have remained on her front porch. Everything was perfect. It was no wonder she was frustrated with me. She didn't want the houses around her to look unkept, and I didn't blame her. She was being kind and knew my situation, but I could tell she was frustrated and didn't like looking at the house falling into disrepair.

"Mary, you might consider adding a fresh coat of paint to the place," she encouraged as I finished mowing and was getting ready to go. Sure. No problem. Like I can afford to take care of two houses! *(Oh yeah, and by the way, I had so much spare time on my hands!)*

"Why don't you sell the place?" she asked. *(Of course; that would be the easiest thing to do, right?)* "Then you wouldn't have to mow or have the upkeep, and it would actually provide some money for you and the kids."

I shook my head in response as tears sprang to my eyes. There were still too many memories. Mama made sure that the house went to me. I believe she wanted it kept in the family and so I planned to keep it.

I pondered what Marley said as the kids and I drove home. Let's face it, buying gallons of paint, even if I went with the cheap stuff, was still expensive. And the last I saw money doesn't just fall from the sky. I knew I had neglected the house and needed to get back to it, and so Marley's call was the push I needed to help me get things started. But as I sat at the kitchen table, that feeling of being overwhelmed began to creep over me again. Just to get caught up with the bills for summer, back to school, and what needed to be done on Mama's house was going to take around ten thousand dollars. I blinked at the number and put my head in my hands. With no faith at all, I prayed, "Lord, I need Your help; please bring the cash! Amen."

As the school year came to an end, I knew I wasn't going to be able to put off working on Mama's house for much longer. We could stay there for the summer, and it would give me a chance to fix the house up and reconnect with old memories. I made up my mind—once Jason's baseball season ended late May that would be the perfect time for us to handle some things at Mama's, and I felt I was finally ready.

I came to work early one morning. Clyde was working hard as usual. He was always the first one in and had already sliced forty pounds of potatoes for hashbrowns before I arrived, and the sun wasn't even up! He pointed over to the glass case as I walked by him to grab my apron. A pitiful single piece of apple pie sat all by its lonesome.

"Is this all we have left?" I was shocked. I had made fifty pies the day before.

"Yes, Melvin picked up the last ten pies for a family reunion."

"Well, I better get to baking," I said as I washed my hands and hurried off to the kitchen. Melvin was one of our regulars. He was eighty years old and ate at the diner every night.

He ordered the same meals each week. Monday was pot roast. Tuesday, turkey dinner with all the fixings. Wednesday was breakfast for dinner. Thursday, liver and onions *(which made me sick just smelling it)*. And Friday was fish and chips with extra tartar sauce and sliced lemons. Saturday was the only day he didn't have a regular order and said he was up for anything. But with every meal he never forgot to order a slice of fruit pie.

Normally we wouldn't allow somebody to clean us out of all our pies, but Melvin was a loyal customer to the restaurant, and we prided ourselves in customer service. His wife had died last year. They had been coming to the restaurant together for twenty years. I could understand why Clyde let him have the remaining batch of pies for a family reunion he was going to.

Now seemed like a proper time to tell Clyde about my idea of going to Mama's house and how I felt I needed to go back to tie things up. "There's a slight problem, though," I told him as I folded up my apron. "This is going to be an all-summer project. I can't afford to hire someone to do it, but I also don't have enough money to take the summer off and not get paid. And I don't want to leave you in a lurch without enough help. Especially since business is really taking off!"

Clyde nodded, letting me know he understood. He had become more than a boss. He was a close friend, and I knew I could count on him for sage advice. As I waited for him to respond I saw him reach in his desk. Then he handed me an over-stuffed envelope.

"What's this?" I asked.

"Perhaps the answer to your question. It's a bonus, Mary. Since you started making your amazing pies, my business income has doubled. I thought that it was only right to give you a bonus for all your hard work and allow you to share in the blessing."

I took the envelope from his extended hand and leafed through it. There were a lot of bills! "Clyde, you didn't have to do this!" I stammered as tears filled my eyes. Could this really be happening?

"Go on. Take it and have the summer off. You deserve it."

"Ten thousand dollars!" I almost fainted after I had counted the contents. It was just what I prayed for. I was starting to think God might not be as far away from my life as I once thought. "Thank you. This is just what I needed," I told him, truly grateful. I gave him a huge hug.

"Okay, enough of all that. Remember, those apple pies are not going to make themselves."

"You got it, boss!" I said as I tightened my apron. The next few weeks would be interesting.

The money from Clyde not only covered our bills for three months, but it allowed some extra money for the kids and summer living. I was excited. I hadn't had the summer off since I was a teenager.

Wilma was happy for me. She knew I needed to deal with the looming issue of Mama's house, but she hadn't pushed me. Immediately after school ended, I did some much-needed spring cleaning around our house and then packed everything I thought we would need for the summer. Just a few days into their school break and we were ready to go.

"Where we are going, Mama?" Gracie Bear asked.

"We are going back to Grandma's old house for the summer." The kids were beyond excited at that news. They didn't care where we were going at all as long as we were all together. In the past we had never taken road trips unless it was bad news. For instance, when someone was dying or had died. But this time was different.

"When are we going?" they asked in unison.

"As soon as school is over and I can get us ready," I responded. But that didn't stop them from asking on a daily basis. They were so excited that every morning and every night they would ask, "When are we going?"

My response was always the same, "As soon as I can get us ready."

And then the sighs began, "But Mama, you said that last time."

"Can I get a consistent timeframe, please?" Jason asked one night. The way Jason articulated his speech impressed me.

"Big words for such a young boy," I replied. "We will get there when we get there," I said firmly. "Is that a consistent enough timeframe for you?" I was being sarcastic.

Gracie Bear kept trying to pronounce the word consistent, but it just wasn't coming out right. Jason patiently tried to help her by sounding it out. By the twentieth time she finally got it, and she beamed from ear to ear. That meant it was the new word of the month.

Another week passed and the reality that we were just about ready to go hit me. It was then I realized that we needed to stay some place other than Mama's house. If for no other reason than we needed a place of rest and solitude at night, and if I was working on the house, it would be in disarray. I remembered a farm not too far down the way where Keith and I had stayed early in our marriage. It was Clarence and Tansy's place. Back then they had named it Tansy's Dairy Farm.

Tansy and Clarence were high school sweethearts. After they wed they bought over five hundred acres of land. Pretty heady stuff for a young couple just starting out. The scenery was beautiful, with various kinds of foliage and a brook running through the property with natural springs and rolling hills along with wild turkeys, deer, rabbits, birds and more.

When Tansy first walked on the property, she fell in love. It was like a slice of heaven, pleasant to the eye and sacred to the heart. They never had any children, so the cows became their spotted babies. Farming wasn't easy. The couple quickly discovered how much work it truly was. But they didn't quit. Year after year they pressed on, adding to their livestock and the number of acres they could plant. In their prime they grew a lot of the food not only for the city, but for other markets. But as the years passed, and with no kids to help, it became too much.

Eventually Tansy's husband, Clarence, became sick and passed away. Like me, Tansy was widowed too early. It was then Tansy decided to retire. So, she filled her freezer full of meat, hamburger, steaks, and beef bones for soup, and then sold most of the beef cows and farm equipment, fences, and such. She kept a few cows for dairy, the chickens, and enough land to plant some fields of corn and also a decent size vegetable garden for herself, because she liked to can. Since it was no longer a dairy farm or working farm, Tansy changed the name to Tansy's Acres. The thought crossed my mind for the kids and I to offer to help Tansy for the summer and see if we could live there. It would be nice to have some company, and it would be great for my kids. Most of all I wouldn't be alone with my thoughts and memories.

We pulled down the road past the blue county sign and made a right-hand turn down an old gravel road. I fixed my hair and put on some lip gloss. It had been a long time since I had seen Tansy. I told Jason and Gracie Bear to wait quietly in the truck, I would only be a minute.

I walked up to the back of the house, which she always used as her main entrance, and knocked on the screen door.

"Hello, is anybody home?" I yelled. I heard Tansy's footsteps as the old farmhouse floorboards creaked under her weight. The door opened and there she was, Tansy Collins—Mama's best friend. In true fashion, she had berry-stained hands and an apron covered in flour, butter, and oil stains. I smiled at the sight. Some things never change, I thought.

"Mary Ann, oh, it's good to see you, darling!" she exclaimed. "Give this old and tired woman a big hug." She peered around the house toward my vehicle and said, "Are those your babies in that truck?"

"Yes, ma'am, they certainly are."

"How old are they now?"

"Jason is ten and Gracie Bear is already seven years old. Can you believe it?"

"Oh, Mary, bring those precious babies inside." After the kids piled out of the truck, Tansy welcomed them with open arms and a big hug for each.

"Well, look at your babies. They is beautiful! She exclaimed. "Gracie Bear looks just like you when you were a little girl," she said as she handed the kids a glass of cold lemonade. "Guess what just came out of the oven?" she asked with a twinkle in her eye. "A cinnamon apple pie. And if your mama says it's okay, I'll get all three of you a slice while it's still warm."

Gracie Bear squealed and jumped up and down. I relaxed against the seat cushion and let out a sigh. It felt good to feel safe and in a welcoming home again.

We sat down at Tansy's dining room table. It was an oak farm table and was beautiful. Tansy set plates of pie in front of each of us. Jason didn't wait for anybody. He began eating his immediately.

"Now baby, put that fork down," Tansy instructed. "In my house we say grace before we eat."

My cheeks grew red. I hadn't said grace at the dining room table since I was a child. And I was embarrassed that we hadn't made it a part of our home, although we certainly prayed at other times.

Tansy asked, "Now who's going to say grace?"

"Me!" Jason said emphatically.

We closed our eyes and Jason said, "Lord, let's eat."

Tansy giggled. "Well, that is one of the fastest prayers I have every heard at suppertime. You keep praying, boy. As you get older, those prayers will get longer and longer. Trust me," she said. Wise words that I knew came from her heart.

"It's so good to see you," she began, "but this isn't just a casual visit, is it?"

"Mama's neighbor wants me to fix up the house. I actually haven't done anything to it since I boarded it up," I began. "It needs paint and repairs badly. I think I'm finally ready to go back into the house, but I don't really want to stay there. But I don't have a choice . . ." I let the sentence trail off.

"What do you mean you don't have no choice?" she asked. "Why don't you and the kids stay in my barn? You remember there's a loft up there. It needs some cleaning, but it's a nice space for you all. I could also use your help as I have some boxes I need someone to carry up there. I'm too old to be taking those stairs anymore. Whatever is in them you can have."

"That would be amazing. I was hoping we could stay here!" I was excited. "Kids, what do you say about staying with Tansy?" I asked as Jason stuffed his mouth with another piece of pie. Already they seemed pretty content at Tansy's, but I had to ask them anyway. I needed to know what they thought about it.

"Can we have pie for supper every day?" Jason asked as he let out a loud belch.

"Why sure you can. If you help me make them," Tansy replied.

"Yes!" Jason gave his hearty vote of approval.

"How about you, Gracie Bear?" I asked as I turned to my daughter. A little on the shy side, she leaned over to whisper in my ear. Only when she so-called whispers, it is never truly a whisper.

"Mama, we need to make sure this woman is consistent," she said in a voice we all easily could hear. I stifled a chuckle. I knew that word would come up eventually.

"You can trust this woman, Gracie Bear," I told her. "The only thing that hasn't been consistent in my life is the men, and they aren't around here anymore."

"Mary!" Tansy scolded. But she smiled. She knew what I meant.

When Keith and I first married, Tansy and her husband had let us stay in an apartment above the garage. But that was many years ago. Her second husband, who hadn't stayed around long, had turned it into a wood shop. She said, "Come on, I'll take you and the kids to the loft and let you check it out."

We walked around back to the barn and went up the stairs. The kids, of course, ran up in front of us. "Careful now. No running. You don't want Tansy to fall over. I need my hips for making pies," she told them with a laugh.

"Slow down, Jason and Gracie Bear," I scolded. "I know your excited, but we don't want anyone getting hurt."

"Sorry, Mama. We will behave," Jason replied.

As we climbed into the loft, I was thinking about Keith. Tansy didn't know it, but Keith and I used to come to the loft to dream and discuss our future together.

I recalled one night by the moonlight, Keith had his arm around me. "One day, we will show our kids all of this," he said.

"What if we don't have any kids?" I asked as fear tried to creep into my heart.

"We will. Don't you worry. God won't let us down. He knows I want children and you're the mother for them."

I laughed. "I hope so since I'm your wife!"

"I am not joking about this. You're the only woman for me and the only mother for our children. I know it to be so." His words echoed in my heart as the kids and I completed our move into the spot that held so many memories. I ached to have him here with us now.

"What's the matter, Mary? You seem sad. Is everything okay?" Tansy asked, correctly reading me.

"Yes, Tansy. It's just memories. All I have are memories."

"It's Keith, isn't it? I'm so sorry, Mary. Some things just don't work out the way we plan them." Tansy was sweet. I knew she deeply cared for my heart. As a widow herself, she knew my struggle.

Being back at the same place Keith and I started our lives together brought back wonderful memories of the two of us. The only problem was he was gone, and I was alone.

"I never told you, but we used to come up here to the loft often."

"Honey, Clarence and I knew that. Where do you think the blanket in front of the window came from? There is nothing we didn't know about on this property!"

"Sometimes I just want to let go, but my heart won't let me," I said honestly. "I often dream we are together again, and this was all a bad dream!"

Tansy put her hand on my shoulder. "There is nothing wrong with dreaming and nothing wrong with remembering."

"Sometimes, I wish I could forget," I said with a sigh.

Tansy paused before continuing. "Mary, every one of us has a past we need to get through. The past is in the past for a reason. Don't let it ruin the joy you feel today. You were made to move forward. It's okay to look back, but don't stay there too long or you'll miss what is right in front of you," she said with a knowing look at the children.

I knew Tansy was right. It was okay to look back as long as we remember what we need to help us move forward. I knew I could not live in the past. To do so would steal our future.

"I know it's hard. When you look at your babies, you see Keith. But I believe the bigger issue is you got to get rid of the pain from your daddy."

I almost jumped as the words came out of her mouth. But I knew Tansy spoke truth. There was still grief from losing Keith, but there was pain from all I had endured with Daddy due to his addiction. I loved my daddy with all my heart. But his alcohol addiction complicated our relationship. It deposited uncertainty and fear in my heart. I always felt protected by Daddy until he was drinking. Then he became unpredictable and left me feeling scared. Mama and I were constantly walking on eggshells. She never left my side and was always comforting. She always reassured me that things would be all right. That was her faith in God talking, but things hadn't always been all right.

"Your daddy is gone now. It don't bother him none, but you, Mary, your young and vibrant. You have your whole life ahead of you. And don't forget about those babies. They're looking to you for love and affection."

"I know," I replied in almost a whisper.

"You've got to get your clarity of mind back and let the past be the past," Tansy instructed.

"I told myself for years there was no point in returning to these memories. It's why I boarded up Mama's house. I just couldn't face them. But now I feel like I have lost who I am, who

I was, and who I want to become. I want to dream again, Tansy," I confessed as tears slid down my cheeks.

"Well, you have come to the right place," she said, giving me a hug. "God will help you get through this, Mary."

"I wished I had your faith." I was feeling somehow a little stronger just being there with her.

"Well, your Mama prayed for you every night. She prayed with her window open, crying out to God for you, Mary. For you! Sometimes the breeze would carry her voice across the field as she talked with God. On those nights, I just closed my window and let her and the Lord talk things out," Tansy recollected.

"Yes, Mama believed in the power of prayer," I was remembering how strong Mama's faith in God had been.

"Now you need to believe it too! Just open your heart and let faith in again," Tansy encouraged.

"Thank you, Tansy." I hugged her back and let go. Oh, how I missed Mama even more at that moment and burst out in tears. The kids turned at my outburst. I quickly wiped away the tears, trying to make light of it so as not to concern them. "Well, we better get to cleaning this loft so we will have a neat place to sleep tonight," I told them and began to give instructions.

"All right then, I'll leave you to it," Tansy said as she turned to go. "I'm looking forward to having you and the kids for the summer. Anything you need in the house is yours. All I ask is that you clean up your own mess, and if you eat all my pie, then bake another one." She was laughing now.

"You got it, Tansy." She made me laugh too.

Later that night after the kids were asleep, I lay in bed and pondered Tansy's words. When I was a child, I would pray to

God. But after losing Keith, my daddy, and my mama, I was plain angry with God. It was hard for me to understand why He does what He does. I know God didn't cause it to happen. But in my mind He could have stopped it. But then again, I cannot even understand why I do what I do. So, what is the sense of trying to figure Him out?

I don't know why we try and figure out death. I don't understand it, and I don't like it. With Daddy, he was older, and he drank. For years he poured poison down his throat into his body. Obviously, it was toxic for him. So, while I was angry that he was gone, there were reasons. But with Keith and my mama? That was different. Especially Keith.

Mama was older, and eventually we all die. But Keith was only twenty-seven years old. We had only been married a few years. We had two beautiful babies. Why, just why? I asked God to save my husband and He didn't. I'll never know why He didn't, and that is where I struggled with the pain the most.

Why didn't God save him? Wasn't He supposed to be the most powerful and all knowing? I asked many people that question after Keith died. No one had an answer that settled my heart. Some even responded with their own question, "Why ask why?" Others simply glazed over the question altogether, telling me everything happens for a reason. Mama said, "We don't always have the answers, but one day when we're in glory, God will show us." She's probably right, but that doesn't help me here and now.

Being on the farm with Tansy made me feel like Mama was close to me. Tansy and Mama were as close as sisters. They did everything together. As much as I missed Mama, I know Tansy did too. I had stuffed my feelings away, but I was starting to awaken, and I was feeling again.

The kids loved being at the farm. This would be a whole new adventure for them. They loved hearing their voices echo in the loft. The space was vast and the two of them chased each other around every square inch of the place. I was nervous at first, as the floorboards were rickety. But they were having the time of their lives. Despite my frustration with God, I was thankful for these two children, which I adored. They brought so much joy to my life. I couldn't imagine life without them.

I struggled not to let worry get the best of me but tried to do better at enjoying the moment with my kids. I thought about Keith and what it would be like if he were with us. The truth is, I never wanted to be a single parent let alone a widow. Regardless of the situation, my babies always had a way of drawing me into their shenanigans.

Gracie Bear was my tidy one. She enjoyed dusting and straightening things. She liked things in order. For her, everything had its place. I couldn't believe a seven-year-old would be so concerned with order. Now Jason, on the other hand, didn't care. He liked the appearance of clean. That is why I never looked under his bed. I would probably have a heart attack!

I loved antique furniture. I saw there were several pieces at the farm, which Tansy had done an excellent job preserving. One piece up in the loft was covered with a bed sheet. I pulled it off and sent a layer of dust flying. Gracie Bear coughed lightly. "I'm sorry, honey! Are you okay? By the way, where's your brother?"

"I don't know," she replied.

I called his name, but there was no response. At times, he could be strategic about getting out of responsibilities. Suddenly, I heard glass shatter. Oh no! I thought. I ran over to the window and saw Jason running away from the house. In a few moments he was climbing the stairs to the loft.

"What did you do?" I asked as he got to the top. He was obviously upset.

"Mama, Tansy is going to kill me," he said as he tried to make up an excuse. "I went to the bathroom and then decided to throw my baseball. I hooked it the wrong way and it broke a window on her green house."

I could tell Jason was embellishing his story. He gave himself away by stuttering as he spoke. I got down to his level so I could look him in the eyes. "Listen. Calm down and take a deep breath. Tansy is not going to kill you. I'll talk to her about it and let her know it was an accident."

"Okay, Mama," he replied wiping his face with the back of his hands.

"Now, if you would have been cleaning with Gracie Bear and me, then this would have never happened."

"I know, Mama. I'm sorry."

"I forgive you. Now go get a broom and sweep off that area rug, so we can be done cleaning this place."

A moment later the kids and I heard footsteps coming up the stairs. It was Tansy. Jason looked at me with pleading eyes. "I'm not here, if she asks."

"Yes, you are!" I whispered back. "Stop worrying about it."

Tansy crested the stairs and stood their looking around. "I saw what happened to the green house. Where's Jason?" Hesitantly, Jason came from under the beams of the rafters where he had been hiding in the shadows. The expression on his face was that of pure guilt. I could tell he was just going to go for it. He knew how I felt about telling the truth—don't hesitate, just do it! Here was his moment.

"Sorry, Ms. Tansy," Jason stammered, making no excuses. Now, that's my boy, I was thinking. I stood back as a proud Mama.

"Don't you worry about it," Tansy told him. "One time I did the same thing."

Jason perked right up. "You did?"

"Yes, I did. I was winding up my garden hose and cranked the wheel too hard. The metal sprinkler hit the window and shattered it." Tansy smiled at him.

"We will replace it and take care of the cost," I told her, grateful she had been so gracious.

"No, you won't. I have plenty of money to take care of it," Tansy answered. "I don't want to hear another word about it."

Jason had expected a scolding but instead experienced grace. He ran to her and threw his arms around her.

Tansy hugged him back and looked around the loft. "It's looking pretty good," she said with admiration. "Can you believe this old barn has survived four tornados with winds so high that the shingles on the roof nearly blew off? We lost a couple of strong trees that year too. I hate losing trees.

"Oh, I also forgot to tell you that there is an antique lamp in a box behind the dresser. It's one of my favorites. You are welcome to use it if you like."

I went around behind the dresser and pulled out the box. Carefully, I unpacked the contents. The lamp inside had leaded glass and flowers and a bronze base. I plugged it in. It was absolutely beautiful. There were so many treasures in the loft, as Tansy had collected many things over the years. I wondered what else we would discover.

"Take what you need and make this place your own," she finished as she turned to go. "If you need something, I guarantee you'll find it somewhere in these boxes." She was laughing.

"I sure will, and thank you," I said, my heart bursting with gratitude. "Things are coming together. It will feel like our place in no time at all, right kids?" But the kids were nowhere in sight.

"Oh my, I better see what they are up to now!" In my brief time as Mama, I learned when they are quiet, or when they disappear, something's brewing somewhere.

We slept well our first night in the loft besides the occasional mosquito that swooped by my head. They say you cannot hear them, but I did! There was a full moon, and I was thinking about Keith. We loved watching the moon together, holding hands, kissing each other's cheeks. It was so romantic. How I missed being held. Exhausted as I was, my brain still wouldn't shut off. I finally rolled over and fell asleep. The questions I had with God would have to be resolved another day.

The kids and I quickly adapted to the schedule of life on the farm. The chickens needed food, water, and constant care. Work started at four o'clock in the morning. Now, Gracie Bear was not a morning person at all. So, Jason and I decided we would let her sleep in, at least the first morning. It made no sense to have her up too early and then we would be dealing with her cranky self all day long, which could include sudden emotional breakdowns. Plus, I could use some time with my boy. Some Mom and son time. We headed outside to help Tansy while Gracie slept.

Living on a farm was mostly about working all day in the hot sun and coming in late at night. I was glad the kids would get a chance to help take care of the chickens and help Tansy with some of the chores. It was good responsibility for them. There is something about a hard day's work that makes you tired, but in a good way. We were all going to get a chance to be outside in the sun and work in ways that the school year didn't allow.

The next thing I knew Tansy rang the bell. You know what that means, don't yaw? A southern cooked Kentucky breakfast! Ah yes! Kentucky breakfasts are known for every unhealthy food you can imagine. The menu included fluffy cornbread pancakes with maple syrup, fresh cut strawberries, crumbly biscuits with sausage gravy, egg omelets stuffed with cheeses, bacon, and fried potatoes with onions.

Lord, I thought I died and went to heaven. I was extremely glad I packed extra sweatpants; living with Tansy I was sure going to need them. I know gaining five pounds doesn't sound like a lot, but you should have seen my plate! It felt good to be back home at Tansy's Acres!

The phone rang. "I'll get it, Tansy," I said as she and the kids cleared the table. It was Clyde. He was checking in on me.

"How's it up there?" he asked.

"We are down there, Clyde," I replied, laughing.

"Well, we sure miss you here. I have people wanting your delicious pies."

"Aww, that is sweet." It felt good to be missed. Clyde lingered on the phone. I could tell he wanted to say more and that he missed me. I was his most valuable employee.

"Well, have a great summer and don't forget to come back home," he said.

"I won't. Goodbye."

Honestly, I needed the break from work. I had been a waitress for a long time. But I did miss Clyde. He was like a father to me, but I certainly didn't miss work!

Waitressing is being on your feet all day and dealing with grumpy old men and women who are not always the nicest people on the planet. Then, there are those who don't tip. We have a name for them in the service business, but I think I'll keep that word to myself.

After we ate and were about to head back outside to work in the garden, Gracie Bear finally rolled out of bed. She was still rubbing her eyes and in her nightgown as Jason and I gave her a wave. We both grabbed another piece of bacon as we headed out the door. "I saved you a plate," I informed her. "Come join us in the garden for weeding and picking vegetables as soon as you are done."

The zucchini came in fast thanks to the spring rains, Tansy told us. We all were working together to cut off the slender dark green vegetable from the vines. Gracie Bear soon joined us, and we picked as much as we could before I had to leave to head to Mama's. We placed them in wicker baskets. If felt good to have one project done.

Tansy asked if I could run into town for her and pick up some goods before I headed over to Mama's. Merle's Market was the only makeshift grocery store in town and the prices were, let me say, a bit expensive. Merle had a daughter named Nancy.

Nancy, who never married, ran the store. She had a snotty attitude, crazy hair, and never brushed her teeth. Whenever I would stop in, which I tried to avoid as much as possible, she said the same thing, "Mary, Mary, Mary."

I couldn't help myself and usually responded sarcastically, "Nancy, Nancy, Nancy." She was a nosey gossip and always wanted to know if I knew anything about anyone. "Are you dating anyone?" she asked every time. Like there was anyone to date in our small town. The funny thing was that in this little town everyone already knew everything about everyone. Gossip travels at the speed of light!

"I keep telling Tansy to let me sell her pies here," she said as she made a production of filing her nails. "I could make her lots of money, but she just won't listen and just gives those pies away." She was a complainer too. I let out a sigh. Some people never change. Nancy was always meddling in other people's affairs.

"I'll make sure I let her know how you feel, Nancy," I responded as I put the items Tansy had requested in my basket and walked over to the checkout.

"That will be thirty-five dollars and seventy-two cents," Nancy said as she totaled the items.

I let out a low whistle. "Really? I only bought five things. I see you have the same high prices as you've always had."

"Well, you know, it's the convenience. And you pay for convenience." She looked at me and smiled. Looking at her teeth, I wish she hadn't.

"Right," I said shaking my head.

I couldn't wait to get out of there. Same old Nancy. She hadn't changed a bit since our days in school together. The thing I loved about this town was the scenery always stayed the same—beautiful. So were the people—at least most of them.

I headed back to Tansy's to drop off the groceries she had asked for and to check on the kids. "I'm headed over to Mama's house," I told them.

"I want to go!" Gracie Bear begged. I pondered that for a moment. "Tansy, is it okay if Jason stays with you while we go? I have to see what needs to be done and get started," I stated with a sigh. I had been dreading this part.

"Honey, you just go do what you need to do," she instructed. "We will be just fine. You stay as long as you need to. There will be a hot meal waiting for you both when you get back."

I gave her a hug. I was so grateful for Tansy's support. I couldn't have imagined doing this without the emotional and physical help she was providing. We got changed into work clothes and headed out immediately. It wasn't far. I pulled into the ribbon driveway and began accessing the yard even before the car came to a halt. The grass was too high. No wonder the neighbor complained. I got Gracie Bear out of the car, and we walked up to the porch and I unlocked the door. Almost at once the memories came flooding back.

I remembered a particular day from childhood. I was no more than eight years old, with pig tails, freckles on my cheeks, and the top of my nose sunburned. (Mama always told me to put sunscreen on my nose, but I never listened. So, my nose was peeling.) The weather that day was hot, humid and sticky as it always is in the south. Daddy arrived home from work, barely pulling into the driveway before white smoke began to billow from his truck. It had overheated. I watched as he slammed the door and said a few swear words out of frustration. I didn't understand what life was like as an adult.

Daddy went inside, grabbed a beer, and came back outside. I was hiding in the grass on the side of the house hoping he wouldn't catch a glimpse of me. That is the last thing I wanted. I saw him open the hood of the truck and begin tinkering on something near the engine. The stick under the hood fell and it hit him hard on his head. Daddy kicked the tires and threw his beer bottle across the yard. The bottle broke and shattered in a hundred pieces. He had such a fit of rage it scared me.

I ran to the safest place I knew—the willow tree. Nothing or no one could get me under that tree. It was my safe place. I checked to see if Mama was at the kitchen window. She certainly was. Mama was my constant. No matter how crazy Daddy acted, Mama was my rock.

Mama had seen Daddy's outburst. I didn't want to go into the house no way, and Mama knew it. So, she did what any good mother would and brought my dinner under the tree. She didn't come underneath the branches. She just laid it down within my reach. "Mary, here you go."

My heart swelled with love. Mama always knew just what I needed. "I love you, Mama," I replied.

"I love you too" she said as she walked back to the house. She would have to deal with Daddy's anger, but she always tried to protect me from it.

I fell asleep under the willow tree waiting for Daddy to go to bed. The moon was already high up in the sky when I woke up because of an ant crawling on my arm. Ants are such annoying insects! I scurried to the back door, but it was locked. So, I decided to go to the front door.

"OUCH!" I screamed. I had stepped on a piece of broken glass. The shard had embedded deep into my foot. It was bleeding pretty bad. Oh, I did it this time! I tried to gingerly pull it out, but it hurt too bad. I didn't want to wake Daddy that was for sure. I didn't want to wake Mama either, but I needed her.

I limped in the house and knocked on my folks' bedroom door. "Mama," I whispered hoping she would hear me.

I heard footsteps and a moment later the door opened. Mama looked at me and the puddle of blood pooling on her wood floor.

"Oh, Mary! What happened?" she asked as she hurried to the bathroom to grab a rag and some supplies.

"I hurt myself, Mama. Really bad," I told her, starting to cry.

"How did it happen?" she asked as she handed me the rag to stop the bleeding and helped me over to the kitchen. "Now sit down and let me have a look." As she checked the injured area she instructed, "Shhh, be quiet now. I'll get you taken care of, but don't wake Daddy."

"It's a piece of glass from the beer bottle," I whimpered. "It hurts!" I exclaimed as Mama pulled out the glass shard and cleaned the wound with rubbing alcohol.

She waved her hand over it to dry the alcohol and said, "Let it bleed for a minute and you should feel better. That was a big piece of glass." She squeezed my hand to comfort me.

"You know that alcohol stung worse than a bee sting! Whoever invented it clearly hates children," I told her as I wiped the tears from my cheeks.

Mama bandaged me up good. She hugged me, and although my foot was tender, it felt better just being in her arms. There is nothing like the love of your mama. "It's late, but I know you went through a lot today. Come on, I have a surprise for you," she said. Her surprise was the richest chocolate chip cookies you could imagine. There in our living room I sat in her lap as Mama opened a yellow umbrella over our heads. The two of us pretended it was raining as we shared warmed up chocolate chips cookies and a glass of cold fresh milk. To this day they are my favorite. No one can make them like Mama.

As Mama opened our special book, I took a deep breath. Mama said she found it discounted at a thrift store. It was *Why Do I Have to Go to School in a Thunderstorm?* Each time it rained,

Mama knew I wanted to curl up in a blanket and stay home with her. But rain or shine, Mama let me know that unfortunately school came first. Amazingly, that morning when it was overcast, the book was already opened when I heard the thunder followed by a downpour of rain. It was as if the book had a built-in barometer. It was a supernatural literary work for sure because although we were inside, big raindrops hit the umbrella Mama had raised for effect. She let out a deep sigh at the sound. "Daddy sure needs to fix that old roof. It's leaking again."

But in my mind, I wondered if it was the roof or if it was magical.

I asked the question that had become our habit when it rained, "Why do I have to go to school in a thunderstorm?" Then we would follow the dialogue Mama designed.

Why do I have to go to school in a thunderstorm?

Me: I would rather play and snuggle in my blanket.

And stay nice and warm.

Mama: I wish you could stay home, I really do, but

If you don't go to school, how will you learn to tie your shoes?

Why do I have to go to school in a thunderstorm?

Me: The waves crash on the shore.

Lighting and thunder rip through the sky.

I want to stay home and eat a slice of hot apple pie.

Can I have cinnamon on it too, please? If not, I shall surely die.

Mama: You won't die, I promise you that!

Now, please gather your things and don't

Forget your backpack!

Why do I have to go to school in a thunderstorm?

Me: I would rather play outside and rest the entire day long.

Or I could sing a country song.

The sky is grey; that makes me feel mellow.

I'd rather sit and draw a yellow Armadillo.

Mama: It is dreary outside, I completely agree.

Come on and don't make me count to three!

One . . . Two . . .

Why do I have to go to school in a thunderstorm?

Me: Wouldn't it be nice, Mama,

if I could stay home and rub your feet?

Or I could clean the house for you. Now that could be neat!

Mama: You know I love a clean house and floor.

Now, come on, let's grab your coat and don't

forget your hat hanging by the back door.

Why do I have to go to school in a thunderstorm?

Me: I know I must get ready for school.

I'll comb my unruly hair.

Look, Mama, I said to distract her.

Over there, a black Gracie Bear!

Mama knows what I am all about.

Looks like staying home from school today

will certainly not work out!

Mama: I love you and I will miss you. Please enjoy your day.

For soon school will be over, then we can love and play!

Why do I have to go to school in a thunderstorm?

Me: I'm dressed now, nice and warm.

Mama opens the umbrella; oh no, the fabric is torn!

She walks me to the bus, and I don't make a fuss.

I guess it's not so bad, to go to school in the rain.

One more time . . . . Can we go back inside the house again?

Mama: "No," she says, with a silly grin.

We cannot go back in the house again!

Why do I have to go to school in a thunderstorm?

Me: I wave goodbye. She smiles and waves back.

I guess it won't be so bad to hang out on the bus.

With all my friends, I won't make a fuss.

I think I'll sit by the back window,

And finish drawing a yellow Armadillo.

Mama: Oh, my darling, I'll wait for you to arrive.

And when you come home, I'll have a slice of hot apple pie.

The End.

Mama said that night I could barely keep my eyes open. "Mama, can you read it again?" I begged, forgetting all about my hurt foot.

"No, darling, it's time for bed; school comes early in the morning." Mama carried me up the stairs to my bedroom. She laid me in bed and said a prayer for me.

"Dear Lord, protect my baby and heal her hurt foot. Give her strength and show her how much she is loved. Let her never forget who You are. Amen." She loved to tuck my feet into the covers and that drove me nuts. I didn't like my feet all bundled up like that. It made me feel trapped. As soon as she left my room, I pulled my foot out. It was hot underneath all those blankets and I needed to air it out!

Recalling that childhood memory, I recognized I was going to have to face the demons that haunted me. My whole life I had been hiding, scared, and I didn't want to be alone. I didn't want the past to control me any longer. I wanted to live again, start over, and leave this mess of a life behind me. I couldn't believe I was even thinking this, but I wanted to love again. It had been so long since I felt the touch of a man. I missed kisses, movies, talks, and hugs. I felt alone and I desperately wanted someone to share my life with.

We walked through the house, and I made a mental note of all that needed to be done and began to make a plan on where to get started first. Gracie Bear helped me get rid of the cobwebs and sweep the floors. We even started some of the weeding in the overgrown garden around the house, but since we got a late start that day, we decided to call it quits, as our stomachs began to grumble letting us know it was getting close to dinner time.

"You were such a big help! Thank you so much," I said as we took off our gardening gloves and I put them back in our box of supplies. "Are you getting hungry?" Gracie Bear bopped her head up and down "Okay then. Let's call it a day and head back to the farm."

We were both pretty quiet on the ride back. When I pulled into the farm, I saw a beat up old red Ford truck. I squealed my Chevy tires around, kicking up some gravel, and parked right next to it. Daddy always said, "Watch out for a man who drives a Ford." You were either a Ford man or a Chevy man where we lived. Anything other than that and your adulthood was in serious question. Now, I am not trying to offend anyone, especially those who drive foreign cars. That is just how it was back then. Of course, times change and so do car manufacturers.

Tansy came out the back door and hollered over to us, "Slow down, this isn't no racetrack."

I apologized although I did it on purpose to make a show. I was making a clear statement, "Get out of my way," to whoever owned that truck. I didn't recognize it and wondered who was visiting Tansy.

I didn't have to wonder long. In the next moment out walked a tall handsome man. He had rugged good looks with dark hair. I couldn't see his eyes because they were hiding underneath a brown cowboy hat. "Who's that, Mama?" Gracie Bear asked.

"I don't know, baby," I replied. Mr. Cowboy Hat tipped his hat and said, "Ma'am" as he walked over to the Ford truck.

Ma'am? Boy, that made me feel old. What's wrong with men these days? He may have meant to be polite, but it irked me. I nodded to be kind, but I didn't want anything to do with him.

"Wait! Wait a minute, Timothy," Tansy hollered after him. "I have someone I want you to meet. Timothy Heal, meet Mary Walker." (*I knew what she was up to--matchmaker!*)

"Hey, what about me?" Gracie Bear said with a pout, not wanting to be left out.

"Oh, I couldn't forget you, darling! This is Gracie Bear Ann Walker, I might add," Tansy inserted.

"Well, thank you kindly, Tansy," Gracie Bear replied.

"So, go on," I instructed my little girl. "What do you say?" Gracie Bear pretended to be shy, and she was unless you knew her. "Nice to meet you," she finally said in a small voice.

"Nice to meet you too!" he said as he offered to shake her hand. He turned to me next. So, you are Mary," he said. "Tansy has mentioned you and your mama often to me."

"Yes, Mary—that's my name," I replied, wondering who he was. Tansy may have mentioned me to him, but I had no idea who he was.

"I already met your son, Jason," he continued. "I'm surprised I haven't seen you around before." He was cut off as Jason came running out of the house.

"Hey, baby!" I told Jason as he ran out to give me a hug.

I eyed Timothy with a little suspicion. Then I remembered Tansy had mentioned that one of the cottages in the area was owned by a couple who had recently passed away, and their son had inherited it.

"Didn't your folks have a cottage here?"

"Yes," he responded.

Now it began to make sense. I remembered meeting him years before when we were both younger. "So that is where I know you from," I replied.

He smiled. "You've grown up." I could feel the heat coming into my cheeks. I don't know why that should have made me embarrassed, but it did and suddenly I felt very self-conscious.

"Hey, Timothy, do you have time to play more catch?" Jason asked, holding his ball and glove.

"Na, little buddy. I have to get back to work. Maybe another time."

Jason told me that he and Timothy had played catch and release, throwing the ball back and forth, while we were at Mama's. I could tell it had made him happy. Being without a father figure in his life was tough on him, and he didn't have a brother. He and Gracie Bear got along well, but she liked playing with dolls and playing kitchen. She wasn't interested in baseball. It kind of creeped me out that a total stranger had spent time alone with my kid without my permission. The Mama Bear in me rose up.

"Hey, Timothy, next time you want to set up a play date with my kid, please ask me first. Are we clear?" As soon as the words were out of my mouth, I realized how defensive they sounded, but I couldn't help it. I was very protective of my kids, and you couldn't be too careful!

"I'm sorry," he immediately replied. "Tansy said it was all right. I'll make sure I do that next time."

I could tell he knew what I was getting at and was glad that he respected my wishes. "Where do you live?" I asked, curious now.

"Just up the road in a tiny house off Hunter's Creek."

I knew that area. The only people who had lived there were strange back folks who lived off the grid. But that was long ago. No one lived there anymore . . . at least I didn't think so. I eyed him now with even more suspicion. "I didn't think there were any houses up that way. Only an old shanty abandoned years ago," I continued, squinting at him as we stood in waning sunlight.

"That would be the one," he replied. "It's not abandoned anymore. I fixed it up. I even put some new windows in and changed out the siding. Why don't you bring the kids some time and stop by and look around. It's quite different now."

The thing about living in a small rural town is pretty much everybody knows everyone. When Timothy and his folks lived here years ago, I was just a kid; Mama and Daddy knew of them, but I really didn't know Timothy. They were what we referred to as "backwoods people."

It seems that strange people tend to hide in rural areas. By *strange* I'm referring to people who prefer living off the grid and the land and to be left alone. We had our share of them in Kettlesville, Kentucky.

Most homeschooled their children. For some, maybe not even that. In my mind they were a strange brood for sure. Mama had us keep our distance from them. But they felt the same about us. We could be kind, but not involved!

I'm not sure when Timothy and his family moved away. But he was back. I looked at this good-looking stranger who had already captured Jason's attention. He was definitely now a man. There had certainly been a lot of changes from then till now.

"A job brought me to town," he replied to my unasked question. But what kind of job and where? The town wasn't that big. His lack of details showed he was withholding information. But that was his prerogative.

"Well, I should be getting home. Nice meeting you, Mary," he said tipping his cowboy hat. I thought he was handsome, but I wasn't going to let him know I was thinking that! No way! I quickly turned away so he couldn't see the red I felt on my cheeks.

"See you Sunday, ma'am," he said to Tansy, also tipping his hat to her.

"Wait a minute, young man. You don't have to leave. Why don't you stay for supper? Do you have plans? Probably just have to go home and eat by yourself. You know I have plenty of food," Tansy said in her friendly manner. But I knew there was more to it than that. I knew Tansy. She was playing matchmaker!

I could tell Timothy wanted to stay. After all, he was a single guy and who honestly likes to eat by themselves? I certainly don't! The offer of a home-cooked meal and conversation did the trick.

"I would love to," he said with a big smile. Jason was smiling as well. I could tell I had my hands full with this guy. Oh, I could take care of myself. It was actually Tansy I was concerned about. Since Clarence died, she had no one around the farm. They never had any kids, and I could see this guy coming in and possibly taking advantage of her. I was going to have to keep my eye on him for sure. He wasn't fooling me with his polite "ma'am this and ma'am that." And he better stay away from my kids. I still felt the need to protect their hearts from people who might step in and then step out of their young lives. And besides, Daddy always told me you can't trust a man who drives a Ford truck! However, I was interested to see Hunter's Creek and what he had done to the old place. I was going to take him up on that offer.

We all went inside and got busy pulling out some leftovers—which Tansy always had plenty of—to heat up for dinner. Even though it was leftovers, it was still a smorgasbord in my opinion. Gracie Bear and I were certainly tired from our day at Mama's and so I was more than happy to let Tansy carry the conversation once we sat down to eat.

"Timothy works at the mechanic shop that Neil owns," she began as she passed around a plate of fresh sliced tomatoes. I thought on that. Now, Neil is a great guy. But honestly, I cannot believe he is still in business! He has such a compassionate heart it seems he never charges anyone for the work he does.

I laughed as Tansy kept trying to get conversation started between Timothy and me. She was not very good when it came to matchmaking. The more she tried, the more I smiled to myself. But I can read body language pretty well, and it was clear Timothy was as tired as Gracie Bear and me. We finished the meal in record time, as the conversation never really took hold. After we cleared the table, he was ready to leave.

"Nice to meet you," he said again and then thanked Tansy for the meal before heading out the door. As he left, I thought I heard him mumble about my Chevy truck. Of course, I needed to comment.

"What was that you said? I asked. He just waved as if he hadn't heard. Well, if he didn't like Chevy trucks there must be something wrong with him!

"Isn't that Timothy a nice man," Tansy said, watching me for my reaction.

"I think he is, but I am not interested, Tansy. Don't even try your hand at matchmaking with me. I have too much baggage. What man wants a woman who is a widower with two kids? I'm not really a catch!"

"Don't say that, darling. You don't have baggage. You have treasures and any man who don't see your worth is a fool." She smiled and gave me a hug good night.

I got the kids up to the loft and ready for bed. It had been a long day. Once I was in bed, I lay there thinking about what Tansy said. She was right. My children were not baggage. If someone didn't love me, then how were they going to love my kids? I don't come unattached. My family was a package deal. I wiped away a tear that slid down my cheek. I sighed at how quickly the tears could still come. Thinking about the past made me sad because I wanted my family back. I missed Keith and I missed being married.

Marriage for me meant protection and safety. I think that is true for most women. Keith was everything I needed. He calmed my heart because he genuinely cared for me. I could always count on him. I missed that. My heart ached for what I once had. I felt vulnerable now, unprotected, and I built a wall around my heart.

I worked hard at Mama's the next day. The kids stayed and helped Tansy. They were learning some new skill sets and helped her each day getting the eggs and picking the garden. As soon as I walked in the door, Jason came running over. "Tansy's tractor broke down!" His concern was showing clearly on his face. I looked up and saw concern on Tansy's as well. The tractor was essential, even on her small acreage. We needed to get it fixed and money was tight.

Suddenly I had the idea for a lemonade stand along with Tansy's pies. By the slice, of course! The kids and I could set it up and whatever money we made would go to the repair cost. Who could resist Tansy's pies? Certainly not anyone who lived around here that's for sure. Tansy had a generous heart. Most of the time she gave her pies away, but this time a little fundraising was in order to help with the repairs.

CHAPTER NINE

EYES WIDE OPEN

*I*t was time for delivery, and I was ready. There is nothing like being generous and bringing joy to others. It was something that I loved to do, even if I was cranky. Serving others all the time can be taxing, but I made the best of it. It's better to serve than to not serve. Trust me. Everybody wants a piece of the pie.

It feels good to be generous and as I reflect over years past, I can say truly God has been generous to me. I love to bring joy to others; serving them and seeing the smile on their faces makes my heart happy. Mama always said, "It doesn't take much to be kind. Open a door for someone. Give them a hug. Lend an ear and listen. Share a home-cooked meal. Always give with a heart seasoned with generosity. Love more, darling, hate less!" Those were wise words.

It was Sunday morning. The kids and I rolled out of bed, got dressed, and got the early morning chores done before heading to the house to have some breakfast. When we walked in the back door, we were greeted by the delicious aroma of pie! Already there were fruit pies of every kind, still hot and bubbly, cooling on wire racks throughout the kitchen.

"I didn't think we were doing the stand today," I said to Tansy. "Who are all those pies for, and why are you up and around so early?"

"They're for the neighbors," she informed me.

I told the kids to sit down and went to get some cereal out of the cupboard. That's when I heard the squeak of the front screen door and heard Timothy say, "Hello, can I come in?"

"You're already in," I responded sarcastically before turning back to Tansy about the pies. "We don't even have that many people in this town," I told her.

"Not on Mulberry Street, but have you forgotten?"

Ah, then I did remember—clearly.

Mulberry Street was behind Tansy's farm. It was a strip of land with shack-like row housing. The bungalow style houses were built close together. They all needed paint and were in varying stages of disrepair. When Mama was alive, she would help Tansy. They baked berry pies and delivered them to the neighbors each Sunday morning before church. Over the years Tansy's hips worsened with arthritic pain, and then Mama died, but that didn't stop Tansy. Since it wasn't easy for her to get around, she enlisted Timothy's help to distribute her baked goodies.

I self-consciously worked my fingers through my hair. I had awoke with crazy bed hair. You would have thought I put my finger in a light socket. Plus, I had noticed a pimple on my forehead that had formed overnight. It had its own heartbeat! Timothy was the last person I wanted to see this early in the morning. There was an awkward silence, so I figured I might as well say something.

"I don't see your Ford. How did you get here?" I asked.

"I am getting new tires installed today, so I walked over," he replied.

I tried to pull my hair across my forehead to hide the pimple. It wasn't moving. So, I rested my palm against it. I wasn't ready for him to see me without coverup!

"What's wrong?" he asked. Do you have a headache? Or . . .

"Nothing is wrong with my head!" I replied grumpily.

"Are you sure? Because it looks like you have a horn to me." He was laughing. Now, it takes a lot to make me blush, but I did!

"Timothy Header, you have a lot to learn about talking to a woman!" I informed him. I'm sure I sounded upset to him.

Jason and Gracie Bear were watching cartoons on the television as I prepared their breakfast, nothing fancy just cereal with milk. Once Timothy realized my agitation, he quickly changed the subject.

"I saw some puppies down the road for sale. You think the kids would want one?" he asked. Well, strike two, and it was only seven in the morning. First, he makes fun of my pimple, horn, or whatever he called it; and now he mentions a puppy in front of my kids. That is like asking your child, "Would you like a piece of chocolate?"

Oh please! How could I say no now? Timothy had a lot to learn about women, kids, and life in general.

Secretly, I really wanted a puppy. But I didn't tell him that. In fact, I should have, but it was the morning, and I was still trying to wake up! "No, we don't have room to take care of a dog."

"Oh Mama, say yes! Please, let's get a puppy. You know I want one!" Jason begged.

"Please, Mama, please! Gracie Bear chimed in.

"Oh great! Timothy, now you got my kids wanting a puppy."

"Oh, I am sorry, Mary. I need to learn when to shut my mouth."

But as I started thinking about it, I realized it wasn't such a bad idea. "Well, the only puppy I've ever wanted is a golden retriever," I told him.

He looked at my face and I could tell he knew what my heart wasn't saying. That's the funny thing about love. Sometimes you just know that you know. I started to blush again. Why did this man always make me blush? "Let's help load the pies," I instructed Jason and Gracie Bear to get the attention off me. Then it hit me—Timothy didn't have his truck.

"How were you going to deliver those pies without your truck?" I asked.

"I'll use the old wagon. We can load the pies in the back," he explained.

"You know you can use my truck if you want to," I offered.

"Thanks, we'll be fine," he responded, turning to head out to the barn to get the wagon and hitch the horses. At that moment Tansy came out of the bathroom where she had been rolling her hair in curlers.

"Okay, everybody. Let's join hands and pray over these pies," she instructed.

I knew from Mama it was tradition for Tansy to pray over her pies. She spent hours chopping fruit and making pie crusts and then prayed over each pie before delivering it to the neighbors behind her property. It was a labor of love for those less fortunate.

"Jason and Gracie Bear, come on in here," I yelled as they continued to play in the living room.

"What, Mama?" Jason asked,

"Come on, we have to pray over the pies." Gracie Bear followed obediently behind him.

"Now close your eyes and bow your heads," Tansy instructed. Jason squinted his eyes and Gracie Bear grabbed onto the bottom of my skirt. We held hands and Tansy prayed, "Dear Lord, we bless these pies. Guide us as we deliver them to the homes that need them most. Give patience where patience is needed and give love where tenderness is missing. Give joy to a heart that has lost hope. Give peace to those with troubled souls. Give patience to those waiting on You. Give kindness to those who feel forgotten. Bring goodness to the heart that serves You. Give faithfulness, gentleness, and self-control to all who eat these pies. For these are Your fruits and my offering to You. Spirit of God, we thank You. Amen."

"That was a beautiful prayer, Tansy," Gracie Bear said.

"Tansy and your mama delivered pies to my family sometimes," Timothy said a few minutes later as we loaded the wagon. I was stunned. I had never considered that his family was one of the needy families my mama had often talked about.

"I'm so sorry! I didn't know your family was one of those families . . ." I started awkwardly.

"We weren't," he explained. "Actually, we were just the opposite. My dad was a big-time lawyer. He made a good income, which enabled us to have two homes, so we bought the small cabin. It was a place where he could get away from the pressure of the firm and we could be together. We were usually here only in the summertime and stayed pretty much to ourselves. Those times in the cabin are probably some of my favorite memories, as Dad was more relaxed and we did things as a family. That is, until Mom got sick." His voice trailed off.

Over the course of the morning, he explained how his mom died when he was only eleven years old. "She had stomach cancer and, in the end, couldn't eat. We watched as she just sort of wasted away.

I couldn't imagine how hard that must have been, especially as he was so young.

"I didn't know how I was going to make it without her," he said.

Now I understood why they had moved. It was understandable that his dad hadn't wanted to stay in the house after that. Her long-drawn-out illness sounded awful to go through. So that is why the house fell into such disrepair. They just never came back! All those years I had thought it was one of the shanties.

"There is nothing like losing your mama," I concurred. "Trust me, I know firsthand."

"What happened?" he asked. The concern in his voice made me look up. His eyes were full of compassion and love. I could have gotten lost in them. At first, I wasn't sure I wanted to talk about it. But then I thought, *why not?* He told me his story, I might as well tell him mine.

"She had a massive stoke and did not recover," I replied, sharing just a few of the details.

"Mary, I am truly sorry," he said as he put his hand on mine. It touched my heart. His hand was only on mine for a moment before he moved to get more pies, but it showed a kind and considerate side that I would not have guessed.

Timothy grabbed a few of the pies and went ahead of us to deliver them. Tansy took the time we were alone to fill me in on some added details.

"Abigail was one of the most wonderful women you ever had the opportunity to know. We met at church one Sunday," she recalled. "I had arrived late, and the church was packed. There wasn't a seat in the whole place. Just as I was getting ready to leave, she called out to me, 'Come and sit here. You can have my seat.' She got up and motioned for me to sit down.

"Nobody had ever treated me like that before," Tansy said. "Especially a prominent wealthy white woman. They usually treated 'colored folks,' as they used to call us, with such disdain and ridicule back then. I am glad they don't do that today. It would make you sick to your stomach if you even knew how mean a lot of people were back in those days." Then looking at the number of pies we still had to deliver, she announced, "Let's get a move on."

I was so glad we got to be part of it. You should have seen the people's faces! They all looked forward to their pie delivery on Sundays and a special note from Tansy. Each family felt loved, especially those who were shut-ins. And they all expressed how much they appreciated her kindness. It was good for Jason and Gracie Bear to help. It allowed them to see firsthand what serving others is like. Tansy let them both deliver the pies as she and I waved from the wagon. The kids were darling and loved the attention they received.

After we delivered all the pies, Timothy went to unhitch the horses, and the kids ran towards the chicken coup, while Tansy and I went inside to rest for a moment before church. We sat back on the couch where Tansy finished her story.

"Back then some people hated the color of our skin. There is no good reason for people's hate," she said. "I remember one time at school. It was third hour during my science class. I had to pee awful bad, so I raised my hand and asked Ms. Williams to excuse me. She did. I hurried down the hall to the bathroom. I went into a stall and locked the door to do my business.

"I hadn't been in there long when I heard the door open and footsteps on the tile floor. I paid no mind until I saw through the door cracks a group of girls come in there and one of them who was wearing an old white linen dress placed her hand on the stall door, covering it. I stiffened my arms and clenched my fist. Tansy was ready for a fight! Nobody was going to bully me, not Tansy Clair Hopper! My mama raised me to take care of myself! That was that!

"You go on and take your hands off this door. You let me out. Ya hear me?" I shouted. That was my first warning to them bullies. The next time they were going see the back of my hand across their nasty little faces!

"'Did you hear what I said?' I yelled again. I was steaming mad at that point.

"'I heard you just fine,' one of the girls said. 'You're not coming out of that bathroom. You hear *me*?'

"I saw her beady eyes staring at me through the door cracks. I was angry, not at her but at the hate inside of her. Demons. Good Lord, forgive me. I don't know how many there were, but I could hear those girls talking. Then I heard a noise coming from the window. Someone was outside and had pushed a garden hose through the window to one of them. When they gave the signal, she turned on the water. Suddenly I felt the cold well water on top of my head soaking my clothes. I was so cold, shivering.

I begged for help and for them to open the door. But those girls didn't care. They listened to me cry but kept pushing against the door. Hate is so ugly!

"Let me go!" I screamed banging on the door.

"I heard one of the girls utter something that I have never been able to forget. She said, 'You're going to stay in there till that color washes off your skin!'"

"Tansy, I am so sorry," I gasped. My heart was breaking for her that she had endured such cruelty. I imagined what if my own child had been the one trapped in a stall and classmates had done that to him or her. Tears filled my eyes at the thought.

"It's okay, darling. I learned not to pay no mind to those kinds of words. I am better than that!" Tansy continued with the story.

"It took me a minute, but I wiped those tears falling off my face, I breathed deep and then tightened my upper lip, and pushed that stall door open. The hair stood up on my arms and neck. Tansy was looking for a fight, but them nasty girls were gone. I looked up on the mirror at my face and realized I looked just like them. Hateful, that wasn't me. It wasn't. I made a decision that day. No longer would I ever live in fear of anyone, no matter the color of their skin. I stood up taller, threw my shoulders back, and lifted my chin up. I was gonna do what my Mammy and Pappy did, Love more, hate less!

"I decided that just because those girls hated me, not everybody did. Not everyone acts that stupid! I can't change the color of my skin and I won't change or be ashamed of it either! Who

I am and who God made me is beautiful and if nobody likes it, that's their problem! People only fear what they cannot control and baby nobody was going to control Tansy!"

"I was still trying to dry off my hair and dress with paper towels when Principal Harris walked into the bathroom.

"Tansy Clair, tell me. Who did this to you?" she asked. I didn't say a thing. I wasn't going to rat them out. I decided to let the good Lord deal with them. I don't have time for hateful people in my life. I got living to do! However, the principal was not going to let me off that easy," Tansy said.

"You go down to my office and get a towel from the nurse's station," Principal Harris instructed me. "You are not leaving till you tell me who did this to you. It's not okay for anyone to be treated this way, ever. You understand?" she said in a gentler tone. I wish Ms. Harris would have hushed already.

"I knew she was right but telling her who they were would only cause more trouble for me. I knew that much. I walked down to her office with my hair and clothes still wet from head to toe. Even my shoes were making noises. I thought about what she said. I didn't want those girls to do this to someone else. They were bullies. I blurted out, 'It was Miss Missy and Miss Treena!' But immediately I regretted it. *What have I done? They're going to kill me!*" I thought.

"I was feeling sick about it. I thought I would need to leave this town forever! I wondered what would happen when their folks found out. Well, I found out soon enough. The principal called the folks of each of the kids involved and there was a private meeting. Plus, Principal Harris made them clean up the water from the hose and scrub the toilets in the bathroom for one month. Those girls were miserable, and it served them right!" Tansy said, laughing.

I began to understand Tansy better after she told that story. I am so glad that people before us have stood their ground and made a way for all races. It's sad how people can still have such prejudice, but love can eat that hate!

I heard the screen door bang shut and knew Timothy had finished unhitching the horses. He walked into the living room where we were, and I could tell he was still thinking over the loss of his mother and that our conversation had left him with a heavy heart. Life has a way of breaking us down, especially when we lose loved ones.

"I wasn't there when she died," Timothy said, jumping back into the conversation about his mom. He put his head down in his arms as he sat at the table. I could tell he was struggling inside, beating himself up about not being there when his mama passed. I don't know what's worse. Being there and seeing what I saw like with Mama or not seeing anything at all. Either way, everyone feels the pain of the passing and the reality of losing a parent.

Somewhere during our talk Tansy had baked cranberry walnut muffins and made a pot of fresh coffee. The smell filled the kitchen and wafted into the living room where we sat. "Mmmm! For some reason I feel famished," I told her. With a mug of steaming fresh coffee and warm muffin right out of the oven, we all sat and enjoyed the home-baked goodness before continuing. Each of us had things weighing on our hearts and perhaps talking about them was what we had needed. We had bared our souls, forming an unspoken bond. I couldn't remember a time I had been that transparent about how I felt. But the conversation wasn't over.

"You know, it's been almost seven years, but I still miss Keith like it was yesterday," I confessed. Tansy put her hand on my knee and patted it. It felt like exactly what my mama would have done and was so comforting.

"I was in love once too," Timothy said. "But never again. She took my heart and my Chevy."

"What? You are a Chevy man? No way!" I said, breaking the seriousness of the moment.

"Used to be," he said with a laugh. "I know it seems strange, but the day she walked out of my life, I watched her drive down the road in my truck. In a way to protect my heart, I suppose, I vowed I would never drive a Chevy again."

"You need to rethink that," I told him. "Why torture yourself?" We both laughed, although what we faced in our lives had not been funny at all, but tragic. All of us had suffered pain and loss. It was nice to have someone to share with who understood.

"Okay. We better rap this up," Tansy said jumping up and grabbing our plates. "We barely have time to get to church we've talked so long! Are you and the kids coming with me this Sunday?" Tansy directed the question to me. "It's been a long time since the pastor has seen all of you."

Normally, I would say no. I had given up on church quite a while ago, but Tansy had a gentle way of persuading me. Also, she invited Timothy, and this would be a perfect opportunity to see what he was about. "Yes, that sounds great," I said, nodding "I could use some joy this morning."

After the service, Timothy walked back home. He said he needed to ponder some things and get some chores done. I know the Bible says that the Sabbath is supposed to be a day of rest, but on a farm, there is no such thing. There is always something to do, even when you are not fully working. But I was going to take the day off from working at Mama's. I needed a break. I had thought about taking the kids out to ride bikes down the road to

Hunter's Creek and see Timothy's place. *He invited me to check it out, so why not?* I thought.

It wasn't far, the weather was nice, and the sun was shining. It would give us a chance to ride bikes and enjoy the beautiful weather. Timothy had said that he'd been working on their old cabin. The last time I had seen it, it definitely needed some TLC. I was interested to see what he had done to it!

Since Gracie Bear was too little to ride her own bike, she road with me. I had an extra seat on the back. She didn't like wearing her helmet, but as I always say to my children, "Safety first." Jason was trying to race me. I let him get ahead, but when I came barreling beside him, I left a wake of dust in his way.

"Mama, you're supposed to let your kid win," he whined. "That's what mamas do."

"Maybe next time," I responded as Gracie Bear laughed. She thought it was fun to go superfast. I wasn't about to show it, but my legs were killing me by the time we reached the street sign. We slowed the pace slightly and in no time we arrived at Timothy's house.

"Did I forget something?" he said as he walked outside.

"No, you didn't. We just thought we would see the cabin you fixed up is all," I replied, suddenly feeling awkward about just showing up unannounced.

"Well, I would offer you to come in, but I need to tidy it up first," he said. "Why don't you and the kids take a walk with me around the property. I'll show you the creek."

I looked at the kids. "What do you think?"

"Yes," they said simultaneously.

I turned back to look at Timothy. "Well, that answers your question."

We got off the bikes and propped them up against the cabin and left our helmets hanging on the handlebars. Timothy took us around the property. It was heavily wooded, beautiful, and quiet. When we reached the creek, the kids bent down to pick up some rocks and skipped them across the water trying to see who could outdo the other.

"Come again next Sunday and I'll make sure the house is presentable," Timothy invited when I let him know we needed to head back to the farm. Although we didn't go inside, I looked around and didn't see anything odd or out of place. I have to admit, I was still watching Timothy, not quite sure exactly what to make of him. But for now, he was okay.

CHAPTER TEN

A LOT OF NEW

*C*hurch was not always a place I wanted to be. Not because I didn't believe in God, I was just mad at Him for a long time. I felt like religion just wasn't my thing, but I learned God and religion are two separate things. It's easy to get the two confused. But that was never an excuse to not attend church. It's important to be around like-minded people who are walking this life out together. I was thankful for Mama's prayers. She was faithful when it came to Daddy and me. Her faithfulness in prayer and in action helped me see the truth.

I still blamed God for everything in my life. It was His fault! Everyone at church was nice to me, and I knew they secretly prayed for me. Why else do you think all those miracles chased me down? Somebody somewhere was praying me through, that was for sure!

Before I knew it another week had rolled around and Tansy had asked if we wanted to go to church with her again. "Sure, we will go," I replied. I knew it made Tansy happy. I took the kids upstairs so we could get dressed for the service. I had bought Gracie Bear a beautiful yellow polka dot dress and white sandals and Jason a bowtie and a blue stripped long sleeve shirt. He hated the tie, but the shirt made his blue eyes pop. I thought we cleaned up good!

When we walked in the small church, everyone greeted me and the kids. Several people said they missed Mama and that they were praying for me. For the first time in a long time, I knew that they were genuinely praying for us. Although I didn't acknowledge God in my life, I felt his peace. It must have been the constant prayers by the faithful church folks.

We settled into our pew a few moments before Pastor Greg walked to the pulpit. The first words out of his mouth were, "Today we are blessed to have Mary and her children, Jason and Gracie Bear. We are so glad you could join us this morning."

It took a lot to make me turn beet red, but that did it. Pastor embarrassed me in front of all those churchgoers. After everyone finished looking at me and the kids, they turned their attention to the worship leader, who had asked all of us to stand. His name was Duncan. He was a heavy man. Probably weighed about four hundred pounds and must have been around fifty years old by now. He was faithful to serve and never missed a Sunday. I remember him from when I was a girl. One thing I recall is he loved my mama; another thing is he had a laugh that could call the cows home.

Duncan climbed the steps to the front and was slightly out of breath. He opened a hymnal, directed us to page 68, and we all started singing. It was just as I remembered as a kid. He had a powerful voice.

Where I grew up, white folks stayed away from black folks except at church at least that is what Tansy said. Then all the "race cuffs" came off and everyone acted like one happy family because they were serving God. Mama raised me to not judge a person by the color of their skin. Sitting in church now I looked around. Everyone sitting near me seemed happy, and they were not afraid to shout it out to the Lord. The message was brief, and I was ready to get home. Jason was drawing on a piece of paper and Gracie Bear was playing with the offering plate. My mind wandered as I pondered the rest of the afternoon. Both kids needed to take a nap. Then the pastor said, "Tell the person next to you, 'Someone is getting saved today!'"

Timothy turned to me and said, "Looks like someone is getting saved today!"

"It's you who needs the saving," I said laughingly.

After church, we headed back to the farm and Timothy decided to stay for lunch. We talked for a bit. It was clear Tansy was happy we were talking. The kids had both warmed up to Timothy quickly. But even though they had, my heart was still heavy. All of this was too much!

We had finished lunch when Jason jumped on my lap and said, "Someone's getting saved today!" Tansy thought that was quite funny. Well, if someone was getting saved, it wasn't going to be me. The kids could have Him and so could Timothy for all I cared.

Tansy was telling us about the worship leader, Duncan. He was going through a trial in his life. His neighbor was prejudiced against him as she didn't like the fact Duncan was a Christian or "holy roller" as she referred to him. Tansy had told him, "Now, you just never pay any attention to people like that. You loves people for who they are not what you see." I had to agree with her. Tansy was an angel in disguise just like my mama. What is the big deal anyway? Can't people just be worried about themselves? There is always some kind of drama people love to get involved in.

Clyde, my boss, was black and that never bothered me none. According to Tansy, Duncan had a wood fence he built around his garden because he wanted to keep the neighbor's kids out. He grew tomatoes, green beans, onions, potatoes, zucchini, carrots, kale, and green lettuce. The neighbor had three boys and they were wild. They didn't have running water in the house and the boys never showered. They had matted hair and tattered clothing. People felt sorry for them because they were poor and often offered them food. Duncan would buy clothes at the thrift store and set them on the porch for the boys. He couldn't directly give it to them or Leon, their dad, would burn the clothes because he knew who was bringing them over.

Duncan worked hard tilling the soil and watering his plants. It was backbreaking work. One night after he went to sleep, the kids climbed over his fence and ripped his plants out by the root. All that work he did, and they took what belonged to him with no remorse. I don't understand why people can be so hateful to others. Love more, hate less!

Lunch had been over for a good hour. I had a feeling that Timothy didn't want to leave, but he also didn't want to outstay his welcome. I was fighting back my feelings and couldn't stop wanting to ask him if he would stay for supper. It must have been Mama tugging at my heart—Go on darling, Go on. All she wanted out of life was for me to be happy, healthy, and strong.

Finally, I blurted out, "Would you like to stay for supper with us?" There, it was out on the table now. My cheeks flushed, and Timothy looked away. I figured he was playing hard to get. But I caught his reflection in the mirror of the curio cabinet, and he was grinning from ear to ear.

That night for dinner I made my famous mouthwatering meatloaf accompanied by three pounds of sour cream and onion mashed potatoes with no shortage of salted butter. Luckily, Tansy had a big enough bowl to fit them all in. I always made a ton of mashed potatoes because my kids loved them. I completed the meal with sides of pineapple coleslaw, candied carrots, and fresh sliced tomatoes with a dash of seasoning salt added on top of each one.

Mama always told me that men liked women who could cook. Well, this woman certainly could. Timothy ended up eating two full plates of food. He stuffed himself. I was sure his belt buckle was going to bust. They say you can catch a man with a lasso, but you'll eventually hold him down with food. Well, at least that's what I heard someone say!

Suddenly, I was bombarded with so many emotions. Instead of being numb, I started to feel again, and that scared me. I was feeling alive and attractive. It felt like someone wanted to be in the room with me for just being me and nothing else.

Those feelings felt good and odd at the same time. After all, my heart was still Keith's, and I knew it would always be that way.

Breaking into my thoughts Timothy said, "By the way, I'm sorry about mentioning that horn on your forehead. I was just kidding, you know. And thank you for supper. It was really good."

Timothy helped me pack up the leftovers and once everything was put away, he turned and said, "Well, this has been a mighty nice day, but I need to be getting home."

"Do you want a ride?" I offered spontaneously.

"I won't drive in no Chevy truck," he said with a grin.

I punched him in the arm. "Sure, you don't. Then go on and walk home." I was laughing.

"Why don't you walk with me?" he suggested.

"How am I going get home then?" I was rather confused.

"I'll walk you back home." That made perfect sense? Not!

I knew where he was going with this. In a way it was our first date. Only he was just trying to be smooth. "Go on, Mary, I'll watch the kids," Tansy said, enjoying the conversation.

"Sure you will," I laughed. "You're such a matchmaker!"

"I'm not the matchmaker, the Lord is!" she insisted. "He knows my heart, but in the end, He gets the credit!" I just smiled at Tansy. She had a good heart, and she was like my mama. I knew she just wanted the best for me.

Jason ran up to me before I left and tried to whisper in my ear, "Mama, I like Timothy, and I think he's kind to you." That made this mama smile. I couldn't make sense about what was happening? But I was going to live in the moment. I wasted enough time feeling alone.

I gave him a hug and kissed him on the forehead. "That is good to hear. Now you listen to Tansy. It's almost bedtime for you and Gracie Bear."

"I will, Mama," he answered with a big grin.

I said good night to the kids and kissed them both. I knew by the time I made it home they would be in bed.

"See you all later," Timothy said as we walked out onto the porch and started down the dirt road to his house. We were both quiet at first and then he kicked up some dirt with his cowboy boots. I could hear the sound of crickets through the warm breeze "Well, are you going to let me hold your hand?" he asked as he held out his. (*This man didn't waste any time at all.*)

"I don't know about that," I said with a nervous laugh. It had been a very long time since I had held any man's hand. Why did he have to go and say that? My hands started sweating.

"Come here already," he said as he took my hand in his.

"Didn't you just ask me if you could hold my hand?"

"Well, I didn't want to wait all night. It's not a very long walk to my house." He laughed, then asked, "So, what do you want, Mary?"

It was a question that caught me completely off guard. It was such a bold question. We were just getting to know each other, and this was the first time we ever held hands. But suddenly things had gotten very serious.

"I don't know what I want," I replied. To be honest I really had no idea what to tell him. I had never dated anyone besides Keith, and I married him. This whole relationship thing was scary for me.

Timothy stopped in the middle of the road and grabbed both my hands. He began to hum a country song. Then suddenly he asked, "Do you like me, Mary? Come on, tell me." He was looking me right in the eyes.

I took a step backwards but even as I did, he took a step toward me keeping my hands in his. He was coming on strong and chasing my heart. But those where big shoes to fill, and I didn't know if he could love me as broken as I was.

My heart skipped a beat and I felt goose bumps all up and down my arms. I looked into his eyes and just stared. No longer was he simply a kind man who was helping Tansy. Suddenly, he was Timothy, a kind guy who had shown an interest in my kids and was taking an interest in me. He was asking about my future and my desires. He stared into my eyes and moved a bit closer.

I could feel his breathe on my cheek and his body was close to mine. As the sun set the sky was glorious, and he held me close to him. I could feel the strength of his chest against mine and the strength in his arms around my waist. I had not been held this way since Keith passed away.

He continued to hum a love song I was familiar with by Garth Brooks. "Mary, may I have this dance," he asked, continuing to hum. I curtsied and said, "Why yes, you may. I thought you would never ask."

Slowly he took me in his arms, and we slow danced on the dirt road with dairy cows in the nearby field. As we twirled he took his hat off and put it on my head. "I feel your heart beating out of your chest. Are you nervous?" he asked.

"Just a little bit," I replied honestly.

"Mary, give me a chance. I promise, I won't break your heart," he whispered, and then he gently kissed my cheek. I couldn't control my emotions. Tears welled up in both of my eyes.

"I'm sorry," I said as I pulled back. "I'm not ready . . ." I left the sentence unfinished.

"Hush, darling. It's going to be all right," he tried to assure me as he caressed my face with his strong hands. "Don't cry," he said as he reached up and wiped the tears from my eyes. I was embarrassed as I looked down to the ground; I felt like a complete fool crying in front of him.

Gently he touched my chin as he tucked the sides of my hair behind my ears. "Mary, I'm not going anywhere. Take all the time you need."

"Can we just hold hands again and walk?"

"I liked holding you close to me and dancing, but if that is what you want, I'll take it as long as I get to be close to you." With that he grabbed my hand and we continued to walk to the house. My mind was in a jumble. So many things were running through my thoughts. There was no way to sort my feelings at that moment.

As we turned down the pathway to his shanty, I gasped. He had done even more since the kids and I had been there just a couple of weeks before. It looked beautiful. "Oh, Timothy, this is nothing like I remember it when I was a child. It's simply beautiful."

"You haven't even seen the inside yet," he said with a laugh as he opened the door and led me in. It was stunning and certainly not what I had expected. There was beautifully stained wood everywhere. He had added on a kitchen nook for his table with two stools. There was a wood-burning stove in the living room with a cast-iron rooster tea pot. I imagined how cozy it would be on a cold winter's night. "Did you build all this?" I asked, admiring the craftsmanship.

"Yes, ma'am," he answered. "Why don't you come sit down on the couch I built?"

"No way, it's too early for that!"

"Early for what?" he asked. "I just want to be close to you."

"We are close enough," I said nervously, continuing to stand.

"Well, at least let me make you some dessert," he insisted.

Dessert? I couldn't believe after two plates of food he was still hungry. I really had no idea where he stored his food. Lord knows, if I ate like him, I would need a bigger car, a bigger house, and a bigger winter jacket.

He made us ice cream sundaes with a caramel sauce he whipped up from a recipe online. I was impressed. Timothy was obviously a man of many talents. We talked for a while but as it grew dark, I stood up and told him, "I really need to get back." He stood and took my hand, but as we moved toward the door, I noticed a picture on the wall. It looked like a younger version of him in a military uniform.

"Is that you?" I asked, looking closer at the framed photo.

"Yes," he responded.

"You were in the military?" That surprised me.

"Yes, I was." He made no move to offer any further explanation, but as I looked at him I noticed beads of sweat had appeared on his forehead.

"Why didn't you tell me? What is the big secret?" I was curious to know more. "Were you a covert spy or something?" I asked sarcastically. When he didn't respond, I knew he was hiding something from me.

Up to that moment everything had felt right, but obviously the conversation had gone in a direction that he wasn't ready to discuss. Suddenly I was eager to get back to the farm and see my babies. "So, are you going to walk me home?"

"Nah, it's too dark out," he said, laughing.

"You're such a smart aleck," I muttered.

"What did you say?" he asked as he began to tickle me. Then he opened the door and looked out. "It's pretty dark outside. Should I bring my sniper rifle?"

I made a face at him as I joined him out on the porch. The temperature was chilly with the sun going down. We walked back down the road, this time a little faster than before.

"Good night, Mary," Timothy said when we reached Tansy's place, and he bent down and kissed me on the cheek. "I had a nice day." Then he turned and headed back down the road. He had been a perfect gentleman. I breathed a sigh of relief as my mind immediately turned to the kids. I ran up the loft to check on them. Gracie Bear and Jason were both in bed. I gave them each a kiss and headed back down to the kitchen for a glass of water. I thought Tansy was asleep for the night, but I should have known better. She yawned as she walked into the kitchen in her bathrobe.

"I'm sorry, Tansy, did I wake you?" She stifled another yawn. "Want some water?" I asked her as I motioned toward the spicket.

She shook her head. "Why don't you heat me up some coffee and tell me about your date night with Timothy." I poured coffee in a mug and stuck it in the microwave.

"Not too long, please. I don't want to burn my tongue."

I pulled out the coffee mug and set it before her. I could tell by the look on her face she wanted to say something, not just hear about the date. "Okay, what?" I asked. "I know you are trying to set Timothy and me up."

"I just don't want you to miss out on what is right in front of you," she started. "Stop being so cynical. You need to give him a chance."

I knew she was right. I needed to stop overevaluating the situation. I needed to just let Timothy be Timothy, and I would be myself. It's simple in life when we are just ourselves.

"So, tell Tansy what happened," she encouraged as she took a sip from her steaming mug. We sat at the kitchen table and I told her about the walk, the dance, the ice cream sundaes, and even the strange conversation about his military tour. "I know I'm holding back," I explained. "I have been since Keith died. But to be honest, Tansy, while I like Timothy, I sense there is something deep down that he is not being honest about with me. At that moment, a million things flooded my mind. It could be anything. Tansy tried to reassure me.

"Mary, he's a good man, a godly man. Those are the ones to hang on to." Tansy was right because Mama had always said the same thing. Mama told me that there are lots of men to choose from in the world, but you want one who's not of the world. What she meant is a man of God knows how to treat a woman. A man who loves God means he belongs to God. He may be living in the world, but he doesn't love the world. Heaven is his home because heaven is his heart!

"God sent you back here. Don't try so hard to figure it out, baby. Let the good Lord work. He knows what you need. He knows what I need. And if there is something Timothy's hiding from you, He'll let you know."

I finally got a chance to exhale. "My work here is done," Tansy said as she sipped the last of her coffee.

It had been an exciting night and I was ready for bed. "I'm going to try to get a few hours of sleep. Thank you, love you!"

"Love you too baby" she replied. I climbed back up the stairs to the loft and kissed Jason and Gracie Bear lightly again so as not to wake them. I never missed an opportunity to kiss my babies. I stood there and watched them sleep, grateful for them both. Suddenly I felt exhausted. The emotion of the day finally hit. I quickly changed, washed my face, and climbed into bed. But sleep didn't come. I laid there and looked out the window. The sky was clear. I looked at the stars and wondered at God's handiwork. I hadn't prayed to God in a while. But looking out at the night sky I said, "God, if You are there, help me to love again."

I didn't expect an answer, but I heard Him respond back in my heart. I actually heard him talk to me! He said, "I have always been here, and I will help you love again."

I felt like I was being tucked in with a warm blanket and that night I slept like a baby. It had been a long time since I felt that happy.

The next morning Gracie Bear jumped on my bed to wake me up. "Good morning, sunshine," she said.

"Good morning," I said with a yawn. "Did you miss me?" I asked.

"Yes, I did Mama." Gracie Bear held onto me, nuzzling into my chest. Jason was up next and filled with questions. "Where did you go last night? Do you like Timothy? Are you going to get married?"

"Wow. where did all that come from?" I asked as I tousled his hair. "It's too early for questions. I need to wake up!" Their excitement made me laugh.

"I want to know all the details, Mama," Jason said.

"Really? Aren't you too young for adult-themed details?" I asked him.

"Listen, any man who's going to date my mama has to go through me first," he said tapping his chest.

"Oh, is that right? Come here, silly." My heart was swelling with love for this little man. I tickled that boy till he couldn't take it anymore. Then I told him that Timothy was a gentleman and that he walked me home. Jason hid his face under the covers as he asked, "Did you kiss him?"

"Why are you hiding under the covers? You want to know details then you have to take the answers like an adult."

"I think kissing is gross," he said, making a face as he popped his head out from under the covers.

"Well, you're young yet. Give it time," I replied.

"I don't think kissing is gross," Gracie Bear chimed in.

"Okay, enough about kissing already," I told them both. "But to answer your question, yes, there was a small kiss. Well, it was more like a peck and only on my cheek. Not my lips," I emphasized.

"My lips are saved for only you two right now," I told Jason.

"Ok, that's not gross then," Jason said after thinking about it. "I love you, Mama."

"I love you, my sweet boy." I was grateful that he didn't feel threatened by Timothy's attention toward me.

Wilma called me later that evening. She was keeping an eye on the house for me. Everything was okay, but she suggested I return just for the weekend. Empty houses can sometimes get broken into, and I didn't want that to happen.

196

I took her advice and decided last minute that we would go back home, but only for the weekend. Then we would get back to our summer vacation and getting Mama's house fixed.

Tansy walked in as I was packing our suitcases. "Where are you all headed to?"

"Just back home for the weekend," I explained. Gracie Bear is missing some of her favorite toys, and I want to make sure everything is okay at the house. "So, I won't be here this Sunday to help you bake fruit pies."

"That's quite all right. This old woman will figure it out. Have a safe trip and I'll see you when you all return," she said.

Timothy did not have a phone hooked up at his tiny house, and he didn't have a cell phone either. I mean, who doesn't have a cell phone? Well, a lot of people who lived in Kettlesville, actually. The reception here stinks, which is why they make cell phone commercials about places such as ours asking if you can hear anything!

"Will you tell Timothy that we left if he drops by?" I asked.

"I sure will, darling," she replied.

Oh, Tansy, she loved a good love story, and she loved that she introduced us. I could see the smile on her face. She was proud of her matchmaking skills.

It was good to get back home and check on things. The house was fine. No issues. I decided to give a quick visit to see Clyde. He commented about my face.

"That farm sure agrees with you. You look happier and more rested than I think I have ever seen you," he said. "I hope you aren't thinking of not coming back to your job after summer. I miss you and the customers miss your delicious pies!" I knew by the look on his face, he really wanted me back. It's hard to replace someone—especially someone like me.

We talked about the business. "I'm still selling lots of pies but not as many as when you are here!" Because of that profit was down a little, but not by much. He was happy about that!

Truthfully, I didn't miss work. I was enjoying the time off. It was fun spending time with the kids, Tansy, and Timothy. I finally felt like my life had meaning again. And I felt I was making a difference by serving others.

"Did you meet anybody up there?" Clyde asked, watching my face.

I was curious to why he asked me that. "What are you getting at, Clyde? Do you know something, I don't?"

"No, I just can tell when somebody is in love is all," he said, watching me closely. "Believe it or not I was in love once a long time ago. Never be embarrassed about love. Loving someone is the most beautiful gift you can ever have. It's special."

"How do you know, I mean really know, that you're in love?" I asked.

"You know when you cannot imagine one moment without them by your side. They make you better. They bring out the best in you," he said without hesitation. He was right!

We stayed through the weekend but by Sunday night Gracie Bear and Jason were begging me to get back to Tansy's. They really liked working and living on the farm. It was peaceful and quiet. And there we felt like a family again.

Chapter Eleven

While Away

I needed to get my life together. I was a hot mess. For too long I carried issues with trust. It wasn't because I didn't want to heal, but I didn't know how to let go of the pain. It was always with me much like when you carry a backpack. I just never put it down. Relationships were hard and making friends even harder. Life wasn't getting any easier as each year passed. I knew I needed to change, but how?

While the kids and I were gone, I called Tansy to check in. "It's too quiet with you and the kids gone," she said. Sounded like she missed us as much as we missed her! But she also told me Timothy was working out back at her place all weekend long. Now I was curious. I wondered what he was doing there. I mean, how many times do you really need to mow the grass? So, I simply asked.

"Timothy had two trucks of dirt delivered," she replied. "For a project he is working on." I was glad Tansy wasn't there by herself all weekend, but clearly she wasn't going to tell me any more about the project, so I let it go.

"Timothy's sister is here this weekend as well," she mentioned.

"Sister?" I asked. That seemed strange. I don't remember him or anyone mentioning he had a sister.

"She lives in Texas and just came to visit," Tansy explained.

My head was spinning with curiosity about whatever project Timothy was working on and why his sister had suddenly shown up. Was he with someone else? Immediately I stopped myself. I better not even go down that rabbit trail. Jealous? Me? Mary Ann? Part of me tried to convince myself why I should care. I mean, we were not together like a couple. It was weird to even feel jealously at this point. But the other part of me was very jealous at the thought that someone else might be at the farm with him. Someone other than his sister. I had been alone for so long I forgot what it felt like to actually care about someone else.

"So, what does his sister look like?" I quizzed.

"She's slender with dark hair. She is pretty and pretty quiet too. She looks like a female Timothy," Tansy replied, trying to sum it up.

"What's her name?" I asked.

"Her name is Samantha." Tansy replied.

"Hmmm. It's interesting, but he never told me he had a sister."

"Well now, I wouldn't worry about it baby. She seems harmless." Tansy was trying to encourage me.

Well, that didn't help a bit actually and raised my suspicions even more. In my mind I figured if a man could hide one thing, then he certainly could be hiding more. My detective antenna was up! I couldn't wait to get back to the farm, but I had another life to tend to first.

I paid my bills and cleaned up the house. Then I cut the grass and closed everything back up. Boy, doing this all by myself is a lot of work. I missed Keith even more. He always did the outside chores. I packed some snacks for the kids, and we jumped into the truck ready to make the drive back to the farm. The sun was out; it would be a wonderful day for travel.

The traffic wasn't bad overall but due to construction along the highway, I spent more time inching along than actually driving. It certainly turned our short adventure into a long one, as detours took us places I had no intention of going. Because of that it was late when we finally arrived back to the farm. We walked in and discovered Tansy had dinner waiting for us. *Bless her heart,* I thought as we unloaded.

She was happy to have us back. "Welcome home! It's been lonely since you left. I missed all of you," she said, giving us a hug.

"It's good to be back. What smells so wonderful?" I asked, realizing we hadn't eaten anything since our light car snacks.

"I made an Italian feast tonight," she informed us. "Stuffed cheesy meatballs, crispy Caesar salad, cheesy garlic bread, and stuffed mushrooms."

My mouth was watering at the sound of the delicious dishes waiting for us. "Oh thank you, Tansy! We're starving. This looks delicious!" As we started to take our seats, I noticed there were two extra place settings at the dinner table. But there were only the four of us. Then I remembered my earlier conversation with Tansy about Timothy and his sister.

"Who else is coming to dinner?" I asked. The back door opened. Sure enough, it was Timothy.

"Hey there, stranger," he said as Jason jumped into his arms. He absolutely adored Timothy.

Meanwhile, Gracie Bear pouted. "What's the matter?" I asked her.

"Jason is always hugging Timothy first when I want to be hugged too. But I am not that big yet!" She had the perfect pouty face. I had to stifle a laugh.

"Awe, sweetie, there is enough love to go around. Come here," Timothy said as he held his arms out to her.

Timothy took her in his arms and twirled her around. "I have something for you, Gracie Bear," he teased as he put her down.

"What is it?" she asked.

"Now, you have to close your eyes and hold out your hands." So, Gracie Bear did what he instructed, but then she peeked!

"Gracie Bear, no peeking," he scolded jokingly. Once he was certain her eyes were closed, he placed a white teddy bear in her hands.

"Can I open my eyes now?" she asked.

"Yes, go on!" he replied.

You should have seen her face. It was clear that she fell in love with that stuffed bear and Timothy at the same time.

Next, he held out a bouquet of flowers. "These are for you." Of course, I went to reach for them, but he pulled his arm back. "No, they are for Tansy," he smiled.

My face flushed from both embarrassment and anger. I started to get mad until he said, "Now, Mary, this is for you."

He reached in his pocket and pulled out a small, wrapped gift.

Tansy said, "Well, go on. Open it."

I took the box from him and slowly unwrapped the tiny package. Inside was a pair of silver feather earrings. I didn't know what to say.

Finally finding my voice, I said, "Thank you. They're gorgeous!"

About that time Timothy's sister came walking up to the house. "Hello!" she said. She was covered in dirt from head to toe, but she extended her hand to greet me. I just looked at it. It was pretty dirty. She realized it and we both started to laugh.

Introducing herself, she said, "I am Samantha, Tim's younger sister." From the sound of her voice, I could hear a Texan drawl. "Timothy has told me a lot about you and the kids."

"That's funny, because he never told me about you," I replied. Honestly, I couldn't believe it popped out of my mouth. But there it was hanging in the air, making everything uncomfortable. Thankfully, Tansy interrupted.

"Come on in and join us for dinner," Tansy said in her warm welcoming manner. I glared at Timothy as my jealousy got the better of me. What else was he hiding from me.? (*Sometimes I am so quick to judge.*)

Timothy shifted around for a moment and seemed embarrassed. "You never asked me if I had any siblings," he responded.

"What else don't I know about you, Timothy?" I sounded like a jealous schoolgirl. *What on earth had gotten into me?*

"Timothy, we are both filthy," Samantha said. "Do you mind running me back home so I can get cleaned up before we eat, please?"

When they came back about an hour later, they were both cleaned up. Timothy smelled good. He wore a nice dress shirt and shined cowboy boots, which Tansy made him take off before he entered.

Over supper, it was nice to talk with Samantha. I was embarrassed by my previous behavior. She told us several amusing stories about Timothy, such as when he was a young boy and had a crush on a girl named Linda. He used to write her love letters and sneak them into her desk. But one day he came home from school crying. His friend had put the notes he had written in the wrong desk. He discovered they were going to a girl named Olive Jackson.

"Olive had smelly feet and snorted when she laughed," Samantha recounted. "One of the notes Timothy had written for Linda was a poem. It read, 'You are cute. You are sweet. When I think of you and me, I think you have nice feet.' To his embarrassment, Olive ended up reading it to the whole class. Everyone began to tease him and call out 'Olive and Timothy.' The next day he pretended to be sick to stay out of school, but no one fell for it. I had never seen Timothy blush before. I laughed. I know it wouldn't have been funny at the time, but now all these years later, it was pretty funny."

Timothy wrinkled his nose at me. "Do you see why I never told you about my sister?" he commented before turning to her. "Come on, Samantha. Enough already. That was years ago," he pleaded.

The rest of the meal was filled with casual conversation. As soon as it was over Samantha thanked Tansy for dinner and excused herself. It was clear she was tired and wanted to get back home to sleep. It had been a long day for her, which I could see in her eyes.

"I can drive you," Timothy said as he got up.

"Never you mind," she told him. "I don't mind the walk to stretch my legs after that delicious meal. I'll be safe. I won't wait up for you," she added as she headed for the door.

I watched as Gracie Bear played with the new teddy bear Timothy got her. She was so happy. Jason was perched on Timothy's lap watching television while I helped Tansy clean up the kitchen. I was drying the dishes when I realized how much the kids needed a father in their lives. They were doing fine with me, but they needed more! (*And I did too!*)

"Tansy, the kids need a father," I whispered.

"They have a father. A heavenly Father," she replied, drying a plate and putting it back up in the cabinet.

"I know that you know what I mean," I said quietly.

"Now, don't go gettin' yourself all upset. God has a timing for every matter. Rest in knowing that. He will provide for you. Just stop your frettin' about everything. You'll get yourself worked up for nothing . . ." I knew she was right.

"Hey Jason, I have something to show you," Timothy said as Jason jumped off his lap. He wanted us to go out back.

"Not until we've had dessert," Tansy insisted. If dinner was not enough, she made a whipped cheesecake with fresh cut strawberries. I barely had enough room for it, but I couldn't be rude and pass it up! It was delicious. Afterwards Tansy said, "Everyone get your shoes on."

"Where are we going?" I asked.

"You'll see," she replied secretively.

It was already pitch-black outside. I wanted to stay inside, but the kids were excited, especially after Timothy said, "All right,

Gracie Bear and Jason, you both need to wear a blindfold over your eyes."

"What, hold up. Wait one minute," I complained. "I want to know where we are going!" Timothy ignored my questions and handed me a blindfold. "Me too?"

"Just do it, Mary," Tansy interrupted. I hesitated a moment but then slid it over my eyes and tied it tightly behind my head.

"Trust me," Timothy replied as he took me by the hand.

Reluctantly, I let him check our blindfolds and lead us outside. Jason was even more excited and so was Gracie Bear. I, on the other hand, was skeptical. *What was he doing*, I wondered?

I grabbed Gracie Bear's hand tightly as we followed behind Timothy and Jason, gingerly making our way across the yard.

"Can I take this blindfold off? Where are you taking us?" Jason asked. He was so excited now that he couldn't keep quiet. He was bursting at the seams. Not being able to see only heightened his senses. "I smell dirt," he commented.

"Well, of course you do," Timothy joked. "We are outside."

"Me too!" Gracie Bear seconded.

"Well, we *are* in a field," Timothy reminded them with a laugh.

My feet began to sink into the ground. "Where were we?" I had started feeling off balance and was about to remove the blindfold when he asked, "Are you ready?"

"Yes, ready as I'll ever be," I said emphatically, wanting to see.

"Okay, on the count of three," Timothy instructed. "One . . . two . . . three . . ."

We each removed our blindfolds, which actually did very little, as we found ourselves standing in the darkness. "Wait one minute," Timothy said. We heard some rustling and then a surge of electricity and four lights came on overhead. I was stunned. We were standing in the middle of a baseball field.

"What? WOW, just WOW!" I exclaimed. "Timothy, really, this is amazing," I told him. The kids and I were mesmerized.

"YAHOO!" Jason exclaimed. I hadn't seen him this excited in so long. I started to cry. Now it all made sense. The dirt on both Samantha and Timothy from head to toe. And now I felt really bad because I had initially been so mean to Samantha when I first met her. She had given up her weekend to come down here and work with Timothy to do this for my children. (*I need to work on not being so critical.*)

Jason jumped up and down with joy. He couldn't hold his excitement. "This is for you, Jason. Your very own baseball field," Timothy told him. "And Gracie Bear, you can play on it anytime you want," he informed her.

"You did this for me?" Jason replied and broke down in tears. He was so overwhelmed. (*I knew he missed Keith, but he was too young to understand that*) I couldn't believe that Timothy did this for my kids.

"You want to play a game?" Timothy was looking at all of us.

"Right now?" Jason asked.

"Yep, right now! Go grab your mitt."

Watching Gracie Bear laughing and Jason beaming from ear to ear blessed a mother's heart. It was at that moment I realized what a gift Timothy truly was. It's amazing how we can take people for granted and not really take time to see who they truly are. (*Lesson learned.*)

There was no doubt Timothy stole the heart of my kids that night. And to be honest, he was stealing mine as well. We got out on the field and Tansy was our cheerleader. She didn't know much about the game, but she sure had a loud voice.

It was hard to get the kids to bed that night. All Jason could talk about was how he had his own personal baseball field at the farm. I wondered how he would feel when we returned home in another three weeks. I would have to get back to work, and the kids would need to start school. Fall was approaching and so was a new school year. I didn't know how I was going to pry the kids away from the farm, especially Jason. They just loved it here.

CHAPTER TWELVE

SAYING GOODBYE

I hate saying goodbye. It's never easy, especially when your used to things. However, goodbyes are necessary for all of us. It's better to step away and really take a look at a situation than to remain blinded from the truth. Sometimes I would rather believe a lie, but life has a way of making reality smack you in the face and leave you with no way out other than goodbye.

It was difficult to keep Jason on track to work. I had my own worries. I was trying hard to get things finished up at Mama's house. Timothy came over each night after work. He and Jason put the new field to use as they played baseball together. Gracie Bear ran from base to base. She never really played, but she enjoyed being around them. I was always concerned she might get hit by a ball. That was just the protective mama in me. I kept telling myself I

needed to just let the kids be kids. (*Well, I kept telling myself that, and it helped—kind of!*)

With just a couple of weeks left of summer, I had to step it up over at Mama's house to get everything done. I still had some more painting to do. I had put that part off long enough. It was work time. Tansy watched the kids for me, and Timothy volunteered to help scrape the paint off the rest of the house and porch. It was going to be a good three-day job for sure. I was happy someone other than myself was helping get it done.

"It's going to take the entire two weeks to get everything finished," Timothy said after we had put in a hard three days already. I was grateful he was offering to help. That meant I wasn't going to have to do it alone, and that was all right by me!

I worked on the remainder of the things on the inside of Mama's house while Timothy worked on the outside. He scraped the front porch swing and added some new metal reinforcements from the ceiling of the porch and chains. The old ones were pretty rusted, and it really hadn't been safe. I made us some sandwiches and ice-cold lemonade and was about to take it all outside when Timothy yelled to me, "Hey, Mary, can you get me a bottle of water in the back seat of my truck?"

"Sure, I'll be right out!" I responded.

I went to the truck and opened the door. Out bounded a golden retriever. He was wearing a red bowtie around his neck and started licking my face as I bent down to pet him. "Is he mine?" I was stunned.

"Yes, he is all yours," Timothy replied.

"You sneak," I said with a laugh. "Thank you! He's precious."

I already knew his name. "I am naming him Sam," I said out loud, my heart full. I had dreamed of this moment since I was a little girl, when I had asked God to give me a dog while sitting under the willow tree. Now, twenty-five years later here I was standing in my driveway holding the dog for which I had prayed. *(Mama was right. It was a place of wonder.)*

I looked up at the sky and said, "God, You're awesome!" Some prayers get answered right away while others take more time. A long time in my case. "Wait till Gracie Bear and Jason see this puppy," I told Timothy. "They are going to flip out!"

Timothy was smiling, obviously pleased by my response. "By the way, I already talked to Tansy, and she said it's okay for the puppy to stay at the farm."

"Really, even when we go back home?"

"That's what she said. You can go ask her if you don't believe me."

I gave him a hug. I could tell, though, he wanted to kiss me.

"Is that all I get?" he said jokingly.

"Yes, that's all you get!" I responded as I flicked his nose with my finger. We had been working all morning. I eyed our progress and was pleased. Slowly but surely it was coming together. We sat down on the porch to have lunch as Sam explored the garden.

"Thanks so much for helping me. I never would have gotten all this done without you," I said as I passed the plate of sandwiches to him. We both chewed silently as we watched Sam play. He was chasing a cricket. I kept my eye on him so he wouldn't run too far.

"No problem. I have nothing better to do than work my real job," Timothy said sarcastically. "You really needed my help." He paused before continuing. "So, what are we going to do, Mary?"

"What do you mean?"

"About us? About the future?"

I could tell he was a bit impatient with the whole relationship status. It felt like he wanted more from me than I was willing to give.

"Well, everything has happened so fast this summer. I haven't really had much time to think about it." I wasn't being completely truthful. I had actually thought about it a lot but had no idea what to do with this handsome cowboy who had invaded our lives.

Timothy just nodded. He knew I had thought about it. I just was not ready to be honest about how I felt. Keith was the only man I had ever known and loved. I know he died, and I needed to move on. Sometimes I felt I was ready, but other times I spent comparing Timothy to Keith. It is hard to move on when your heart is still filled with love for someone else.

I looked down not knowing what to say but realizing Timothy needed some reassurances. "You said you weren't going anywhere. Did you mean it?" I asked. Timothy took a bite of his sandwich and with a full mouth said, "Yeah, I most certainly did."

That made me feel better, but I could tell my lack of commitment was really bothering him.

"So, when are you leaving?" he asked.

"Two weeks. You know that. I have to get the kids back in school." My voice was soft. "I don't want you to leave, Mary," he said, taking my hand.

"You're not being fair. I can't just uproot our lives for a relationship that has barely started."

"Fair? You came into my life like a whirlwind and now you're leaving the same way."

I knew it was time to be honest with how I felt. But I was still wrestling with the fact that he wasn't being completely honest with me. Now was the time to ask him the question I had been withholding in fear it was something bad. "So, what are you not telling me about yourself?" I was staring at him straight in the eyes.

He looked down unable to keep eye contact. "I'm not who you think I am," he answered quietly. Well, I certainly didn't expect that.

"What is that supposed to mean?" I didn't know where this was going.

"I was in the Army in a secret ops division."

"What? Are you kidding me? You're a spy?"

"Well, technically not a spy," he said. "A special agent."

"Are you running from the law, Timothy Header?"

"No, the law is running after me!" he exclaimed. I had no idea what that meant, and he still hadn't fully answered my question. I stayed quiet to let him speak.

"Why are you quiet? Come on, talk to me." He was trying hard to keep the conversation going.

"I'm sorry. I just found out that you are not who you said you were. I don't know what to say. Please, give me a minute to let this sink in," I told him with a condescending and sarcastic edge to my voice.

"I am still me—Timothy," he said. "The one you're falling for." I have a past, okay? So do you. Can we just move on?"

"Let me be clear. I don't have a *criminal* past, Timothy, and I haven't lied to you. It's not the same thing."

"If you would just let me explain, you would understand." He looked worried.

"Explain what? How you lied to me and my kids, making us think you were someone you're not?" I allowed my voice to raise louder than I intended.

"Mary, I didn't expect to fall in love." *(I couldn't believe what I was hearing. He loved me?)* He continued, "The feelings I have for you and your children are real. I love them. Jason is the sweetest boy, and Gracie Bear has such a gentle heart. I would never hurt them. I care about them, and I care about you!" *(I knew he was sincere, but I was angry and wouldn't listen)* "Won't you listen to me? Can't we work this out?" he pleaded. *(He had a lot to learn about the woman he loved.)*

I can be flat-out stubborn and at that moment I just felt I had been lied to. It triggered some old emotions from childhood when Daddy would make a promise and then not follow through. I hated to be lied to. "No, we can't, Timothy. Not only did you get me involved with you, but you got my kids involved. You weren't honest with me, and that is not all right. You know Jason and Gracie Bear love you. But I have to know I can trust you. This breaks my heart, and it's going to break theirs as well." I felt angry and betrayed. *(How could I have been so naïve?)*

"Look, I'm protective over my babies," I told him. "You stay away from Tansy too. You stay away from me, and you stay away from my kids. You hear?" I was worked up now and the words were out of my mouth before I knew it. My emotions were in a jumble and I felt like a nine-year-old, mad at the world and ready to crawl under my willow tree.

Timothy tried to convince me otherwise, but my mind was already made up. At that point I didn't care anymore. He could leave for all I cared. I was mad and the conversation was over!

I walked into the house and slammed the screen door behind me. Thoughts of Daddy drinking when I was a little girl filled my mind and the betrayal I felt each time he would choose his liquor over Mama and me. Then I was bombarded with thoughts of Keith and Mama. I needed to simmer down and calm my nerves. Sometimes all it took was for me to clean something. Whenever I get mad, you could eat off the kitchen floors. Some people eat, but I clean! Whatever works, right?

About twenty minutes passed and I finally cooled down. The counters never looked so clean. They sparkled. Now that I had become calmer, I realized I had been too harsh with Timothy. I walked outside to say so, but he was gone! On the porch swing was his plate, and Sam was chomping on the rest of his half-eaten sandwich and mud was all over his fur and paws. He needed a bath. Then the guilt set in. If only I would have taken Mama's advice, "Think before you speak, Mary, think!"

I didn't mean to push him away, but what was I going to do? Let him lie to my face? Deceive my children, and break Tansy's heart?

When I got to the farm, I had Jason take Gracie Bear to the baseball field to play a game. Sam ran right behind them, they just adored him. I sat down with Tansy to break the news. I didn't want the kids to hear anything bad about Timothy.

"I have something to tell you about Timothy," I said.

"Yes, go on. What is it, Mary?" she asked.

"Timothy is running from the law." The look on my face was pure panic. But before I could say a word she interrupted me and said, "Now before you go gettin' yourself all fired up. Here me out! I am gonna tell you the story Tansy's way."

"Yes, Ma'am," I respectably replied. But before she could say another word I blurted out, "Tansy, before you tell me, do you trust Timothy?"

"I trust God who made him," she said. Then she began sharing his story with me, how one Sunday at church Timothy's countenance was downcast. He was having a bad morning. She felt she should pray with him, and he ended up telling her everything. After high school Timothy had joined the Army, and after four years of faithful service, he was promoted to special forces. The military sent him all over the world in secret locations on secretive missions. Everything was classified. She proceeded to explain that Timothy came over to the farm to help her from time to time. They would drink a lot of fresh lemonade which got them talking about all kinds of things.

"One morning Timothy woke up," she continued, "but he was in a different place. It wasn't home, he was somewhere else. Somebody gave that man drugs, covered his eyes and dragged him out of the country. Lord, he was in trouble. They locked him in a cold prison cell. He said it smelled awful.

Timothy told me they had plans to kill him. He knew it. After all those years of military training, he was scared. He didn't dare tell them any secrets about the land of the free. No, he didn't. He kept his mouth shut, just like a proper military man would. He's a good man, Mary, loyal.

I couldn't believe what she was telling me. I was skeptical at first but then this was Tansy and if anyone could see through a lie it would be her. Mama always said there was no shortcuts when it came to wisdom.

"He sat in that cell until he got an opportunity to escape. Timothy is smart. He used a butter knife to cut away the bars by the window. It took him awhile though. You know how sharp butter knives are?" Both of us got a laugh from that statement.

"Listen to me Mary. God was with him," Tansy said. "He made it out! They chased him for a long time, but no body caught him. He said bloodhounds couldn't even sniff him out."

"What happened next?" I asked.

"Something happened when he got home. The government did something real bad Mary. They lied to him, erased important papers, and then blamed him for their lies. They made it look like he was the wrong doer. Can you believe the nerve of some? I'll never understand it.

"He didn't do nothing wrong! Here look." Tansy reached in a small wooden box on her coffee table. She handed me a picture of Timothy with five other men and two women. Then I remembered Timothy briefly telling me, in passing, about the others with him. *(I have not mentioned them. It's classified information.)*

"Only two survived and he was one of them," Tansy continued. "As he told me, he broke down and cried like a baby in my arms. The years of pain and grief he held came bubbling to the surface. He needed to get it off his shoulders. He had been carrying the pain around for too long." Anger turned to compassion as Mary realized what Timothy had endured.

"He ran baby and I would have too. He came back home where it was safe and quiet. Back in the woods—back home!

"I told him that we could allow our pain to eat us alive if we didn't deal with it. But when we give it to God, He takes it ALL away. He makes us lighter and gives us hope. "News came that his solider friend died. Brady Tenner, was his name. They were like brothers. There was nothing they wouldn't do for each other," Tansy continued. "Timothy was sad. It sounds like they had been friends just like your Mama and me was."

To make matters worse, from what Tansy told me, Brady was newly married and had a young son named Dylan. At the time of Brady's death, Dylan was only two years old. It left his wife, Clare, a widow, and his son fatherless. I found out much later Timothy was completely undone by his friend's death. No wonder Timothy always seemed so sad. Loss is hard to deal with and I was not stranger to it.

I sat stunned for several minutes. Now I understood why he fled to Kettlesville to the cabin where his folks had brought him and his sister when they were young. He knew that because it was somewhat off the grid, so to speak, it would be a safer place for him. He wanted to put the past behind him and start over. Leaving the military without permission was his only option, or face court martial for things he didn't do.

"Timothy said he had been on the run about three years now."

"So, what will happen if they find him?" I questioned.

"I've wondered that too," Tansy replied. "I have prayed to God for Timothy. I put my trust in Him. Even if that means Timothy goes to jail.

I felt so guilty. If only he has been honest with me from the beginning. But if I were honest with myself I had to wonder if I would have trusted him or turned him in? Hard to say.

"He's not a bad man, Mary. He may be a broken man, but he is a good man, a godly man. And that is what you need. A man who loves God knows how to love you. Can't you see that?" (*Please Lord open my eyes. I want to believe this with all my heart.*)

CHAPTER THIRTEEN

GOING BACK

I'm a curious person and I just can't let things go when they are bothering me. Its better just to face it, get it out of the way, and deal with the matter. Then you'll find the truth and the truth will set you free—or it will break your heart. But even if it does, they say it's better to live in reality. I would rather just deal with whatever I need to. This has often gotten me in trouble because I am willing to confront and speak my mind. But sometimes I wonder if I should stick to dreaming and just keep my mouth shut. I can be my worst enemy.

After I talked with Tansy, I decided I'd walk over to Timothy's. *(I had a lot of my mind.)* Before I left, I gave the kids a bath and a snack and then put them to bed. As I walked the short distance to the cabin, I pondered how to approach the conversation. I could talk some sense into him and tell him I was sorry for how I treated him first off. The guilt was eating me alive. I hated when I got this way. My plan was only to be gone for a couple of hours.

"It's late for a young lady to be walking alone. You be careful," Tansy said as she shut the front door behind me.

"Oh, I'll be careful and be back before too long," I replied. After walking a short distance, I turned back and noticed she was looking out the kitchen window.

Suddenly I heard her yell, "Wait! Why don't you take Sam with you? There is a leash for him hanging up in the garage."

She was right. Sam needed the exercise, and it probably wasn't the best decision to walk alone. The town wasn't the same place as when I grew up, that was for sure. I went back to the house and got the leash. Sam was excited. He took off ahead of me. That dog could never wait for anyone. He's a bloodhound. As we started down the road, I heard some rustling in the trees not too far ahead. It got Sam's attention and mine. It made me jump, but then I realized it was only a barn owl.

When I arrived at Timothy's house, he was not there. I walked around the back hoping to see his truck, but there was no sign of him. Come to think of it, there were no tire tracts on the dirt road to his house either.

I peered through the kitchen window and saw a few drawers open. There were some dishes on the counter, but nothing looked suspicious to me. However, there were no lights on inside or even the porch light, which I had learned was uncommon for Timothy. When he left, he went away either mad or sad at me. And now that I couldn't see any trace of him, I was worried that I caused him to disappear. I began to pray. Strange how I was becoming more comfortable with that. I knew I couldn't change what had happened, but I really hoped he would be home soon. I wanted to apologize for how I had acted. It was not my intention to be cruel to him. In truth, I was trying to protect myself from getting hurt. I walked around the front of the house. Sam had to go to the bathroom. Then I noticed headlights pointed straight at me.

Well, good, it was Timothy. *Perfect timing,* I thought. Now I wouldn't have to walk home by myself, and I could finally get this whole mess off my chest, and we could put it all behind us.

I walked up the road to greet him. But the closer I got to the headlights, I realized it wasn't Timothy. The car stopped next to me, and the driver rolled down his window. There were two men inside dressed in all black.

"Ma'am, what are you doing out this late at night?" the driver asked me. Sam jumped on the car and barked ferociously. "All right little buddy. That's enough," the driver said.

"Get down, Sam," I instructed. He actually listened but let out a low growl. My little protector. "Well, I don't think that's any of your business," I told the driver.

"Do you know who lives down this road, ma'am?" he questioned.

I was scared. Now that I knew Timothy's past, the men looked like secret agents to me. They had their hair high and tight, and they looked out of place in this town. I was by myself and scared being a single woman out in a rural area with two grown men. I glanced at them for a minute and didn't want to take long with the response. "Nope, I was just taking my dog for a late-night walk." I better be getting back though," I said as I turned to head up the road and away from them.

"Well, be careful," the other man said. "We are looking for a fugitive. A man named Gary Gaver." The driver pulled out a photograph and showed me the man in question. I gazed at it trying to keep my expression from giving anything away.

"Never seen him before," I remarked casually. "There is nobody in this town named Gary. Looks like you're in the wrong place."

I kept my game face on and didn't want to give away what I knew. Oh, it was Timothy no doubt. They were coming for him, and I had a sneaky suspicion they knew I knew something.

"Ma'am, if you happen to see him, please call us at once. Our number is on the bottom of this paper," the driver said as he offered his card. "He is armed and dangerous and not to be trusted!"

I took the card, folded it, and placed it in my jacket pocket. "I sure will."

"Good night to you, ma'am, be safe." he said as they watched me walk down the road back the way I had come. It seemed to me that they looked at me suspiciously. They were sure I knew something but were playing it safe.

"You let us know if you see him around here," the driver called out. "We wouldn't want any trouble."

"Thank you. I sure will. You all have a nice night." I started picking up my step.

I heard their car doors slam behind me. Curiosity got the best of me and I turned around to look, although everything in me said *don't look back*. I mean, what if I turned in to a pillar of salt? (*Lot's wife did in the Bible after all!*) *I was being ridiculous*, I told myself. Anyway these weren't biblical times. But my heart was beating as I considered how I was out there very much alone, watching these two men—and they were watching me.

They had flashlights out and were looking into the house windows and around the perimeter. I immediately thought of the soft ground and that they would be able to see my footprints. *Don't freak out,* I told myself. *Just say you were chasing Sam around the house.* Yes, that would be the perfect alibi in the event I was questioned later. My legs were shaking as I continued to walk the road home. I couldn't believe this was happening to me. It was scary and exciting at the same time. I mean, nothing ever happens like that in a rural town and especially to me—a simple pie maker and widowed mom of two. Good Lord!

As I walked back home paranoia set in. The hair on the back of my neck stood to attention, and I kept looking over my shoulder to see if the men were following me. I wanted to get word to Timothy, so he would know they were looking for him. There was no way that someone would not turn him in. The more heat these two men put on our town, the sooner someone would speak up. It seemed as if Timothy's days of running from the military were coming to an end.

It took quite a while for my nerves to settle once I was safely back in the house. I unleashed Sam and gave him some water before I crawled in bed. Tansy was already asleep so I would have to wait to talk to her in the morning. I didn't sleep well; I was up and down all night. Each time, I checked on the kids, nervous that something could happen to us. I also looked out the window and at least twice saw a car on the road. There were only a few cars that ever passed the farm and to see two in the wee hours of the morning? Well, I was sure it was those two men.

A thunderstorm came rolling in around three in the morning. The lightning and the thunder shook the loft. It even woke Gracie Bear and Jason, who could usually sleep through anything. I was already like a wired cat who just ate catnip, but even more so with the storm. The kids crawled in bed with me, and we watched the lightening flash until I heard their rhythmic breathing as they fell back to sleep.

All this mystery had me feeling like Angela Lansbury, the star of the hit television show *Murder She Wrote*. Don't get me wrong, I am one for a good mystery, but I prefer watching it on a television series and not actually walking it out in my own life. (*My imagination was taking over; I needed to stop!*)

I still couldn't believe they said Timothy was armed and dangerous. (*What if he wanted to kill me or my kids?*) He was the kindest man I had ever met. Obviously, they were intensifying the story to get my attention and wanted me to believe he was dangerous so I would turn him in. Then their hunt for the AWOL military agent would be officially over.

As soon as it was light, I rushed to the house to talk with Tansy. I told her everything that had happened. Then I handed her the paper the two men gave me. "Tansy, I lied to them. I told them I never saw him before. I feel really bad about it, like I am hiding information and harboring a fugitive." (*It felt good to get it off my chest.*)

In my mind I pictured myself in a courtroom. The jury listened to the arguments, but by the look on their faces and their shouts of "Guilty!" I had no chance of getting acquitted. The judge, an older man in his late sixties, pressed his bifocals onto the bridge of his nose and glanced at a piece of paper, notarized by a court liaison. It looked like an official document.

"I hereby find the defendant, Mary Ann Walker, guilty of aiding a military officer under Article 27251 or 27352 or whatever. It truly doesn't matter at this point," he continued. What matters is we find her guilty!" Immediately the entire courtroom stood to attention and began to applaud.

I heard shouts of, "Guilty! Give her a life sentence with no parole." Someone randomly yelled, "She is outta here," just like an umpire.

I was shaking. It felt real. All I wanted was my old life back devoid of a criminal background. Then the courtroom turned into a party scene. Everyone was celebrating my pending doom with streamers, party horns, and even cans of silly string. The judge took his gavel made of solid wood and hit the desk. The sound resonated through the courtroom, then silence. All eyes were on the most honorable judge.

"This courtroom shall come to order," the judge instructed. It was hard to take him seriously with a celebration cone on his head and silly string stuck to his black robe, but I fought through it. I didn't want him to think I was making fun of him.

Then he said the unexpected. "Security, would you please remove Ms. Walker from this courtroom and make sure she has extra shackles and heavy weights placed around her arms, neck, and legs?" Was I that guilty that I needed extra shackles? Come on! Somebody give me a break!

The judge concluded, "I was hoping this trial would be over soon. My lunch is getting cold. This court is officially adjourned. Now, let's go in the back chamber and eat some delicious food. My secretary ordered pizza for everyone!"

The court went wild. People were jumping out of their chairs and high fiving one another. "But not you, Mary. Get her out of here!" he said with an evil laugh.

I looked back to my kids as the guards started to shackle my hands. They were crying. I yelled across the room in hopes they would hear me, "I'm so sorry. Mama will get out of prison soon." Gracie Bear and Jason reached their arms out for me, their faces covered with pure agony. "No, Mama, no! Don't go!" they both screamed.

A curvy woman wearing a blue and white flowered bonnet grabbed the kids and with a southern accent and a stroke of her wooden cane said, "I'm their mama now!" Then the court whisked the three of them away. I stood there innocent, wrongfully charged, having an unruly hair day on my way to three miserable sentenced years of incarceration and no human interaction. (*Why do I always have to think of the worst possible scenarios?*) Mama told me that my overthinking would be a problem. She was right! Gosh, I need to stop this!

Tansy interrupted my thoughts as she set a mug of coffee down in front of me. "What is wrong with you? You look shook up!"

"I am, Tansy. I need to tell you what happened last night."

"Okay, but just don't let your thoughts get the better part of you. You know your mama was like that too. There was many a time I had to calm her down. Especially when you were sneaking out of your bedroom window at night."

"You two knew about that?" I asked.

"Of course, we did. I think the whole town did," Tansy said with a laugh.

"Your daddy also knew you were sneaking out at night. He waited until you crossed the creek and then followed you to make sure you were safe."

I was stunned. I thought I had been so secretive. It's a good lesson to learn, someone, somewhere is always watching.

"Oh, yeah, I cannot tell you how many times he slipped on those rocks. You're lucky you didn't go and get yourself killed. Those rocks are dangerous," she scolded.

"Well, let me tell you what happened when I went to Timothy's last night," I began. "Timothy wasn't there, but two men were . . ." I let the whole story spill out along with the fear that had gripped me.

"Now, now, darling. Timothy knew this day would come," Tansy said as she reached over and patted my hand, then told me more about his story.

"One evening Pastor Greg called for a prayer meeting and Timothy decided to go with me. He was helping me with some chores on the farm that day. While we were there, he began to open up about his past. He didn't go into detail, but Tansy knows when somebody's got something heavy on their mind. I don't call it intuition. I call it the Spirit of God.

"He wanted us to pray for wisdom for him, as he didn't know what to do. He didn't feel he did anything wrong, but, of course, that is not up to him to decide. It took him time in prayer to really look at his situation. That's why it is so important we pray. Because when we pray, prayer changes us. It cleans out the garbage and brings things forgotten to the surface for healing."

"So, what do you think needs to happen now?" I asked.

"What needs to happen now is he needs to take responsibility for what he's done. Everybody eventually gots to come clean."

I couldn't have agreed with Tansy more. Everyone needs to own the decisions that they make and the consequences. I remember Mama told me, "Sometimes we are our worst enemy." (she was right!) It's true, we can feel guilty or blame ourselves when we are not even the ones to blame.

"I agree with you, Tansy, but what if we never see him again? What if those men looking for him kill him?" I was letting my imagination run wild again. A vision passed through my mind of me and the kids dressed in black. It was raining. A few people were around the casket at the cemetery. But there was nobody in it. Timothy was still missing. I noticed the headstone read, "In living memory of Timothy Header." As I looked down at the headstone, the date of death read "TBD," which meant "to be determined."

Still, I wondered, what if someone killed him? What if he'd been kidnapped? What if the government decided to drop him completely? As we sat at the table, my mind going in a million directions, it was as if Tansy could read my thoughts.

She blurted out, "Now, listen here, nobody is going to kill Timothy. God has His hand on that man. You're getting yourself all worked up. Go on and have some pancakes. There is butter on the table and strawberries in a mason jar over by the coffee beans."

But I couldn't seem to eat. My mind was going haywire. Where was Timothy? Why did he disappear into thin air? My thoughts were interrupted by a knock at the door. "Who could it be?" I looked at Tansy, my stomach already knotting up. She nodded her head cool as could be.

"Well, there is only one way to find out. You sit here and I'll go answer the door. You let me handle this, you hear? Be quiet and follow my lead," Tansy said softly as she made her way to the door.

"Well, hello gentleman," Tansy greeted. "What can I do for you?" I glanced over and it was them—the two men who were at Timothy's the night before. One of the men pressed his face up against the door screen. He cupped his hands around his eyes to try to see inside the house.

"Can we come in and talk to you for a minute?" he asked.

Sam ran to the door and began to bark. The man looked down and I could tell they recognized him. "No, I am sorry, but I don't allow strangers in my house," Tansy informed him, double-checking the lock on the screen.

"Does anyone live here with you, ma'am?" he questioned as he tried to scan the living room.

"Well, that would be none of your business," Tansy told him matter-of-factly. "Is that all," she asked?

"No, actually it's not. We are looking for this man," and he held up the photo of Timothy he had shown me the night before. "Have you seen him?" Tansy squinted as she looked at the paper and shook her head. "No, I cannot even tell who that is," she responded. "I've never seen him before. You sure you're looking in the right town?"

"We hope so. He's armed and dangerous, so watch out for him, ma'am." He held out a card to her as he had done with me the night before.

Tansy opened the screen door slightly and took it from him. "Thank you kindly for the warning. If I hear anything, I will let you know. Good day!" she said as she closed the door.

She turned around to me and put her finger to her lips. "Hush," she whispered. I knew what she meant and we waited in silence for the men to finally leave the farm. They glanced around the area before they got in their car and pulled out of the drive, leaving a wake of dust behind them.

"That was them," I informed her. "Those were the guys who were being nosy at Timothy's house."

"I know baby don't you worry," she said. "They aren't from around here."

"I don't feel too bad now," I told her.

"And what do you mean by that?" Her hand was on her hip.

"You lied to those men too. When they asked you if you knew the man in the photo."

"No, baby girl, I didn't lie to those men, I told them the truth. I told them I could not even tell who that man was!" she laughed "And that was the truth!"

"Oh please, Tansy. You knew it was Timothy!"

"Now, you watch your mouth. I may not be your mama, but I am older than you," she scolded, wagging her finger at me. "Not only am I older than you, but I am also wiser than you, and don't you forget it!"

"Sorry, you're right. I need to know when to keep my mouth shut!"

"I wasn't even wearing my glasses, Mary. So, you see, I really couldn't see!" she replied with a laugh.

Tansy was a character that was for sure. I laughed too. She hadn't lied. She just didn't give them what they were looking for.

"Would you mind heating up my pancakes?" she asked. "I'm starving." Suddenly I was as well. *(It's amazing how a little laughter can take away stress and change your attitude!)*

CHAPTER FOURTEEN

PACKING IT UP

*I*t's hard when your kids are sad. They have feelings too. The Mama Bear in me just wanted to take all their pain away and never see them suffer. But that is not what happens. They feel just as much as we do. Only they can't understand or see the full picture. I am so thankful for grace, not only for me, but for my children. They make me smile when I am sad and they show me how to never give up. They believe.

Summer was ending. The kids and I weren't happy about it either. We hadn't seen Timothy since the incident with the two military men. I hadn't finished fixing up Mama's house. The painting was only partially done. With Timothy gone, things moved much slower. I resigned myself to the fact that it wasn't going to get finished and cleaned up before I needed to close it up for the winter. At least the lawn was mowed and the look of disrepair was gone so the neighbor couldn't complain any longer. It's amazing what we do to make other people happy. Sometimes you just can't please everyone, so you must figure out how to be happy yourself.

The kids and I didn't want say goodbye to Tansy. But I had to get back to my job and our own home. My boss was eagerly waiting for my return. It was time to leave the farm. Jason showed his sadness more than Gracie Bear. He desperately wanted to say goodbye to Timothy before we left. He admired him and looked up to him like a father figure. I never told the kids what happened. It was too much for them to process at their young age. I simply told them Timothy had to go away for a while. They're smart so I figured they knew something had happened, but they didn't pry. That made me feel good. I didn't want to lie to them, just protect them is all. While Jason didn't want to go because of Timothy, Gracie Bear didn't want to leave Sam. She was crazy about that dog and didn't want to go back without him. The closer we got to the time to head out, the harder it became.

The truck was packed, and I stepped back for a moment. Where did all this stuff come from anyways? *We didn't bring this much when we got here,* I thought. Gracious Tansy made us chicken salad sandwiches, dills pickles, and potato chips for lunch. I was truly going to miss this place, especially her home-cooked meals. I looked around the house again before walking back out to the truck. It felt surreal. It had been a wonderful summer. I had come heavy-laden—Mama's house had needed repair, but so had my heart. I recognized that just like Mama's house my heart had come a long way. I certainly wasn't expecting to meet Timothy. Leaving both Tansy and Timothy behind was probably the hardest part about going home.

"I really enjoyed having you and the kids here for the summer," Tansy said as she gave us all a hug.

"We so enjoyed being here," I told her. "We are going to miss you."

"I hope you can come back and stay," she said as she wiped a tear from her eye.

"We would love that," I told her. I suddenly felt I would burst into tears. This had been the closest thing to having family again since Keith, Mama, and Daddy had all passed. It was going to seem very lonely to get back to a life with just the kids and me.

"We shall see. I don't always have time off work being a single parent." Now I was wiping a tear from my eye too. I was going to miss this place, that was for sure!

It didn't seem right leaving without saying goodbye to Timothy. My heart was broken. It was hard to forget that day when he left without a trace. I still felt guilty. I wish I wouldn't have been so hard on him.

"I know it isn't easy leaving without being able to see him again. But have faith, Mary. God works in mysterious ways," Tansy said. "If anything else happens, I'll let you know."

I knew she was right, but it didn't change things. And I needed to end that topic of conversation because I didn't want Gracie Bear or Jason catching on to what we were talking about. When they were little, I could get away with a lot. Keith and I could spell words out, or mouth a sentence over their heads, but now? No way! Those kids were smart and they figured stuff out quickly.

The kids kissed Sam a hundred times. I thought his tail was going to fall off, he was wiggling it so fast. "Please can Sam come home with us?" they both begged. But that was not going to happen. I worked full time and they went to school full time. It wouldn't be fair for him to be alone all day caged up. At least at the farm he could roam free and give Tansy some much needed company and added protection.

Before we left, I told Tansy we would try to be back for Christmas. I certainly didn't want to spend this Christmas alone. Being around Tansy made me feel like Mama was in my life again. Although Tansy could never replace Mama, she was like a second mom to me! Sigh...I hate goodbyes!

The ride home was a long one, but in a strange way it felt good to be going back. The memories of Keith were at our home. The first home we bought together.

We made the trip back safely. With just one weekend before school started, we needed to go buy school supplies and pick out some clothes. It had been a while since I had seen Wilma and I missed her. It would be nice to get back to our morning visits.

Monday morning came in a flash. Clyde was very happy to see me. He ordered double bins of baking supplies. I was officially back to my old life, but deep down the wistfulness I experienced for the farm and Tansy was intense. I felt like I was falling into depression. I still had heard absolutely nothing from Timothy. Mary and I didn't know if they had found him or if he was in hiding. It had been three weeks since I left Kettlesville. How the kids and I missed the farm!

While I was gone Clyde hired a new employee. His name was Ralph. I could tell when I met him that he was a nice guy, but I so was not ready for another relationship. I arrived at six o'clock each morning to begin the baking. Clyde wanted Ralph to shadow me and learn how to bake pies. I gave Ralph the heavy job moving the flour sacks and then the more tedious tasks of sifting flour, cutting in the butter, blending, mixing, rolling, and filling. Meanwhile, I chopped berries, sliced apples, and made custard.

Clyde allowed me to figure out the pie menu for each week. Only certain pies were available on certain days and when they sold out, I would remove the sign. Clyde was easy to work for. He had his own way of doing things, but we worked well together. Plus, he was easy to talk to. Ralph also seemed that way.

"So, tell me about yourself," Ralph asked one day.

"Well, I have two kids," I replied as we got into the groove of the morning.

"What are their names?"

"Gracie Bear and Jason," I told him as I washed some berries.

"That's cool. A boy and a girl? That's the best of both worlds," he said. "Are you married? I don't see a ring."

"Boy, you ask a lot of questions," I responded. "Well, I once was, but my husband died a few years ago. I'm a widow." I could tell by the look on his face he felt embarrassed for even asking.

"Oh, wow, I am sorry to hear that! Yeah, I do ask a lot of questions. I just like to know who I'm working with is all," he said as he started rolling out the dough for the pies.

"How about you?" I asked.

"I have a boy. His name is Darren. I haven't seen him in a few years though."

"Why not?" It was my turn to be nosey now.

"His mom and I broke up. She split to another city with him. I don't have a super reliable car right now and haven't made enough money at my former job to replace it. That's kind of how I ended up here with Clyde and you baking pies; and then I work another

job at night. I am saving my money. I plan to send my ex-wife my first check, which should help her out with all the school supplies and clothes she bought for our son. It's always expensive when school starts."

"You're not kidding," I agreed, thinking of how much I just had to spend on my two.

He seemed like a fairly good guy. I had to work with him, so I gave him the benefit of the doubt. Before too long we were in the swing of things and actually worked well together. But soon I could tell someone was beginning to like me a little bit more than just a friend, and I wanted nothing to do with it. It seemed to me that men always like to chase something.

We were finishing up for the morning and washing the utensils when he finally asked me out. After a long pause he got up the courage and said, "Do you want to go on a date with me tomorrow night?"

I cringed. I was not interested in him in that way and knew it could mess up the good working relationship we had developed. "Ralph, you know I like you, but I am not interested in dating anyone." I was trying to let him down gently.

"Oh, come on, Mary. Live a little. Look, it's okay if you just want to be friends."

I threw some flour in his face trying to lighten up what had become a serious conversation. It looked like a trail of white smoke. "Who said anything about being friends?" I started laughing.

Clyde walked in about that time and didn't find the mess in the kitchen very funny. He was mad and felt I was wasting the baking supplies he bought.

"I'm really sorry, Clyde!" I was glad that he quickly forgave me, and Ralph and I cleaned up the kitchen for an extra hour. Oh well, we deserved it!

I was beyond exhausted when I arrived home. But the kids weren't! They were wired and sleep was not on their radar. I will never understand the amount of energy they have. I need to figure out how to bottle it up and sell it. I would be a millionaire and wouldn't have to work anymore! I reclined in the chair and put my feet up for the first time since that morning. I was sore and desperately needed some me time, which in my mind involved a hot bubble bath and a cucumber mask. But when I finally got the kids down, sleep was calling. Maybe tomorrow night.

CHAPTER FIFTEEN

OPPORTUNITY MEETS DESTINY

*H*ave you ever been in that moment where you know you have an opportunity in front of you and have a choice on whether to take it or not? Sometimes you just don't want to jump especially when life is in coast mode, but you know you need to because your destiny may just depend on it.

I turned over and looked at the clock. It read 8:00 a.m. *Oh great!* I thought as I started to holler at the kids. I'm supposed to be at work by seven thirty and I still needed to drop them off at school.

I hurried into their room. "Get up you guys! We all overslept. Hurry and get your clothes on. We need to go!" I felt more like a drill sergeant than their mom. Thankfully, they weren't cranky because God in all His mercy let them have a few extra hours of rest that morning. Still, it was like waking up bears in hibernation. Gracie Bear will grow out of it, or so I kept telling myself.

I made a quick mental checklist—coffee, car keys, kids, backpacks. Check. Check. Check. We hopped in the car. Fortunately, the traffic wasn't bad on the way to school.

Oh darn—it suddenly hit me I had forgotten to make their lunches. "Okay, here is five dollars for both of you, but I want the change!" *Yeah, right, like that was going to happen!* Since we were late, I was thankful the other cars had already cleared out so I didn't have to parallel park. I never did it right.

"Bye, Gracie Bear. Bye, Jason. Have a good day!" I said as they ran away from me to the school doors. There is nothing more beautiful than watching those two kids God, Keith, and I created.

Work was a madhouse when I got there. Clyde was busing tables and Ralph ran the counter and was the cook. "Sorry I'm late," I said as I tied on an apron. Then I washed my hands and started to help, cleaning the lobby and wiping down the tables. Every table seemed like it was dirty from the morning rush. It was a lot of work. I refilled the salt and pepper shakers, wrapped silverware in napkins, and restocked the coffee cups and glasses. Just as I finished an unexpected visitor came in. It was Tansy.

"Well, what in the world are you doing here?" I asked as I gave her a big hug. I breathed in deeply. She smelled like home to me! "It is so good to see you, Tansy!" and I really meant it.

"Oh Mary, I have missed you baby. How are the kids?" she asked.

"They are doing good. Busy. Learning a lot in school—more than I ever did. How are you doing, Tansy?" I asked.

"Good, darling. Pie baking has never been better, though, and from the sign out front, you're making some good pies, too. How about you slice me a piece of your apple pie?"

"Now, they are not as good as yours, but you got it!"

There were many questions running through my head as I cut Tansy a slice of pie and heated it up in the microwave. I had been wondering about Timothy. Had she heard anything? I wanted to ask but Ralph was close by, and I didn't want anyone to hear our discussion. So, I devised a plan to get rid of him for a little bit.

"Hang on a second, Tansy," I said as I placed the warm plate in front of her. I then yelled in the back of the kitchen, "Hey Ralph, do you mind going over to the supply store and grabbing me a ten-pound bag of flour?"

"Sure, let me finish making the salads." He was always helpful.

It would be better that Ralph didn't overhear. Although he seemed content with just being my friend, I knew he still liked me. The less he knew about my past the better was my way of thinking.

"Thanks," I responded as I poured Tansy a cup of coffee. I pulled out a second mug for myself. The diner was slow. I could take a coffee break. Plus, it would be nice to get off my feet for a few minutes.

"Do you have time to talk with me for a bit?" Tansy asked.

"Sure, I was just getting ready to take a break," I replied, filling my own mug.

I was itching to find out if she had heard anything from Timothy, which was the first question that popped out of my mouth.

"No one has seen him or heard from him since the day he left," Tansy said. "People talk lots, gossipers and such, but I don't pay any mind to them."

"I still regret not listening to him, Tansy. How could I be so dumb?"

"Don't go beating yourself up about it, dear. Timothy's a grown man, and he got to do what he has to do."

"But I feel so guilty about it." Whew, I had said it. It felt good to let it out and confess. I had been carrying so much guilt, and it was eating me up inside.

"Now, you need to let this go, Mary. If the Lord wants that man back in our lives, then back in our lives he will come. But only when He's ready, though. You got to believe that! And stop tearing yourself up about it," she scolded gently.

Boy, I needed to hear that. I was so glad she was here.

"You're right. I need to stop," I agreed.

"Things will turn around better someday. You'll see." Tansy was always an encourager.

I sat across from her truly wanting to believe her words. Would it turn out for the better? Then it dawned on me—I had no idea why she had suddenly just showed up without calling. Curiosity was getting the best of me about her impulsive visit. My mind raced with negative thoughts. What if she was sick or dying? I couldn't bare losing her after everything I had faced with my folks and Keith. Then I berated myself. Why did I have to always think the worst! The suspense was killing me. But Tansy was a storyteller, and telling stories takes time. I tapped my foot with impatience just at the thought of the delay to get to the good part.

Tansy knew me well and I could tell by her facial expression that she knew I was wondering why she was there. Without delay she said, "Now, you know I want something, don't you?

I nodded my head, "I figured as much."

"Your Mama didn't raise a fool. I'll tell you that. Well, I gots a proposition for you." She let the sentence hang in the air for a few minutes.

What could it be? Knowing Tansy, it could be anything. I was all ears.

"Well, since Clarence died, I have saved some money from the farm and his insurance policy. I thought about going someplace nice and warm for the winter. You know, somewhere with palm trees and tropical drinks, but I got to thinking I may miss the farm and all the people I love. You understand what I am saying?"

"Yes, I do! You can't take the country out of the girl," I exclaimed as we both laughed.

"Here me out. You know Bob's Diner has been closed for years since he died. I started thinking that if I go and buy the building, maybe you can fix it up and start your own business? That way you and the kids would be close to me and could help me on the farm. These bones are getting old, and I could use a healthy, strong, smart woman to help me. I can't do this by myself anymore. Would you do it?"

I paused for a minute, picturing my life in ten years, and it wasn't at this diner that was certain. I blurted out, "Yes!" It must have come from the depths of my soul. Mama always said that in life opportunities can come quickly and if we jump, they can shape our destiny.

"I knew you would say yes, darling. I am so excited I could have another piece of pie over that news! Come here, girl," and she gave me the biggest hug. I hadn't felt that loved in years. I was going home. In that moment I knew I made the right decision. I served Tansy another piece of pie and a hot cup of freshly brewed coffee. Why is it at the most incredible time of my life I started to think of the past?

Thoughts of Keith flooded my mind—the love of my life. To remember him was to honor him. But sometimes it's hard to remember especially when you've lost so much. I shook the thoughts from my mind. Now was not a time to go backwards, but forwards. (*I needed to let go.*)

Tansy was so excited. I was, too, until I thought about poor Clyde. I was going to have to break the news. This wonderful man was going to be heartbroken, but what could I do? I had my two babies to take care of and a future to look after, not to mention a dream to chase. This restaurant was Clyde's dream and now I was going to have mine.

"It's going to take some time to sell the house," I cautioned.

"Don't worry about that. I have a good friend who is a realtor. He can help you," Tansy offered.

"I don't know if I am ready to go back to my old house and live. There are still too many memories," I said as tears suddenly spilled over onto my cheeks. That's another place in my life that I know I am not yet healed from.

"Now, don't you go worrying about that," Tansy replied. "You can deal with that when you are good and ready. You and the kids can move back into the loft. And you don't need to worry about the financial end. I will handle the money. There is no charge for lodging, love, and food with Tansy."

"Oh thank you, Tansy. That is such a relief," I gushed. Then I started to ponder everything that had happened and how God had orchestrated my future in just thirty minutes. Truly He could pull that off.

I exhaled not even realizing I had been holding my breath. What a relief that someone was standing with me, and I didn't have to do the whole adult thing by myself any longer. Sometimes that is all it takes. Someone to believe in you and believe you are capable to do the task set our before you and *BOOM*—it can happen!

Mama and Tansy had been the best of friends and now her best friend was helping me, Mary Ann Walker, become the woman I was destined to be. People are certainly placed in our lives for a reason.

There was no doubt that just a few years before, life had come at me fast. I had almost forgotten about my dream from when I was a little girl. I always wanted to be married and to have my own business and make pies. And suddenly when it seemed that the dream had died, here it was again.

"I'm going to go over to see the banker in the morning," Tansy said.

"Do you need me to do anything?" I asked her.

"I will take care of everything. Don't you worry, honey," she replied.

Tansy slipped her coat on and then placed both her hands on my face to look me in the eyes. "Oh Mary, it would do my heart good if you could come back to the farm for Christmas. I want to spend it with you and the kids. I even bought a cute Santa outfit for Sam."

"You did?"

"I think he might hate it, but he's going to be a good boy and wear it for Ms. Tansy. Christmas only comes around once every year after all!" she laughed. "I know you need to get back to work," she said as she stood and gave me a hug before she left the diner.

I still had plenty to do before I could leave for the day—a till to sort and a dining room to clean—but I think my mind was busier than my hands. What had just happened?

CHAPTER SIXTEEN

SOUTHERN ROOTS

*W*all have roots deep in us from generation to generation. My heritage was from the south and everything that came with it. I thought I would escape its grasp when Keith and I moved away to the cities, but, low and behold, God was sending me right back to the place I always wanted to leave. Go figure! You know, I am starting to think God has a sense of humor.

You will never guess how the kids reacted when I told them. Well, maybe you will. Jason jumped as high as a kangaroo, and Gracie Bear ran around the living room twirling and singing. That did my heart good. You never know how your kids are going to react to stuff. But I had a good idea that they were going to welcome the news. They loved Tansy and they loved the farm. Plus, Jason wanted to get back to his baseball field because, as he kept telling me since we came home, he had a game to win.

Daddy always said that there are two kinds of people in this world. Those who love baseball and cows and those who really love baseball and cows. Southern roots were in the heart of each of us. You can't get any more country than me, and my little girl, Gracie Bear, was cut from the same cloth. She even tried to wear her pink cowboy boots to bed! It might just be a sign, you think? She was just like me—free and wild.

Later that night after I put the kids to bed I still felt like I was in a daze. I looked around the house as the decision I made really sank in. It wasn't going to be easy to leave this home. Keith and I built the start of our lives here, and this was where we brought our newborn children. At least I still had his truck, and I wasn't selling that anytime soon! But the house was also the place I found out that Keith was dying. It was where, for the first time since we were married, I got used to sleeping alone. The memories I carried in my heart were bittersweet.

Tansy's real estate guy, Jacob, called me a few days after her visit. I made an appointment for him to come by the house on Friday. I was going to need to take the day off, but I hadn't yet told Clyde the news. I needed to wait until just the right time to gently break it to him. He had been so good to me. I didn't want it to feel like I was dropping a bomb on him.

Wilma came over several times to help me get the house cleaned and packed up. "Are you sure you want to do this?" she asked more than once.

"Yes, I am. To be honest I didn't take long to think about it. I just knew it was the right thing," I replied.

"Well, you're right about that. Sometimes you just have to stop thinking about things and jump in," she said. "But how are you going to get the money to do all this? Are you a secret millionaire and just not telling me?"

"Yes, I am a secret millionaire who works at a diner and bakes pies," I said sarcastically. She looked at me with a twinkle in her eyes, and we just laughed. Wilma was my girl. We had become quite fond of each other, and I knew she was going to miss me. But it wasn't like we would never see each other. It would just be a longer drive.

"Do you think there is room for me in the truck?" she asked.

"Oh, Wilma, you wouldn't want to leave all this, now would you?" I was surprised by her response.

"You're right. I got it good here. My house is paid for and everything I need from toilet paper to corn flour is close to me, along with the town mall and the grocery store."

"Well, living in a small town isn't for everyone," I told her, wondering if it would be hard for me to readjust to it.

"Girl, you got that right!" Wilma snapped her finger like a woman who knew what she knew.

Friday came and went and in no time at all, thanks to Wilma's help, we got the house ready and up for sale. Jacob listed it on the internet and did a walk-through video of the house for social media.

Within three days someone wanted to see it. I was nervous. It was one thing to get the house up for sale, but I was not prepared for it to happen this fast. I had never sold a house before. It was nice to have an agent working on my behalf. Honestly, I didn't want to share the percentage; can you imagine how much money I would be able to put in my savings account for a rainy day? But I was grateful for his help and ability.

I decided to take the kids to Clyde's diner for dinner soon after the house was listed. I still hadn't told him, but now that the house was officially up for sale, I needed to before someone else did. I had the night off but figured after the dinner rush I could sit down and break the news to him. I thought having the kids with me might make it easier. Besides, there was a showing scheduled for that night, so it would give us somewhere to go while they showed the house.

"So, what do you want to eat for supper tonight, Jason?" Clyde asked as we looked over the menus.

"Let's see . . . I want pie," he answered.

"Now, you know you can't just have pie for dinner," I interrupted.

"Please? Tansy let me a few times," Jason pleaded.

"No, you have to get something else with it." I was unwavering.

"Okay, how about some fries and a cheeseburger with no onions," he told Clyde, finishing out his order.

"Can I have meatballs? I really want meatballs," Gracie Bear said, bouncing in the booth. You would have thought Clyde was Italian because *meat a'balls* was his specialty.

"Yes, you certainly can," he spoke up before I could. The one thing I loved about Clyde is he never skimped on portions. If you came hungry, you definitely would leave over full!

Clyde served us our food, but he could tell I had something on my mind and lingered after he put our plates in front of us.

"I have something to tell you, Clyde. Can you sit with us for a moment?" I asked.

"Hang on, let me grab some dessert before I sit down," he replied. He not only brought some for himself, but he brought an entire caramel apple pie and dinner plates for us all, along with a can of whipped cream. He sat down. "Okay, I'm all ears now. Just let me slice some pie for us so you each can have a piece once you've finished your meal." He was smiling. Clyde was pretty serious about pie.

Jason and Gracie Bear ate quickly so they could have their pie. With all the eating going on, it was pretty quiet until Clyde asked, "What is it, Mary? What do you need to tell me? You look worried. Please, just get out with it. I've known you for a long time, and there is no need to beat around the bush. It's me, Clyde, remember?"

I felt horrible. Clyde was such an amazing boss, and he was like a father to me. He also gave me a lot of money to go away for the summer, and I promised him I would return. I did keep my promise, but now just a couple of months later I was about to tell him I would be gone permanently. Just as I opened my mouth to tell him, my cell phone buzzed. I looked at the text. It was Jacob, my realtor; he said, "They want to make an offer on the house."

My eyes got big, and Jason asked, "What is it, Mama?"

"Oh, nothing, baby. Don't you go worrying. It is good news," I told him as he continued to shovel in bites of pie.

"Clyde, I don't know how to say this, but . . . I am going to move back home." I closed my eyes afraid to look at his face. But surprisingly, Clyde was calm.

"I knew it!" he said.

"Really?" I was amazed.

"You're not a city girl. You've always been a country girl and that is where you belong," he said. *(I took a deep breath. Why was I getting so worked up about this again?)*

I reached over the table and gave him a big hug. What a relief! Clyde was okay with me moving. In my mind I had pictured him standing on the rooftop of the restaurant holding a pie in each hand, screaming, "If you quit, Mary, I'll jump."

I could see myself screaming up to him, "Clyde, don't do it!" Instead, he threw the pies one at a time. Suddenly I heard his voice, bringing me back into the present.

"Mary, Mary, snap out of it, will you?" He was looking at me rather strangely.

"Are you sure that you are not mad at me?" I asked.

"No, I am not. Really. But you will certainly be missed. Where am I going to get a pie baker like you?" he said. "I'm going to miss you but so will my customers!"

I went ahead and told him the text was from my realtor. "They want to give me two thousand dollars more than my asking price. But here is the kicker. I need to be out of the house in thirty days."

"So, what are you going to do?" he asked. "Are you going to take the offer?"

It was the third of November. I really wasn't interested in moving in the dead of winter. When Jacob listed the house, he warned me of two things: "You may sell your house quickly, or it may take the entire six months we have on our contract agreement." But what he didn't tell me was that it could sell in just days. It was all happening so fast!

"I think you should take it, Mary," Clyde said, offering some of that fatherly advice I had come to appreciate from him. I finished telling him about Tansy's offer to buy the old diner so that I could start a business and have a place similar to what his restaurant served.

Immediately he offered to help me with business advice, supplies, finances—whatever I needed to make my dream happen. I deeply appreciated his offer because he had been in business for a long time and knew all the dos and don'ts. Plus, he told me he wanted to upgrade his machines and equipment. "I could give my old machines to you to help you get started, Mary, if they fit your space and needs." It was great to get good news for a change after everything I had faced.

I called Tansy later that night with the news of the sale of the house and Clyde's offer to give me some of his used equipment. She was ecstatic. "Everyone in the town is excited you and the kids are coming back home," she told me. And she filled me in on her trip to the bank.

"Everything is taken care of. I have a few papers to sign next week after they get the paperwork done," she explained.

I still didn't know what I was going to do for money to move yet, but I did have some money left over in savings from Keith's insurance policy when he died. The company he worked for was paying me small dividends to keep finances afloat. I knew I would be all right, but I didn't want to always use Tansy as a resource. Even so, she insisted I did.

I had packing to do. The kids were so excited it was hard to get them to go to sleep. "It's a new season in our lives and we are all in this together," I told them. The next couple of weeks were beyond exhausting. Coming home from work, getting the kids dinner, and then packing late into the night. I have to admit that sometimes I was a little short with the kids, as time was running out and I was feeling the pressure to get everything done. One morning I woke up and Jason had done the sweetest thing for me. He had written me a note that said, "I'll go wherever you go, because my heart is our home." You know, kids are an absolute blessing from God. A treasure for sure!

Jason and Gracie Bear were given two simple jobs. One, to box up all their toys. Two, to box up everything else in their rooms. Sounds easy for them, right? Wrong! Those two were driving me nuts. They found more time to goof around and play than they did work. So, I called in a reinforcement. With just one week left Wilma came over to help me pack up the rest of the house. I still had so many things to do. We made a checklist. Then she helped me with the garage. I was certainly dreading that garage part because it was filled with Keith's belongings and car parts. Wilma said she was happy to do it. I was blessed to have a great friend like her by my side. (*Don't let go of good friends. Especially those who help you in times of need!*)

CHAPTER SEVENTEEN

TIME TO REBUILD

*M*iracles do happen. I can testify to that. They are all around us if we take the time to see them and believe for them. Sometimes they come from others. And even though we didn't work to get them, they are given to us. It's amazing what God can do! But just when we think we have it all figured out . . .

As I left I looked back at Wilma. She waved us good-bye. I was truly going to miss her. God had sent her into my life at a time I needed it. She was an angel in disguise. It took us longer than normal on the move back home. I must have stopped ten times for bathroom breaks as Jason felt the need to use every rest area we passed. I guess I shouldn't have given the kids a pack of twelve juice boxes! I never understood Jason's fascination with public rest-rooms. I hate them!

Once we arrived at the farm, it didn't take long to get settled in. We quickly slipped back into the same comfortable routine as summer except the kids were now in school. Tansy was glad we were back, and Sam almost did a somersault just greeting the kids. I was sure he would have a rudder tail in no time at all. He couldn't stop wagging it. Sam was one happy dog! And with Thanksgiving only one week away, I was optimistic that we could get everything completed for the business before then or in my worst-case scenario, shortly afterwards.

We still had unfinished business with the banker. There were tons of papers to sign to make the transaction complete. I never knew being an adult was so much responsibility.

Before long, the banker stopped by the farm to drop off some papers for Tansy. His name was Glen, and he was glad that she was buying the foreclosed restaurant that I was going to run. No one in town was happy about a vacant building. When Bob owned the diner, Glen was one of my weekly customers; I waited on his table many times. I remember he was always a good tipper!

Glen brought the final paperwork with him, along with the deed to the property and a second set of keys to make the transaction official, which he handed over to Tansy after she finished signing what seemed like a hundred pages!

"But I still need to buy the liability insurance," I told Tansy. She was purchasing the property, but we were in this together and the insurance was to be one of my responsibilities.

"I'll take care of the first year," she said. "Just get me the policy and I'll send you the check."

"Wow, that's an unexpected blessing. Thank you, Tansy." Boy, that was a relief. I was grateful how much she was helping me so that we could do this. I didn't have much money left after the move and my part of the start-up expenses. I could have never done this without her help.

After Tansy signed her papers, the banker turned to me. He had about fifteen sheets I needed to sign. I didn't quite understand but started signing my name when I suddenly realized it was a release putting the deed to Tansy's Acres in my name. I turned to Tansy not knowing what to say. Not only had she given me a partnership in the restaurant, but she also had just given me the farmhouse and her property. I looked at the paper; I couldn't believe it!

Teary-eyed I told her, "Tansy, you didn't have to do this. I cannot accept it."

"Yes, you can, Mary Ann, and you will. It's yours. It's the kids. It is where you belong."

Then I began to panic inside. "Tansy, is there something wrong that you're not telling me? Are you going to die?"

"Baby, I'm not going nowhere soon," she reassured me. "But when the time comes, Jesus will let me know. And when He does, I'll let you know. Now, come on and let's get this paperwork signed. I got pies to bake!"

Glen and Tansy finished the paperwork. He checked it over one last time to make sure every *i* was dotted and every signature was in the correct spot. Grinning from ear to ear he handed me the deed to the farm and to the restaurant; it was official—I was a business owner and a farm owner all in a matter of hours. Who would have thought this could happen to me, Mary Ann Walker? *Whoosh! That was a lot. I think I'll faint now! Someone, smelling salts, please!*

Tansy was not going to let Glen leave without giving him a slice of heaven—her cherry pie with a crumble topping. It was to die for!

"Glen, take this pie home to your wife. I know it's her favorite—my cherry crumble," Tansy told him as she put it into his hands.

"Oh, thank you, Tansy, she's going to love it! That is mighty kind of you," Glen replied.

"Well, I appreciate our friendship over the years. You are good people. God bless you, Glen, and please tell Cheri I said hello and blessings too!

"I sure will, Tansy. Oh, before I forget," Glen said as he fished in his pocket, "here's an extra set of keys to the diner," as he handed over the keys. "Congratulations, Mary. Bob would have wanted you to have this place. He would have been proud of you! I know your mama and daddy are as well. They are smiling down from heaven, and Keith is too!"

"That is very kind of you to say," I told him. *I still could not believe that Tansy gave me the diner; I couldn't believe it—PAID IN FULL!*

"Best of luck to you," he replied as he headed out to his car.

"Thank you! It means a lot!" I hollered after him.

After he left, I thought about what he said. Almost everyone I loved was in heaven. No wonder my life was turning upside down in a better direction. They were my angels, and they were looking out for me! I still missed them every day, but I was learning to live again and understand that even though they may not be here in the flesh, they were with me in spirit.

I couldn't wait to see the old diner again. It had been years since I had worked there. "Well, why don't we take the kids and go check it out?" Tansy asked.

"That's a great idea!" I felt excited as I called for the kids to put their shoes on. It only took a few minutes before we were all walking out to the truck. I helped Tansy into the passenger's seat, made sure the kids were buckled into the back, and then drove us down to the diner.

"It's all yours, Mary, my gift to you!" Tansy said.

I couldn't believe what was happening and felt like I was going to burst!

I cried and hugged her so tight, what a beautiful gift she gave me. Tansy was like Mama to me; God knew what I needed. I could have never dreamed this could happen to me. It was God's grace.

When we arrived, I parked in the third parking spot. Keith used to always be waiting there to pick me up when my shift was over. I had vivid memories of him sitting in the truck with the windows down. I could hear the country music playing from the minute I walked out of the diner. In that moment of nostalgia, I remembered how much I loved running my fingers through his thick brown hair. He had great hair that made all the girls jealous!

From that parking spot he could get glimpses of me as I worked. He always got there at least thirty minutes early just in case I could get off early, but that was rarely the case. Finishing out the shift I had to wipe down the tables and booths, clean the floor, fill the salt and pepper shakers, and prepare the silverware and napkins for breakfast the next morning. Working at a diner there is always something to do. He always waited patiently for me and drove me home. I let out a deep sigh. I sure missed those days, and I missed seeing his beautiful face.

At the time of Bob's death when the diner closed, it was decorated in a '50s style theme. The pictures of the red and yellow retro cars and black and white checkered floors were all as I remembered them. I tested the old jukebox in the corner that had played music from the '50s and '60s. Even though the place had been closed for a while, it was in fairly good shape. I was no building inspector, but I examined the ceiling tiles and didn't notice any water stains. It appeared the roof and inside were in rather good shape. Everything just needed a good cleaning.

Now, the appliances were old, but Clyde had already offered his. Even though they obviously were used, they were newer than what was already in the diner.

"Well, what do you think?" Tansy asked. I still couldn't get over it. This was really happening! My dream of being a business owner was happening.

"I need to get this place fixed up and then deal with Mama's house," I told her as I took inventory of what had to be done to reopen the diner. In my heart I was dreading dealing with Mama's house, but it was time, and I couldn't put it off any longer. Timothy had helped me get a lot of things done, but it was time to deal with the rest.

"I absolutely love it!" I exclaimed. "I am still in shock!" I looked down under the counter and was surprised to see something from when I was a teenager. "Look at this, Tansy. It's my old name tag! Can you believe it?" I was stunned as I held it up to the light.

"See, Mary, it's meant to be," she replied.

I asked Jason and Gracie Bear what they thought about the place. Pure joy was written all over their faces. It was cool to see the excitement in their eyes. "Is this really ours, Mama?" Jason asked. This was the happiest I had seen them in such a long time.

We had suffered much loss over the years. But now instead of tears I saw smiles and that made my heart leap with joy!

"Now, don't you worry about the cost of fixing this place up. I have some ideas," Tansy reassured me.

"Tansy, you have done enough. Letting me live with you, keeping Sam, and now buying me this place. You have no idea how grateful I am. Thank you from the bottom of my heart. Thank you!"

"You're most welcome," she told me, her eyes beaming. "It's God's blessings. He provided the money. I just said yes to His plan."

The drive back to the farm was quiet. I think we were all exhausted. I got the kids ready for bed and said a prayer with them before tucking them in for the night. *Yeah, I had started making prayer a regular practice again.* Finally under the covers myself, I thought I could sleep, but yeah, right. My mind was racing with ideas to reopen the diner. I was running over the name in my head, thinking about what the menu would look like and the dishes I would make and how much I should charge, decorations, pictures on the walls, color schemes, lighting, a new mirror in the bathroom, and curtains for the front windows. I figured I would make those myself. I am not going to lie. It was overwhelming.

The plan was to spend every spare minute I could over the next two weeks to work on the diner and get it reopened. Tansy helped me get material for the curtains. Together we planned what would go on the menu and one of her friends was able to typeset and design it for us so we could get them printed. Most everything else just needed elbow grease.

"I'll be over at about one o'clock today to help you and the kids," Tansy said the next morning as we were about to head out to work on the diner. It was Saturday and the kids were out of school and wanted to come help. I think they were as excited as we were to get the diner reopened.

"No, Tansy, we got it. Just take it easy," I replied.

"No, I want to help! I insist!" she told me as she sent us out with sack lunches, snacks, and water bottles.

"If you insist. We would love to have you," I told her.

She showed up at one o'clock all right along—with over ten more people all dressed in work clothes with paint brushes, paint cans, and brooms in hand. "Surprise! We are ready to go!" they shouted as we opened the door.

"What? No way!" I exclaimed, completely stunned. Over the next hour or so additional people showed up as well. It seemed like the whole church congregation, including Pastor Greg, had come to help. Not only were the church members there, but also others in the community came ready to work. I was completely overwhelmed and humbled at the outpouring of love for my family.

But the surprises weren't over. Toward the end of the afternoon a large moving truck pulled up in front of the diner. It was my old boss, Clyde. As he had promised, he brought his appliances that he was replacing and gifting to me.

"How am I going to pay you for all this?" I asked.

"You are not going to pay me for anything. It will be a business write-off," he said. "This is a gift from me to you. Plus, you know I needed new stuff anyway."

Ralph waved as he opened the back of the truck and started rolling out some of the equipment on a dolly. Together they hauled all the old stuff out and replaced it with the new—well, technically used but new-to-me appliances. "You know I have been wanting to remodel and upgrade my restaurant anyway and who better than you to take this old stuff off my hands," Clyde said warmly.

"Get over here," I said giving him a huge hug.

The diner was transformed in no time at all. It was astonishing how everyone worked together to bring it alive again. They worked tirelessly to help me and the kids; it was a labor of love and a community affair. Just when I thought it couldn't get any better, it did. Wilma pulled up outside with a gift of her own. It was a big one.

"Come out to my truck," she instructed. The bed of her truck was covered with a blue tarp. "Go on, pull it off," she coaxed.

My forehead wrinkled. What could it be? I pulled the tarp cover off revealing a new sign for the business. It read *Mary's Pies* in large black letters, along with a hand-drawn apple pie with cinnamon sugar on top and a few red apples on the side.

"Oh, Wilma, I love it! Thank you so much."

Tansy and Clyde were already prepared for Wilma's surprise. An electrician had volunteered to help and had a truck with a crane already there to lift the sign into place. By the time everyone finally left that day the diner had been transformed. It would have taken me weeks to accomplish what they had all helped me do in a day. It was astonishing how everyone had worked together to bring the diner back to life. It was truly a labor of love and a community affair. I looked around at how things sparkled, and it all looked fresh and new again. It was like the diner had been completely resurrected from the dead.

The diner was officially finished. It didn't take as long as I thought it would with so much. It brought tears to my eyes at how wonderful everyone had been. How can we ever succeed unless others help us? Mama always told me, "We were never meant to be alone; we need each other." I now understood what she meant.

I wanted to give something back to them. I knew that many who had come out to help me weren't wealthy themselves. They didn't even have much of anything but still offered their time and hard work. I wanted to treat them with love and show them just how much I appreciated their contribution to help Tansy and the kids and me.

I was hoping to get all the inspections and licensing done so that we could be opened before Christmas. I never realized how much work goes into owning a business. I was grateful for all of Clyde's guidance and help in that area, as he talked me through everything I needed to do. I don't know what I would have done without him. This whole adult thing is no joke! I also had to buy extra insurance just in case someone fell or hurt themselves. The insurance agent told me stories about how people get hurt. He told me someone sued a restaurant after they spilled hot coffee on their pants and got burned—not the waitress, but the customer spilled the coffee on themselves! Welcome to business ownership, I guess. I'm in it to win it now!

Clyde helped me get through all the necessary legal mumbo jumbo needed to bring the kitchen up to code. He also gave me two stainless steel sinks. They were deep and perfect for dish washing. Plus, he gave me small appliances and supplies for baking to get started.

I had used an old mixer at Clyde's restaurant to mix the dough for the pie crust. I had loved it. It mixed the butter into the flour perfectly. Clyde said he really didn't even know the date it was made, but it was failproof and he gave it to me—what a gift! It was like the icing on the cake.

I wanted to surprise everyone who helped me get this business dusted off, revamped, and built up again. I couldn't have done it without them. So, I had decided to throw a party for the entire community as a thank you. I asked them to bring a specialty dish they were known for and it would be a sort of potluck, but Tansy and I planned to bake turkey and make mashed potatoes and, of course, a ton of pies. That included pumpkin, apple, cherry, and lemon whip pies. Tansy said she would do all the pies. I was so grateful for her contribution.

The only thing missing with all the excitement and wonderful things that had happened was that Timothy wasn't there to share it with us. I missed him and wanted him to be here. We hadn't seen the men who had come looking for him. They never returned to the farm, and his house was still empty. I went by his place often hoping he had returned, but nothing. No one had seen him or heard from him. It had been over three months since he disappeared. I hadn't heard anything from his sister either. I couldn't help thinking the worst—that he had been arrested.

The next morning the mail carrier came to the door. Normally he just placed the mail in the mailbox down at the road. But today he knocked on the door. "Hi, Mary. I have a certified letter for you, and I am going to need a signature," he said as he handed me a pen. I signed on the dotted line. He tore off a copy and handed it to me along with the letter. "Here you go. Have a good day," he said as he headed back to his mail truck.

I glanced at the return address. The United States Military office. There was an American flag and a batch number in the lower right-hand corner. Now I was really curious. I pulled the flap open and pulled out *the letter inside.*

Dear Mary, I sent this letter certified so it would reach you and only you. I am sorry that I left the way I did that day. There is no excuse for what I have done.

I decided to turn myself in. I knew we could never make a life together if I didn't face my past. I couldn't go on forever pretending that it didn't exist or forever be looking over my shoulder. I needed to take responsibility and honor the United States of America and my commitment. Based on the circumstances and after much consideration, rather than court martial me, my superiors have allowed me to finish out my term on a probationary period. I have to say, I was shocked. They did take some disciplinary action against me and have added that to the time I need to serve. But at least once I get out, this will all be behind me.

I promise I will see you and the kids as soon as I can. I miss you, Mary. I should have told you the truth about everything. I must take responsibility for my actions as a military officer who is to uphold the law. I needed to do what was right, and I hope you understand. I never told you how I felt about you and how I still feel. I am in love with you and the kids. I loved you from the time I first saw you in that Chevy truck. There has not been a day when I haven't thought about you!

I hope you can forgive me. And I hope you will wait for me. I promise I will come back to you!

It was signed, "All my love, Timothy."

I almost fainted. I was not expecting this at all! I yelled for Tansy.

"Good Lord, Mary. What's wrong?" Tansy said, concerned. I was slumped on the floor but handed her the letter. I just didn't know what to do!

"Read this," I told her.

"Come on, Mary. Gets yourself up off the floor and come sit on the couch!"

"Tansy, you have got to read this!" I was shaking the letter at her.

"Now, give me a minute; I don't have young eyes. Let me get my glasses."

Tansy got her glasses from the coffee table and sat down on the couch to read. She leaned over the arm to be under the lamp light but said nothing as she digested the contents of the letter. "Well, I'll be. He finally did it!" she exclaimed once she finished. "God is going to take what is broken and make it right again! Glory to God, this is great news!"

I was overwhelmed by the news and began to cry. "Oh, Mary, come here. It's going to be all right. Don't cry, God will make a way for him, just like He made a way for you and the kids." She attempted to comfort me; I was a blubbering mess as I tried to process my feelings and deal with everything going on in my life!

It was a lot to take in, but I was actually relieved. I finally knew where Timothy was, and he was finally doing what he needed to do. He was dealing with his past, and so was I. There was more I was dealing with—the reason I came back in the first place was to let the past be the past!

I decided to go to Mama's house. I still had unfinished business to attend to there, and it seemed like the time to deal with the emotions that I had stuffed down for so long that were attached to the house. I took a deep breath and walked in with tenacity as

Mama would say. Afterall, my name is Mary Ann Walker. The ghosts of the past, my father's addiction and unhappy memories, were going to be dealt with once and for all. I realized I hadn't been up to my bedroom since I married and moved out. Even when Timothy and I had worked on the house during the summer I had avoided going there. I walked up the stairs. The wood steps still creaked. There is no place like home.

A wave of emotions flooded over me as I walked into the room. I closed my eyes for a moment and reassured myself. You can do this, Mary! I went to my bedside table and opened the drawer. Inside was the penny necklace Daddy made for me that I risked my life for. It has been there all these years. I placed the special necklace around my neck. It was like a little piece of home and a reminder of my adventure to the train tracks that night!

I thought about Daddy and how he struggled with grief and disappointment through his entire life. He had used alcohol to hide his feelings and pain. I had always felt Daddy walked away from Mama and me. Emotionally he checked out after my brother died. He was just never able to deal with it. And what we don't deal with will deal with us. My brother's death had affected us all, but so had Daddy's alcoholism.

I knew God didn't want me to feel depressed anymore. He was tugging at my heart and helping me understand and forgive. He was giving me a new perspective. As I sat on my bed remembering He spoke to my heart, "Mary, you walked away from Me. But I never stopped loving you. Even though your daddy walked away from you, he never stopped loving you either."

It was then that healing finally left my head and reached down into the depths of my heart. As tears slid down my cheeks I whispered, "Daddy, I forgive you, and I love you." Instantly the weight, depression, and fears that had been bottled inside lifted and I was free. I felt it! Now, why didn't I do that years ago? I really could have saved myself a lot of unnecessary problems.

I spent the rest of the day upstairs organizing and packing and then left for the farm. The kids were dying to make Christmas cookies with me. I had promised them we could make sugar cookies with sugar icing on top just like Mama and I used to make! I love carrying on her traditions with my little family.

Gracie Bear had the dye and Jason made six cups filled with vanilla frosting. "What colors are you going to make?" I asked Gracie Bear as we pulled out the small bottles.

"Green, pink, and yellow," she said, clapping her hands in excitement.

"And what about you, Jason?"

"Blue, orange, and red," he answered, ready to begin.

"That sounds good to me. Don't forget to read the instructions and stir in the dye until the color is mixed evenly throughout," I instructed. "Let's get our first batch of cookies in the oven. They need to cook for ten minutes, then cool for another ten minutes before we can ice them." It had been quite a day of healing for my heart, putting to rest the things of the past between Daddy and me and bringing the past into the present with Mama's sugar cookie tradition. My heart was full. This was going to be the best Christmas ever.

I had some finishing work to do as far as decorating the diner before it could open. I'd found a box of fabric while organizing Mama's stuff. It was an ivory-colored linen that I thought would be perfect to use for the café-style curtains I had in mind. Mama had all kinds of accessories for sewing, which she had collected over the years. Everything I needed was already right there as if she had prepared it in advance.

Tansy and I got all the food bought and started to get ready for the big thank you community meal. The curtains were finished and hung, and the final details were ready. It was going to be like a big grand opening event. All the while Sam never left my side. He followed me everywhere and looked so cute in the red and black checkered bandana Tansy had bought for him and tied around his neck. He wore it proudly. He was such a gift to our family and always reminded me of Timothy.

Jason prayed every night to see Timothy again. It broke my heart how much he missed him. Gracie Bear agreed with us in prayer, but she wasn't tied to him like Jason was. I was not sure how long the military would hold Timothy, and I didn't want to tell the kids something and get their hopes up and then have their hearts broken again if it didn't turn out the way we thought.

I called the church to talk with Pastor Greg. I thought I would get the church answering machine, but to my surprise he picked up the phone. I told him of the plans Tansy and I had for a Christmas surprise party for the community. If you want to tell a secret to someone, tell a pastor; they are a vault with any information.

"Mary, that's a wonderful idea. I would like to help. We can use the church's benevolent fund to donate the turkeys if you will cook them." Boy, that was an offer I couldn't refuse!

"Thank you so much, Pastor Greg!" That was a load off my mind and budget for the event, and now I could pour more money back into the diner. Pastor Greg also said I could use any decorations I needed from downstairs in the storage room at the church from the various plays and parties they had hosted over the years. He was such a generous man, always serving others! I had one more thing to ask him before I hung up the phone. "Pastor, would you mind being Santa Claus at the event?"

"I would love to. Thanks for asking!" He sounded excited as we said goodbye. I was too!

Things were coming together nicely. I was checking off all the items on my list of what still needed to get done. There was plenty left to do, but I knew I would get it all finished. I decided to enlist Jason and Gracie Bear to sing a song for everyone at the dinner. They were excited about it! You can't have Christmas without Christmas music—it's like a BLT without bacon! That's not happening.

Even though Tansy was older, you sure couldn't tell it. She never slowed down. Some mornings, she was up before me! Together we were getting all the final details done and ready for the big event.

Christmas truly was my favorite time of the year! I enjoyed all the seasons especially fall. But Christmas time? Well, that is the most enchanted season of all. Jason and Gracie Bear loved it too. The teachers at their school helped them make many craft projects, which they brought home. I realized I was going to need a bigger fridge to display their handiwork! There were so many magnets, stickers, coloring pages, and paper cut-outs filling the front. That is where we displayed everything, as I think most families do. I know when I was growing up Mama saved everything I ever made her at school. She never threw anything out. I could attest to that, as there were still about ten more boxes I had yet to go through downstairs in the basement. I knew I was going to have to do a better job of picking and choosing what I was going to keep from all of the kids' wonderful arts and crafts projects. But for now, they were proudly displayed. Gracie Bear beamed as we found room for her most recent school Christmas project.

Our town may have been small, but our hearts were filled with much love for Christmas! Red, green, white, gold, and silver lights decorated the houses and our downtown—it was a wonderous wonderland delight. The more shimmer and sparkle the better.

We also opened the farm for people to come visit Santa. We made white puffed divinity candy, hot chocolate, and hot apple cider. Santa (aka Pastor Greg), always said a prayer for each child and family who visited and invited them to church to remind us of the true reason for the season, which was the birth of Jesus, a sweet baby boy.

Tansy made Christmas amazing. There were stockings with each of our names hung by the fireplace. There was Mr. & Ms. Claus statues resting in the corner, surrounded by small stuffed animals sitting on decorative boxes.

I helped Tansy decorate the tree. We put so many ornaments on that thing, I was sure it was going to tip over. At night when everyone was asleep, I would sneak in the living room and lay on the couch just to stare at the Christmas tree lights. It was dreamy!

Tansy turned her barn into a winter wonderland. She decorated the barn with lights strung throughout the ceiling. And she allowed the high school band to practice there. They liked the acoustics. They played Christmas carols like "Silent Night," "Drummer Boy," "We Three Kings," and "We Wish You a Merry Christmas." I loved the classics. The music floated across the field and into the house and lent a perpetual air of Christmas. This was especially true when it was accompanied by a dusting of fluffy white snow!

On Christmas Day, it was tradition for Santa Claus to visit the farm. I couldn't wait for Jason and Gracie Bear to experience that! I took them to see Santa at the mall, but that was just creepy, and they hated it. They thought the Mall Santa had bad breath and a weird laugh. (*P.S. they were right!*) I went back and looked at the pics I had taken on my phone of that day. I quickly deleted them. The kids were right. He was indeed very creepy!

They were getting older and more in tune with what was going on around them. Since I was a girl, Mama and Daddy never discouraged me from believing in Santa. The kids at school said he wasn't real. But for me, while I knew the true meaning of Christmas—the birth of Jesus—I also liked the imagination of believing in Santa. It was fun to think of him bringing gifts to all good boys and girls.

Gracie Bear wondered how he was able to slide down a narrow chimney being as big as he was. That took imagination all by itself to figure that one out. I love how honest kids are and how they think of everything!

Jason assumed his large belly was due to eating cookies and drinking milk at every home. He guesstimated Santa had to deliver toys to one million homes by Christmas morning. He eventually brought it up one night to let me know what he was thinking. "Mom, if he visited one million homes in one night, well, that's a whole lot of cookies! (*And pies, of course, from our home!*) How does he make it to all those houses in time?"

I love the wonder of children! Oh, if only life could remain that simple.

One night I had them work on their Christmas list. Both were excited, of course. Gracie Bear asked for a doll with blond hair, blue eyes, and a pretty dress. She also asked for a teddy bear, but it had to be a big one with soft fur, eyes close together, and a big nose so she could kiss it! She was incredibly detailed and descriptive with her list.

Jason, on the other hand, wanted a new baseball glove and baseball bat, a red cap, and new tennis shoes. I noticed on the top of his list was Timothy's name.

"Why do you have Timothy's name on your list?" I asked.

"Because I want Timothy to come back to the farm for Christmas!" he explained in simple childlike faith.

"Oh, Jason," I started. "That's probably not possible. In fact, honey, he may not come back here ever again."

"Don't say that, Mama!" Jason cried in my arms. "I know he'll come back. I just know it."

I said nothing more but held him and stroked his hair. It broke my heart to hear his sobs. It also made me angry at Timothy. I knew he needed to fix his past, because if he didn't, he would never have a future in the military or with us! But he had added trauma to our lives, and my kids certainly had already had enough of that.

"Mama, I am going to keep on believing that God can do it. He can send him back. You told me that God does miracles," he said with expectant eyes.

I held his gaze and nodded. "Yes, He does. You know, you are a miracle," I told him. "You and Gracie Bear are both my miracles."

While I tend to doubt from time to time, the reality is that miracles do happen even when we don't see them. Mama used to tell me, "You can't see miracles unless God opens the eyes of your heart."

That is what I needed now. "Lord, open the eyes of my heart," I prayed that night after I put the kids to bed. Jason's faith was strong when it came to believing. I needed my faith renewed. I needed to see that God could do this for my son. Mamas don't like to see their babies hurting. God knows that!

"Lord, please don't break Jason's heart," I said as I fell off to sleep dreaming of twinkling lights, a family holiday, and a hope that maybe, just maybe, it could include Timothy.

CHAPTER EIGHTEEN

CELEBRATION TIME

*T*is *the season. That means Christmas carols, cookies, pies, cakes, dinners, friends, gifts, late nights, Christmas cards, Christmas trees, beautiful bows, and lights, wreaths, and candies. And a little snow, Lord, PLEASE!*

Christmas Eve arrived. The weather was cold, and the forecast hinted at snow. I was hoping for a blizzard, but a good dusting of snow would do fine as well. Tansy invited us to a candlelight service at church. The kids and I were excited. There was going to be a play about the birth of Jesus and after the performance, cookies, hot chocolate, and hot tea in the basement fellowship hall!

The church drama team put on quite a skit. It was about Jesus's birth and the three wise men who came to see Him in a manger and brought him gifts. Pastor Greg talked about the meaning of Christmas. He shared why

we celebrate it, and what the birth of Jesus means for us and the entire world.

"It means new life," he began. "It means God sent His Son, born of the Virgin Mary, as the Savior of the world. Jesus was sent to save the world from death. He left heaven to come and make a way for us! Jesus our Savior, the Christ child, is born!

As his message ended, Pastor Greg asked if anyone needed prayer to come up to the front. It was an invitation he always gave at the end of each service. There were times in the past I had wanted to go, but each time I talked myself out of it with one excuse or another. But not this time; I was ready! I needed prayer that God would help me deal with my pain and the things holding me back so I could move forward and walk in the path He destined for me and my babies! "What I really need is to start over. I want to rededicate my life to His will and surrender everything to Him. I don't want to be a prisoner to my past anymore!" I said to Pastor Greg as the tears started to flow. "I want to be free!"

Pastor Greg prayed for me as I asked God to be the Lord over my life once again. Immediately I could tell a difference. It was truly as if someone had lifted a huge weight off my shoulders. That Christmas Eve I truly understood the meaning of Christmas. It was Christ in me. I was changed and it was all because God sent His Son to the world to save me!

We sang "Silent Night" together as a church, holding our candles. It was peaceful, and I felt free for the first time in a long time. But I couldn't help watching Jason and Gracie Bear as the candle wax was melting down the sides of their candles. I looked up to God and said, "Don't let them burn one another. I don't want their hair to catch on fire, God. Amen."

When the service concluded, Pastor Greg invited everyone downstairs for Christmas cookies, hot chocolate, hot tea, and fellowship. As we waited in line, I thought of the many blessings that had come our way like the fresh start we had been given by Tansy inviting us to live with her and the start of the new business. Now I had also been given a fresh start in my spiritual life. Finally, I was getting back on the same page with God. I wanted to learn how to believe in the impossible like my children did.

God had done so many wonderful things for me and my kids despite all the tragedy and pain we faced. He turned things around and gave me a fresh start at life. He gave me Tansy, who helped me grieve over the loss of my mama.

Once we got home, Tansy had Jason and Gracie Bear set out a piece of pie for Santa. We didn't leave him cookies. No sir! In our house he got pie and milk.

That night as I tucked the kids in bed Jason told me, "Mama, I cannot wait to see Timothy tomorrow. I know God will answer my prayer. I can feel it!"

My heart sunk. I certainly didn't want to discourage him. I could see he believed it and deep down I wanted to. But to be honest, I was not sure!

"God will answer you," I told him as I kissed him good night and smoothed out his covers. There was a part of me that was skeptical. But I didn't want to listen to that voice any longer. I remembered what Mama had said repeatedly, "All things are possible with God. You just have to believe it!"

There are people who don't know God who will never understand that kind of thinking. Or they think He is something other than who He is. Tansy believed in Him with all her heart. She prayed every morning and every night before bed for me and my kids. It was a blessing.

I spent most of the night wrapping gifts for the morning. Tansy had gone to bed when the kids did. So, I was alone with a pile of gifts, the Christmas tree, and my thoughts. I talked to God as I wrapped with a heart overflowing with love. I wanted to keep this joy in my heart always. It was going to be a great Christmas. I could feel it! When I finished wrapping the last gift, I laid down on the couch and enjoyed the peace and glow of the tree lights. I must have fallen into a deep sleep because, boy, did I have a dream.

I was walking through a field with my hands down, feeling the grass as it went through my fingers. In the dream I was wearing a white dress and my hair was flowing down my back. I heard Keith's voice calling for me in the distance, "Mary, Mary, keep coming. Don't look back." I kept going toward his voice.

"Where are you?" I asked, squinting to catch a glimpse of him.

"Keep coming. I am here," he said. It sounded like he was directly ahead of me. I began to run, afraid that I would lose him. At first, I couldn't find him and began to panic until I saw him sitting by a willow tree.

Never had I seen such a beautiful tree. It was unlike the one at my house. From a distance it looked like it had silver branches. Keith seemed peaceful. He was overjoyed to see me, but I couldn't touch him or even hug him. It was as if a barrier was placed between us, separating us from two different dimensions—this world and the supernatural world. I saw thousands of bodies faintly in the background. They were all around us. It looked like people mountains. Some were even in the clouds.

"Why did you call me here?" I asked.

"It is time that you let me go," he said.

"But I don't want to let you go!" I told him and began to weep. I reached for him with everything inside of me. Even though he was right in front of me, I could not touch him. The grief and pain in my heart bubbled up to the surface and my chest felt like it was going to cave in.

Keith started to fade into a brilliant light. "I will always be with you, Mary. It's your time to live again. I speak hope to you, and life . . . Don't look back. There is no point of return." In an instant he was gone.

I woke up wondering if it were real. But the deep abiding peace that remained told me it was. It took my eyes a bit to adjust to the glow of the lights on the Christmas tree. I smiled. Keith had loved Christmas as much as I had. But now I realized it was time. Time for me to live again.

No one really knew the secret pain I had lived with except God. He knew my heart. I needed to move on. I needed to be free from all that still chained me to the past. God was showing me that it was my time!

There are moments in your life where you know a change is about to happen, and this was that moment for me. Something happened in the night hours in my dream that changed my whole outlook. I fell back asleep in no time, exhausted. When Christmas morning finally arrived, the kids were up at five o'clock in the morning. I really hoped they would have stayed in bed a few more hours at least. But I remembered as a child I never did. They were just like their mama.

I need coffee. Lots of it, I thought to myself as I filled the coffee pot with water. "Shhh" I whispered to the kids so they wouldn't wake Tansy. They couldn't contain their giggles and excitement. It was Christmas morning after all.

"Mama, why didn't you sleep in your bed last night?" Jason asked as he saw the blanket on the couch I had used.

"I was tired, baby, and I fell asleep on the couch." I told him as I rubbed my neck. *I must have slept on it wrong, but that's what happens when you don't sleep in a bed,* I thought.

"Can I go and wake up Tansy?" Jason begged.

"No, sir! You both go eat some breakfast first. Tansy will be up soon enough," I instructed. They both obediently marched over to the pantry and pulled out a box of cereal. I watched as Jason got bowls for the two of them along with the milk. Then he got them both settled at the kitchen table. They said a quick prayer and I heard him ask God to wake up Tansy. I stifled a laugh.

They shoveled the cereal in their mouths as quickly as possible. Between bites Gracie Bear asked, "Can't we just send Sam in there to lick her face?"

I laughed at her creativity but before I could answer, God answered Jason's prayer. Just as he was about to eat his last bite Tansy came out of her bedroom.

"I heard that, Gracie Bear," she said with a laugh. "Now, don't you go sending that animal to lick my face in the morning."

"Merry Christmas!" Gracie Bear exclaimed, running to give her a hug.

"What are you all doing sitting around?" she asked. "We have some gifts to open!"

That was all the encouragement the two needed. Jason and Gracie Bear ran to the pile of gifts. They began tearing the paper off their presents and then would hold them up for us to see. It was precious to watch them with such wonder and excitement! I hadn't opened any of my gifts yet. I was content to observe them.

Gracie Bear got that doll she had wanted, and Tansy bought her a lot of jewelry and dress-up clothes. Gracie Bear was in heaven.

Jason got a new bat, glove, and cap, among other things. But once the presents were all opened, I could tell he was bothered by something. "What's the matter, Jason? Didn't you get everything you wanted?"

He came and sat on my lap. "Well, I did get everything I wanted but one thing!"

"And what would that be?" I was dreading his response.

"Timothy is not here. I asked God to see him on Christmas!"

"Mary, let me handle this," Tansy said as she knelt and looked him straight in the eye. "Jason, you prayed to God, right?"

"Yes," he answered.

"And you know that God hears us and answers us, right?"

"Yes, ma'am" Jason replied.

"Then you got to know that sometimes our prayers don't always get answered in the time we want them. But He does answer them when in *His* timing," Tansy explained gently.

"I know, but it's Christmas!" Jason insisted.

"I've been walking with God a long time, baby. He's never let me down, and He won't let you down," she said. "Now, come on. What do you say Tansy gets her boots on and watch you use that new bat and glove you got for Christmas!"

Jason nodded his head, and we all went outside. Tansy watched. Jason was the pitcher, I was the batter, and so that left Gracie Bear to be the catcher. Sam didn't know what position he was playing, but he sure had fun running around the place and trying to take the ball from Gracie Bear.

Tansy sat down in a lawn chair and became our cheerleader! I was thankful for Tansy's timely distraction. In no time at all Jason forgot about Timothy and enjoyed his new gifts and the field he now had on which to play. After our baseball game, the kids helped me set up chairs for the barn dance. The school had let us borrow some tables for hors d'oeuvres and fruit punch. I loved fruit punch, and it was easy to make. Tansy had a huge punch bowl. I loved the red color; it was perfect for the party. The school also let us have about forty chairs. The kids and I placed them around the corner of the barn walls to make the center a dance floor. I hoped it would be enough. I had no idea how many would show up after the dinner. We had to hustle though if we were going to get the food cooked and everything ready. We loaded the car and headed over to the diner.

We had been looking forward to tonight and from what I heard from others, they were too. It was to be our thank you to the community for helping us get the diner restored. Gracie Bear had helped me cut out cowboy boots and red and white Santa hats as the invitations. We had invited all who had helped me, which was a significant number of people! They were asked to bring their favorite side dish, and we were providing turkey and Thanksgiving type fixings to go along with it.

When we got to the diner, I had the kids help me put up just a few more Christmas decorations and lights to add a festive air for the occasion. I needed to start cooking the turkeys immediately to have them ready. Fortunately, Pastor Greg met us there soon after with several of them. Boy, those birds were big. They were going to take no less than four hours of baking time each. I turned the ovens on and was thankful again for Clyde's donation of the equipment. After I got the birds seasoned, Pastor Greg helped me lift them into the pans. They were so big that it took two people!

We were going to have one entire table just for Tansy's pies. She had been preparing and baking for days. Mama taught me and Tansy had taught her how to make pies. There are tricks to baking and making the perfect crust. Pie making was in our blood. We were born to do it! Those pies were going to be the pièce de résistance to the meal. After all, the sign did say *Mary's Pies*, right? So, what would a thank you dinner be like without pie?

The kids helped Tansy and me cut up the potatoes so I could boil them and turn them into my famous mashed potatoes. It was a lot of work, but we went fast! The diner smelled heavenly of turkeys and fresh baked pies when everyone started to arrive around 5:30 p.m. Soon the table we had set up for the side dishes was filled. By 6:00 p.m. the place was packed. I thought I would say a speech before we started and then have Pastor Greg say a prayer before we ate.

The tables were filled with all kinds of scrumptious goodies. I had cooked two twenty-pound turkeys and ten pounds of sour cream mashed potatoes with lots of salted butter. Several of the church ladies had brought green bean casserole, two kinds of gravy, candied yams with brown sugar, cranberry chutney, cornbread stuffing, collard greens, cheesy baked macaroni, creamed spinach, banana pudding with vanilla wafers, and sweet potatoes with marshmallows. It was quite the spread. And, of course, the entire table of pies for dessert!

Clyde and Wilma even drove down to come to the event! They were going to join us at the barn dance afterwards as well. I asked Clyde ahead of time if he would run the fake snow machine. He said he would. I also wanted Wilma to sing an old classic, a song written in 1958, entitled, "Rockin' Around the Christmas Tree" by artist Brenda Lee. Wilma wasn't sure at first, as all she had ever sang was karaoke, but she figured since I lived in a small town no one would make fun of her. Mama loved that song and every year I played it over and over on her vinyl record player.

Even though it was Christmas Day the diner was filled with people. I looked around and my heart felt full. It looked like everyone I had invited had come. It was such a wonderful surprise! While everyone was greeting one another, I propped myself up on a five-gallon bucket I used for mopping the kitchen floors. I raised my glass of fruit punch and spoke.

"Welcome everyone! Merry Christmas! I am so glad you made it to celebrate with us! Thank you for what you have done for me, Tansy, and our children. Each one of you has sacrificed your time, finances, and resources to help us, and we are so thankful!

"Christmas is a time when we receive extraordinary gifts, and this Christmas I realize that this community and everyone present here is my 'extraordinary' gift. Each one of you has brought light into my life. This diner would not be the way it is if it weren't for your hard work and dedication. So, it is with a grateful heart and a hungry belly that I say, 'Thank you for coming. Merry Christmas!'"

"Let's eat!" Jason yelled.

"Not so fast," I told him. "Don't you and Gracie Bear have a song you prepared?" I said with a nudge, nudge, wink, wink. Jason and Gracie Bear had been practicing "We Wish You a Merry Christmas" for weeks. They were a little nervous once they climbed up on one of the tables, but they sang the song and the hearts of my family melted. It was the sweetest thing.

Afterwards, Pastor Greg gave a heartfelt prayer: "Dearly beloved, we gather here on this Christmas Day to celebrate the birth of our Lord Jesus Christ and to thank You, God, for His birth. We celebrate together, united as a community who believes in helping one another achieve their goals and reach their victories. We gather together and partake in a feast of thanksgiving to remember, God, what You have done. Not only did You give us Your Son, but You have given us eternal life. For that we celebrate! Bless this bountiful food to our bodies and continue to touch this community with Your love and grace! Amen!"

Everyone ate until they were stuffed! The jukebox was playing festive Christmas tunes and there was much laughter and talking. After we finished eating, I asked them all to write down what they were thankful for on the new curtains I had made. I had plenty of fabric markers, which I spread across the table. Most people just signed their name. Others signed well wishes. I thought it would be a perfect reminder, as the signed café style curtains hung on the windows, that this was indeed a community diner, that each person here could feel they had a special part of the business.

Afterwards, everybody pitched in and helped clean up! Clyde and Ralph cleaned the kitchen for me and did all the dishes. That was such a blessing. Jason and Gracie Bear wiped down the tables and booths. Tansy left to go back to the house to greet people and let them in for the barn dance. We finished putting the rest of the food away and then everyone headed over to the farm. It was going to be a fun ending to a very full day. We were going to have a great time. "Santa Claus has just finished making his deliveries for Christmas Day," I told Jason and Gracie Bear. "This will be his final stop before he heads back home to the North Pole."

CHAPTER NINETEEN

THE CHRISTMAS BARN DANCE

*C*hristmas is my favorite time of year; I have always *loved it. There is nothing like Christmas! Passing around cookies, cooking familiar family dishes, and spending time with dear friends. Having the barn dance on Christmas seemed like the perfect way to finish out the day. The barn was magical in the winter with lights, candles, and fun. It was the dreamiest place to be especially with the ones you love.*

It was 9 p.m. and the party had officially started. Tansy had the high school band play while we all joined in and sang Christmas carols. It was magical! Clyde ran the fake snow machine since we didn't actually get our white Christmas that year, so we made our own. The barn

felt like a fairy tale as I watched the Christmas lights glisten! Surrounded by friends and seeing the children who were all expecting Santa filled my heart with joy. I looked at my watch and noted that Santa should be arriving any minute!

I calmed everybody down to make the announcement. "Quiet everyone! We don't want to miss the arrival of Santa! He has traveled a very long way to get to the farm tonight!"

Jason added his own wisdom. "Everyone, listen. Santa is going to be burned out, okay? He has been traveling all night and visiting many countries in the last twenty-four hours. If he is late, we understand so don't be upset with him!"

"Thank you, Jason," I said with a smile. "That was very kind of you and I speak for all of us when I say, we will take that into consideration."

We heard sleigh bells and the horses whinnied. "I think Santa is at the barn door!" I announced.

Everyone began to cheer and clap, shouting, "Santa, Santa, Santa."

"Well, come on, everybody. Let him in," Gracie Bear said excitedly.

Those near the front opened the barn door. There was Santa (aka Pastor Greg) decked out in full costume. He was in a sleigh with horses since reindeer are hard to come by. "Ho, Ho, Ho, Merry Christmas!" he said. He gave me a wink as he got out of the sleigh. "Shush, it's our little secret!" he whispered.

The kids gathered around him, talking with him and sharing in some fruit punch and Christmas cookies. "Don't you get sick of eating cookies all the time?" Jason asked.

Santa laughed and gave a mighty "Ho, Ho, Ho," as he patted Jason's head.

The band kicked in to start the dance. Most everyone had on their cowboy boots and Santa hats. The high school band played their hearts out and Wilma sang the lyrics to the song, "Rockin Around the Christmas Tree," as I had asked. She really surprised all of us. She is an amazing singer!

Around eleven o'clock everyone was ready to get home and call it a night! But before each person left, they helped clean up a bit. Most of the high school band members had already left as well. However, a flutist, violinist, and guitar player were still there playing softly.

"Merry Christmas, Mary! I'm going to get to bed. This old woman is tired," Tansy announced.

"Good night, Tansy. Thanks for all your help. It was a wonderful Christmas!" I said as I hugged her and watched her walk out into the night. A light dusting of snow had begun to fall and shimmered in the moonlight.

"Mom, I need to run to the field and get my baseball stuff," Jason insisted. In our hurry to get to the diner, he had left his baseball Christmas gifts in the field. He felt he couldn't live without his bat, mitt, and hat nearby.

"Jason, can it wait till the morning?"

"No, Mama, I don't want them to get ruined by the snow. Please? I won't be but just a few minutes!" He sounded insistent.

Gracie Bear was already curled up and asleep on one of the hay bales. She was exhausted from all the dancing and playing. It had been a big day. "Jason, let me take your sister upstairs and put her to bed. Then we can go and grab them. Okay?"

I picked her up, carried her upstairs, and laid her in bed. I took her shoes off and started to cover her when she said softly,

"Mama, will you say prayers with me?" (*She knew how to keep me there with her!*)

I laid down next to her and began to pray. Then I kissed her good night and tiptoed out of the room. I headed back downstairs. People had continued to leave until it was just Wilma and a couple of band members, and Clyde, of course. I looked around for Jason, but it appeared he had gone ahead to the baseball field and grabbed his stuff without me. *Oh, well, it's Christmas; I'll let it slide,* I thought.

I walked out to the field in time to see Jason looking up at the stars and heard him pray. "God, will you send Timothy back here? I miss him. I think he is supposed to be my daddy." Then he said, "Daddy, if you are with Jesus, can you say it's okay?" My heart swelled with pride and how God had let me hear his prayer. I said one of my own before I took Jason's hand and led him back toward the loft.

"It's time for bed, honey. Go on upstairs and get ready. I'll be there in a minute."

"Merry Christmas, Mama. I love you. Thanks for everything. This has been the best Christmas ever!" He had a big smile and threw his arms around me.

"I love you too. I'll be there in a bit," I told him. "I just have to finish cleaning up and close up the barn. Merry Christmas, Jason."

I looked at my watch. It was 11:30 p.m. Only a half hour before Christmas Day was officially over. I let out a sigh of relief and satisfaction. It was one of the most amazing Christmas Days that I had ever had! I started to sweep the dance floor with a broom, enjoying the music from the three who still remained. They were enjoying the magical night as much as I.

A familiar song began to play and I started to hum along with it—"Bless the Broken Road" by Rascal Flatts. It was the song that Timothy sang to me on the road to his house when I first began to fall in love with him. Wilma was still there waiting on Clyde and picked up the mic and started to sing. I began to sing along with her. I thought we harmonized pretty well together! I closed my eyes and swayed with the music when suddenly someone came and put their arms around my waist. It was Timothy. He moved in close and turned me to face him as he pulled me nearer to him. I could feel the stares of the three band members along with Wilma and Clyde. They all smiled. "Timothy, everyone is staring at us," I said stunned that he was actually standing there in front of me. I giggled nervously. I never liked being the center of attention.

"I don't see anyone but you," he whispered into my ear. I could feel his breath on my face. It sent goosebumps all over my body.

Although Jason was supposed to be in bed, he walked back into the barn looking for me and suddenly saw Timothy.

"You came back! You came back!" he yelled.

Wilma stopped singing and the room grew quiet as Jason ran to him and jumped in his arms. "God answered my prayers, Mama. I asked Him to bring Timothy back on Christmas and He did. He's here!"

"I missed you, Jason," Timothy told him as he held him tight.

"I missed you so much, Timothy," he responded and then turned to me with a most surprising announcement. "And, Mama, it's okay with Daddy. He's okay!"

It was all I could do to keep from crying as I looked at my precious boy whom I loved with all my heart held by the man who I felt sure was going to be his new daddy.

"It's a Christmas miracle. God did it! Merry Christmas, Mama," Jason said.

Then I saw Tansy appear as well. "I thought you were going to bed," I said, surprised.

"And miss all this? No, ma'am, no way," she replied with a laugh.

"You mean, you knew about this?" I questioned.

"Well, yes, I did actually. Timothy called and told me he was going to be released on Christmas. Now, I didn't know what time, but he said he would come, and I believed he would."

"Come on, Jason. Let Tansy put you back into bed. I think your mama and Timothy got some catching up to do," she said with a grin as she walked with him up the stairs.

"Good night, Mama. Good night, Timothy," he hollered back. "I am glad you are back, and you are surprisingly good for Mama. Merry Christmas!"

As Tansy led Jason back to the loft, Wilma began to sing again while Clyde turned on the snow machine. They were going to turn this into a moment for us. Timothy held me tight and moved in close. "Mary, I'm in love with you," he whispered.

"Well, can I know your real name first, Gary?" I asked, still a little perturbed.

"My real name *is* Timothy," he replied. "Gary is a name they gave me. It's a long story; maybe we should talk about it over dinner sometime."

He leaned into kiss me when I noticed he had something around his neck. I pulled back. "What? What's the matter?" he asked.

"Let me see that necklace you have around your neck," I told him.

He reached in his shirt and pulled it out so I could see it clearly. I about lost my mind. "Where did you get it? I asked him.

"Well, you remember the day we were at your mama's house eating lunch on the porch?"

"It was where we had our first fight. How could I forget?" I said.

"Well, I left mad and stomped around the side of the house. Sam ran out to the field and under the willow tree, and I followed him. He was playing there, so I sat down to think. I saw something reflecting the sun; Sam had it in his mouth. I pulled it out and looked closely at it. It was a penny necklace! I don't believe in magic, but there was something about that penny that compelled me to make the hugest decision in my life. Perhaps you could call it luck? A feeling rushed across me. I knew this was my one chance. As I held this one penny in my hand, I had to do what I has been dreading. I knew I had to turn myself in. That's why I left so suddenly."

Timothy couldn't have known how special it was that he had heard God's voice under *my* willow tree. (*He was the one I prayed to God for under that willow tree when I was just a little girl. Don't you ever try and tell me God doesn't answer prayers! He certainly does. Now, it may not be the way we think it should be, but He always makes sure it's everything He thinks it should be.*)

"You are the one!" I said with tears of joy filling my eyes. "You are the one God chose for me." I reached around my neck under my sweater and pulled out the matching penny necklace. As I looked into his eyes I said, "You came back."

"I promised you I would," he replied.

We stood there in that moment staring into each other's eyes. This was it. Clyde watched our smitten-by-the-love movement and kept hitting the button on the fake snow machine. It was truly magical and I finally kissed Timothy for the first time!

What would the future hold for us? Only God knows that! But I was sure of one thing I was holding in my arms the answer to my prayers. Does it get any better than that?

EPILOGUE

*I*t's good to look back on life. It's good to reflect on the greatest lessons we have learned. It makes us stronger when we remember what we have been through and how God got us through it. That is, if we are open to see Him at work in our lives. I choose to remember!

I cherished the moments Keith and I spent together. He will always have a special place in my heart. He was the first man I ever loved, my husband, and the father of my children. I will always miss him. I miss the way he held me, the way he looked at me, and the gentle way he had to calm me down. I will never forget who he was or who he is. And every day I see him increasingly in the faces of our children. His memory will always live on in my heart!

Love is a crazy thing, and I never expected I would find it again. God brought me someone who loves me for me, just like Keith did. That is the best part. I wasn't expecting a thing and then it showed up! Sometimes we must learn to sit back and enjoy the ride. There is a journey all of us must take, and there is beauty in the pain if we just keep our eyes from looking down.

Love will come to you. Wait for it; don't rush it.

Life for me wasn't always easy. I have always wondered why some people get all the breaks and others make all the mistakes. It was hard to lose my husband, Daddy, and Mama. I wouldn't wish that pain on anyone. But also, if I could go back, I wouldn't change a thing.

Pain has refined me and I have become stronger than I ever was before. The secret is to become stronger, not harder. I had to go to the darkest places inside myself to find out who I truly was. I had to heal even though I didn't want to at first. I needed to take control of my pain, not let it control me. I realized that I could not do this on my own; God had to help me.

I found a treasure in sorrow for there is hope in pain and there is freedom in forgiveness. It took me a long time to forgive my daddy. I knew he loved me with all his heart, but his drinking made me feel abandoned and sad! We don't get to choose the circumstances we face. Sure, we can make mistakes and sometimes we are treated unfairly. We can never get through a tough situation without remembering God's faithfulness. He is building a history with us, and part of that history is His provision!

The broken road was the best road for me. It wasn't always easy to walk through. At times, the twists and turns seemed unbearable. But every time I wanted to give up, hope would increase in me. (*That was when I could feel the prayers of Mama and Tansy for me.*) It wasn't by accident. When Mama was alive, she prayed for me every night and that's the reason I could make it through the dark times I faced. Then when she passed, God gave me Tansy. She stepped into that role in a way I could never have imagined.

We need to never forget that others have sacrificed their time for the freedoms we enjoy today! Sometimes we only look to who the world says are heroes, but grandparents, moms, and dads are heroes behind the scenes, praying us through.

At one point I took out a pen and a piece of paper and began to remember and write down all the things that God did for me. It is important to do this because God is faithful and He does work in our lives. It's important that we acknowledge that and keep a record, so we don't forget! I remembered wanting to get married since I was a little girl and be the best pie maker on the planet. God made sure that happened in an unconventional way.

I remembered when I asked God for a puppy and my folks wouldn't let me have one. He gave Timothy the idea of getting us a puppy. I had to wait for a while, but Sam came into our lives at the right time. It was divine.

I remembered when Jason had a dream about a baseball field and God sent Timothy, who also loved baseball, to build him a baseball field. Jason had such faith. I wondered how God was going to use him and use that faith in his future.

I remembered when I prayed that God would bring the person to me that I was to spend the rest of my life with. And he did. He brought Timothy. He took my penny necklace and gave me the most precious gift any woman could have. These were just a few of the many things God had done in our lives. No, it hadn't been easy, but the growth had been worth it.

There were things that I prayed for and things I believed for that I didn't receive in the timing I wanted. In fact, some of the answers I waited for many years until those prayers were finally answered. At times I wanted to give up, but I didn't. Sometimes we ask God for things and when He doesn't give us what we ask for we can become disheartened, disenchanted with life, depressed, or even fall into self-pity. Instead of being honest with Him and telling Him how we feel, we hold everything inside. Like my daddy.

He bottled up his pain and never healed from his grieving heart. What I learned, as I watched him become trapped in depression, is if you are going to live, then live! Don't let doubt and sadness consume you.

Love deeply. Why act like you're dead before your time? Be present.

Sometimes others hurt us. They don't mean it, but it is a result of their own pain, and they take it out on us. As a result, we can get wounded and hurt and then shut down and stop loving. However, we need to do the opposite. When someone hurts us, we need to love them even more!

I finally forgave my daddy. But most of all, I forgave God. I was mad at Him because I felt He took my husband, my daddy, and my mama from me. I didn't understand why. Why did I have to endure so much heartache? As time passed, I began to realize that sometimes there is no answer why. God knows the answers and He knows the reason, but often it is not for us to know. It's hard to accept that, but every day I am learning to let go!

It was hard for me to walk away from the past! I spent a lot of time there and missed what was right in front of me. I decided I needed to change that! No more was I going to let pain and unforgiveness rule my life.

God helped me. When I finally was willing to talk to Him, He changed my perspective. That is what I needed to move on with everything. I needed to be free of my past, which haunted me. Timothy had to do the same.

I learned that you cannot do things on your own. We were never meant for that. It takes a community of believers to make things happen. If it weren't for my community and the people from my church, I would never have been able to finish the restaurant. Our families, our friends, and even strangers can play an intricate role in our lives if we let them.

Too often we let the worries of this life or the circumstances we face blind us from seeing what is profoundly important. So, what is important? Waking up in the morning with love in your heart, and knowing no matter what we face, God will give us the strength to overcome it. We need to honor and appreciate the people the good Lord has blessed us with. We need to be thankful for them and pray for them often. Because everyone is facing a battle and sometimes they just cannot talk about it. We need to learn to be gracious and love them anyway.

I also learned that we need to take time to spend with the ones we love. We need to serve others while we have them in our lives. We need to take them a homemade pie or a plate of cookies or even a card made with love and deliver it to their door. And one of the most important things is that we need to go to church and fellowship with others. We were never meant to walk through this life alone.

Let me encourage you, if you're mad at God, get to praying. Don't stay mad for long. All of us need Him in our lives. He is a constant friend. Don't give up dreaming and don't give up on your dreams. Remember that when it seems like nothing is going to happen. In one moment, everything can change. So, never give up!

Be quick to forgive and love passionately with all your heart. Never let others ruin your joy. You have a choice to live. So, choose life and choose love over hate. Tansy taught me that.

Never let people try to change who God created you to be. You are perfect just the way you are; whether that is a different skin color or not, it doesn't matter. Be you. Each one of us has a purpose in life. Find yours and live!

Count your blessings and enjoy every moment you have breath in your lungs. Tomorrow is not promised to any of us. So, let's make the most of today. Be present, stay awake and don't forget to dream!

Don't wait to do something. Do it now. Tomorrow may never come. Live in the moment and laugh till your stomach hurts. Dance in the face of adversity and sing in the times of great joy! Pay attention to those treasures whom God has placed in your life. I have shared many seasons of love with beautiful friends who have made me a better person inside and out.

Pain may remind you, but don't let it define you. We must learn to let go of the things that hold us and learn to embrace it. Running away from what hurts us never solves a thing. Trust me, it's better to face it head on! I've decided that I am never going back to the place I was before. I'm on a new journey now. I have been given a chance at life, and I've made up my mind I am not going to waste it. The past is in the past for me. I'm not going to let it control me. What's done is done.

I have learned many lessons and I have many more to learn. I am going to keep pressing on and moving forward. I am going to live life to the fullest, cherish every moment, and make the most of every opportunity and situation. Life is a gift, and I intend on living like it is.

Like Mama said, "Love with all the strength and all your heart that the good Lord gave you. Love more, darling, hate less!"

ABOUT THE AUTHOR

Holly Szurpicki was born in Detroit, Michigan, the car capital of the world. Long before she could drive, her imagination had a way of taking her wherever she dreamed to go.

At one time, Holly wished to be a princess, a park ranger, or an entrepreneur. She says, "Two out of three is not too shabby."

Holly is enthusiastic about creating stories, screenplays, and writing songs. She began writing her first manuscript in 2001. It lay dormant for several years as she focused on raising her two children. But in 2008, she teamed up with a virtual animation studio out of New York. That is when the dream came to life, and the story of Shorty Bean became her first novel. Today it is a series.

Art and individual creativity have tremendously inspired her throughout her career. Holly has tremendous visual creativity, which takes her to places beyond words to live animation in her mind. Being able to envision her characters and their environments is a true gift, and she recognizes this as supernatural.

Despite many tragic circumstances she has faced throughout her life, Holly has always kept a cheerful outlook and loves to encourage others to pursue their God-given dreams.

Her goal for writing books is to make faith-inspired yet impactful stories for both adults and young children. All of Holly's novels reflect a childlike imagination in her creative process which result in inspiring and meaningful stories. Holly believes we all have a divine destiny and wants everyone to know that they should never be afraid to pursue their dreams.

Holly lives in northern Minnesota with her husband and two children and a water dog named Klause. She loves the outdoors, photography, and fishing, to name a few of her passions.

For more information about the Shorty Bean series, other works and future works, or general inquiries, check out her website at:

www.hollykszurpicki.com

www.ingramcontent.com/pod-product-compliance
Lightning Source LLC
Chambersburg PA
CBHW020944260626
47169CB00006B/1817